ALSO BY KAT & STONE BASTION

No Weddings Series

No Weddings · One Funeral

Two Bar Mitzvahs · Three Christmases

For Valentine's

Unbreakable Series

Heartbreaker · Rule Breaker · Lawbreaker

Forthcoming: *Ball Breaker · Icebreaker*

Highland Legends Series

Forged in Dreams and Magick

Bound by Wish and Mistletoe

Born of Mist and Legend

Found in Flame and Moonlight

THE TRAVELER: Initiate Years

Veil of Realms · Secrets of Alexandria · Panther Rising

Stones of Power · Highland Magick

Half-Baked Holidays

Half-baked Holidays:

A Romantic Comedy Holiday Collection

Comic Book Date Series

The Accidental May the 4th Comic Book Date

The Unbelievable Made on a Dare Comic Book Date

The Irresistible 4th of July Comic Book Date

Standalone Novels & Novelettes

Brand New Year · The Espionage Effect

Romantic Poetry for Charity

Utterly Loved

PRAISE FOR KAT & STONE BASTION

No Weddings and
THE NO WEDDINGS SERIES

"One of the best romantic comedies of the year!"

— AGENTS OF ROMANCE

"The No Weddings series is one of the best I have read that follows one couple. Cade and Hannah are both lovable characters, the storyline is real and entertaining, and the banter is fun and witty."

— LIVES & BREATHES BOOK BLOG

"I loved it, and I mean REALLY loved it!"

— ORCHARD BOOK CLUB

"This is an exceptional series... You find yourself fully engrossed in their world and can't put the book down."

— BOOKS -N- KISSES

"The No Weddings series has a group of such amazing characters; you can't help but relate to them and feel the emotion in every situation they encounter. It has been a long time since a story has made me feel that way let alone an entire series!"

— *UNDER THE COVERS BOOK BLOG*

"The story of Cade & Hannah's relationship is realistic, heart-warming, and filled with real-world connections that shook me in a way that few titles I've read this year have managed...I have loved every minute of the No Weddings series."

— *THAT'S WHAT I'M TALKING ABOUT*

Heartbreaker

"This book has definitely earned its five stars and I am just floored right now. The passion is explosive, the story itself is beautiful, and the emotions are so real my heart is ready to burst. Beautiful book. Absolutely breathtaking."

— *ONE PAGE AT A TIME*

"Heartrending, passionate, and captivating! *Heartbreaker* is a riveting page-turner that will leave you breathless with raw emotions, and the need to hold tight to the ones you love!"

— *BENEATH THE COVERS BLOG*

AWARDS & PRAISE FOR KAT BASTION

Forged in Dreams and Magick

First Place – Unpublished Beacon Award
Best Paranormal Romance

First Place – Hold Me, Thrill Me Award
Best Paranormal Romance

Chosen by FreshFiction.com as their
Fresh Pick for October 22, 2013

"A beautifully woven tale about love, choices, courage and destiny, *Forged in Dreams and Magick* is one of the best time-traveling novels. Fans of Gabaldon's *Outlander* will love it."

— *BOOKISH TEMPTATIONS*

"I was gripping my iPad like a crazy woman and fanning myself from the smoldering romance. Lawdy!"

— *THE FLIRTY READER*

"Bastion's debut is pure perfection, a combination of romance, magic, emotion, adventure and surprising twists and turns. This is a truly unique romance that should not be missed!"

— *THEBOOKQUEEN*

"HOLY HELL!!! I am so... um... wow! FABULOUS-NESS. *Forged in Dreams and Magick* definitely makes my BEST OF list for 2013..."

— *THAT'S WHAT I'M TALKING ABOUT*

"A story guaranteed to enthrall with lushly detailed travels into times long gone by. Woven with love, passion, magic and legend, the story had me hooked from the very first chapter."

— *READ-LOVE-BLOG*

"Kat Bastion's wonderful debut brings a new voice to the fore. Her voice is strong and unhesitating, very human and real, sometimes young and delicious in her treatment of intimacy and relationship development."

— *FANGS WANDS & FAIRYDUST*

"OMG, Bastion hits all cylinders in this supernatural tale. The layers in the book were fascinating, and I devoured the fun, adventuresome read."

— *LITERATI LITERATURE LOVERS*

Bound by Wish and Mistletoe

"I LOVED it! *Bound by Wish and Mistletoe* is, to my mind, a perfect entry in the historical / paranormal fiction genre and has quite a bit to offer."

— *FAB FANTASY FICTION*

"Kat Bastion has done it again! ... Excellent holiday novella, perfect for a cup of cocoa and snuggling under a blanket in front of the fireplace this holiday season."

— *THAT'S WHAT I'M TALKING ABOUT*

"Move over, Julia Quinn and Sabrina Jeffries! Kat Bastion is an absolutely gifted author and deserves to be recognized for her talent."

— *LOVESHISTORICAL BOOK REVIEWS*

NO WEDDINGS

NO WEDDINGS

KAT & STONE BASTION

No Weddings is a book of fiction. Names, characters, places, occurrences, and theories are the products of the authors' imaginations or are used fictitiously. Any resemblance to persons, living or dead, locales, events, or theories is wholly coincidental.

The authors acknowledge the trademark status and trademark owners of products, names, and/or phrases mentioned within this work of fiction, which have been used without permission. The publication of the trademarks is not authorized by, associated with, or sponsored by the trademark owners.

No Weddings

For those of us who've been brokenhearted...

PROLOGUE

The Last Weekend in June

"...And special thanks for making our bar, Loading Zone, look as awesome as it does goes to my sister Kiki. Our resident artist insisted on keeping all the brick and repurposing the steel. She gave it a name." I searched the several hundred guests, trying to spot her. "Grunge. Or..."

Kiki cupped her hands around her mouth. "It's Industrial Grunge, Cade!"

I raised my beer bottle to the spirited one in our family while she kissed her fingertips and blew me kisses from across the crowded room. Several people broke out in laughter, and I glanced down at the guests. "Don't worry, I'm told the surfaces are sealed. Any actual rust is for effect, not because the warehouse is still decaying. I hope."

"Quit hogging the mic, man." With a grin on his face, my best friend and business partner, Ben, grabbed the microphone from me and nudged me off the DJ platform.

I grinned back at him, letting him have his earned moment in the spotlight too.

Our time had come. After almost a year of planning, our dream was now a reality. The idea of opening a bar in Philly's Old City Arts District had finally been realized.

Ben bowed his head at my sister. "Thanks, Kiki. Your design skills are incomparable. Speaking of design skills, the cake you see up at the bar was custom-made for our grand opening tonight by up-and-coming baker Hannah Martin. Thanks, Hannah. I'm sure it tastes as good as it looks."

At Ben's introduction, Kiki gestured her arms to the brunette on her right, who I had yet to officially meet. Then Kiki turned, speaking with a friend of ours from the country club.

I made my way toward my sister and Hannah through the crowd. The last of Ben's words echoed and twisted in my head while I stared at Hannah. *I'm sure she tastes as good as she looks.*

As I approached them, my focus remained on Hannah Martin, whose features had been pulled straight out of my fantasies: wavy dark hair, expressive eyes, pouty lips, and mouthwatering curves.

On the edge of my awareness, Ben raised his beer high as he finished his speech. "Enjoy the celebration. Drink, dance, eat cake, and tell all your friends about Loading Zone."

A thumping bass rhythm began to vibrate through the room as I once again dragged my gaze from Hannah's high heels, up her shapely legs, to the bottom hem of a black dress that clung to every curve, dip, and gorgeous swell.

My gaze lifted to her face and locked with hers right as I

stepped within talking distance. Happily caught in the act, I smirked.

Hannah's expression hardened, eyes narrowing.

Okayyy. Clearly she didn't like a man appreciating the assets she'd put on proud display.

I glanced at my sis as she took a sip of a frozen strawberry daiquiri. She was just now turning my way, oblivious to the frosty reception I'd gotten.

"Cade!" Kiki side-lunged into me, giving me a half hug. "Have you guys met yet? Hannah, this is my brother, the one I've been telling you about. Cade, this is Hannah, the baker from my art class."

I reached a hand out toward Hannah, but instead of shaking it, she crossed her arms over her chest and gave me a curt nod.

The one I've been telling you about? I wondered what Kiki had said about me.

Setting my jaw, I pulled my hand back.

When one of our waitresses rushed by, I stopped her with a gentle hand on her forearm. "Hey, Jillian, do you have a drink menu?"

"Sure, boss. I mean, Cade." Jillian smiled and gave me a slim menu from her pocket before continuing on toward the bar.

"Would you like a drink?" I held out the laminated list of specialty drinks to Hannah.

Her gaze drifted down. She glared at the menu like it had teeth and might bite. After a sigh, she unlocked one of her folded arms and took it from me.

Kiki glanced around the room. "You two good? I'm going to find Mom and Dad."

I nodded behind me. "Try the bar. Everyone was back

there a few minutes ago." Everyone being our parents, our other two sisters, and a few close friends.

I stood alone with Hannah, who now wore glasses balanced low on her nose. The librarian look did nothing to mar her beauty. If anything, it enhanced it.

"See anything you like?" Loaded question. I know.

She shrugged, glancing up from the menu to give me a hard stare. Taking her time, she scanned her gaze down my body, then shot it back up to my face and tilted her head. She handed the menu back to me before crossing her arms once again.

"Not really."

Oh, so that's how it is.

Hannah Martin was a contradiction in the flesh. Tempting cleavage swelled over a low neckline, guarded behind crossed arms. Her toned body was held rigid, her full lips pressed in a firm line.

Beautiful, but clearly unattainable.

She was a hotter-than-fuck...Ice Queen.

1. THE START UP

Six Months Later

"Thanks for kicking my New Year's off with a bang."

Firm breasts were pressed into my chest. She leaned further into me as we stood off to the side of the dwindling crowd, her hands clasped around my neck. Fingers slid through my hair, tugging, gripping.

She didn't want to let go. I could hardly blame her. *That* was one hell of a ride.

"Anytime, Amber. I'm a full-service host."

With care not to topple the girl who already teetered on four-inch heels, I untangled us and propped her against the bar. She stretched her talented fingers out for an untouched Champagne glass, but I quickly lifted it out of her way. She'd had plenty of fun for the night.

"Ben, grab her a cab ride home?" He had agreed to help with my family's party tonight which was held in a converted backyard barn.

He shook his head. "Nah, I'll take her."

"Thanks, man." We bumped knuckles before he grasped her elbow and led her out.

Did it seem cold not to take the girl home? Maybe. But she knew the score with me. Not that I knew what the hell was up with me, but I needed no-strings-attached therapy to be able to deal.

Shoving my fingers into my hair, I rubbed my scalp and turned around—then grimaced. Three blue-eyed brunettes stood across the room, glaring at me, as my sisters often did.

How long have they been watching?

Long enough, I decided on a heavy sigh as the magnified strength of their glares tried to strip the skin off my hide. I grinned wide, pissing them off even further.

Glitter and confetti covered the maple floor. Blue and silver balloons floated around, dragging their ribbons. Someone at the main control panel silenced the music and turned off the giant flat-screen TV which had been streaming post-ball-drop Times Square footage. The lights went off seconds before amber security lights came on. My oldest sister, Kristen, had done a great job renovating the abandoned space on her country estate, and tonight's party had made excellent use of it.

As I made my way toward my judge, jury, and execu-tioner, they turned in unison, shaking their heads and muttering while they opened the door that led up to the house. I quickened my stride, weaving through two clean-up crew workers who'd begun sweeping up. I heard a distinct "fuck" from one of my sisters as I caught the edge of the door before it slammed shut.

I chuckled.

Riling them into swearing amused me to no end.

The bitter cold of the first few hours of January bit into

the skin under my black dress shirt. Its rolled-up sleeves and untucked hem over dark jeans had earned a couple of rolled-eyed sighs from the sisterhood. Hey, the shirt had a collar. Which was as close to dressed up as I was willing to get on New Year's Eve.

By the time I opened the French doors and stepped into Kristen's living room, the three had commandeered the best seats: the overstuffed suede chair and the dark, broken-in leather couch.

All taken.

I ignored their judgy looks, angling toward the fridge.

"Cade!"

I smiled, taking my time in silent defiance to "decide" on what to confiscate. Of course, the Fat Tires in a neat row on the second shelf had been stocked specifically for me. Spreading three fingers, I lifted two of the bottles and popped the door shut.

"Kincade Joseph Michaelson! Get your ass in here now!"

Feeling more than a little devious, I pretend-snuck up behind Kendall—the one with the lungful of attitude—and gave her an open-mouthed ear kiss, finishing with a slobbering lick. "Really?" I rounded the chair, arching a brow at her. "We're using full legal names now?"

"Uckkk." The half word lodged in her throat, like a stuck cat hair ball.

Kristen narrowed her eyes at me, growling. "You get full, middle, and last name with plenty of attitude when you fuck a guest while we're doing a trial-run party."

I gave her a tired look. "Please. The party was over. I'd put out half a dozen fires, more than all of you put together. At twenty minutes till midnight, with Champagne pouring and guests dancing, if the party wasn't already a success, my eleventh-hour absence didn't make a bit of difference."

With raised brows I met her calculating eyes and waited for the rebuttal. None came.

I knew they had more important things to pick apart, like tonight's inaugural Michaelson-planned event, which I thought we'd successfully hosted. I moved with purpose toward the seat I wanted, regardless of the impertinent ass currently warming it.

Kiki's big blue eyes widened, locking on to mine as I stalked *my* spot on the most worn corner of the couch. Those eyes narrowed in challenge, and her arms and legs spread out. She gripped the arm and back cushion, as if her slight mass would make a difference in my tossing her aside without a strained breath.

"No." Kiki braced her legs, defending her stolen territory.

I tilted my head and placed my beers out of harm's way on a safe corner of the side table. Their clinks on the glass surface were the last sounds heard before her earsplitting squeals. In a fluid movement, honed from years of practice, I yanked her up by the waist, swung her around, and threw my weight back, landing on the couch.

Kicking and screaming, she landed on my lap.

"Hey, watch the elbows!" I shoved my arms over my groin to guard against cheap body shots.

Kiki extricated herself from my lap in a dramatic huff and glared at me while she planted herself in the uncomfortable wing chair, as far away from me as possible. She crossed her arms, silently hating me with her body.

I winked at her. She loved me.

In fact, all my sisters loved me, their baby brother, no matter how pissy they got over my behavior. Kristen's the oldest. Katherine, or Kiki as we all call her, the next. Kendall is the youngest girl, two years older than me. They were the only people on the planet who got to call me Kincade. And only ever when they were pissed as hell. Or impatient. Or PMSing, which was pretty much all the time.

I had asserted my independence from the cutesy "K" names at the age of three and a half. A defiant toddler learning to spell his name, I only wrote the last four letters in black crayon. To a chorus of *awww*'s and sighs, the girls took to the nickname, and Mom pinned up my artistic masterpiece under a Hello Kitty magnet on the refrigerator with pride.

In a household dominated by pink, I came along and colored their lives in bold black lines. Their world has never been the same.

Dad hardly noticed. Busy in investment banking at one of the world's largest firms, he was gone seventy hours Monday through Friday. And that was a good week. But he had a large family to support in the style Mom had grown accustomed to. I got decent father–son time on sporadic occasions: a tossed baseball in a glove for a couple of stolen hours; a Mets game once for my birthday. So rare were our "guy times," I remember every one with clarity.

Was it any wonder that these rowdy girls had become my world? My life's mission was to have as much fun as possible while simultaneously disrupting theirs. Over a couple of decades, I turned the technique into an art form.

I sprawled out, hogging as much space as possible. I practically owned this couch. I actually would, if squatter's rights applied to furniture.

Kendall scraped the bottom of a tub of Ben & Jerry's that she'd defeated; Kiki plucked silver sugar balls off a chocolate frosted cupcake, popping them into her mouth one at a time; and Kristen reclined her head on the back cushion at the other end of the couch, fingertips massaging the pressure points above her brows.

Bored with the heavy melancholy hanging in the room, I took a long draft from my beer and stretched my right foot out, pushing the toe of my boot onto Kristen's jean-clad thigh. She grunted, but I was disappointed with the dismal reaction.

"What a disaster," Kendall proclaimed, giving voice to the apparent thickening consensus. She tossed the demolished ice-cream carton onto the cocktail table. The container toppled, the spoon clattering onto the glass surface.

"I don't know." Kiki shifted forward, bracing her forearms on black pants. "At times, everything went smoothly. We could break down the problems and streamline things."

I watched Kristen as I finished my first beer and twisted the top off the second. As I relaxed further into the couch, everyone grew quiet. The two girls who'd spoken now focused their attention on our silent older sister, who remained with her head tilted back on the cushions, her body slouched down.

Kristen's eldest status wasn't the only reason the group deferred to her—this country estate was her property. And throwing a party in the refurbished barn out back had been her idea, even if none of the three remembered their excited conversation over breakfast a month ago.

In a calm voice, Kristen finally broke her catatonic state. "Cade, what do you think?"

And there it was.

For all the years of experience and wisdom these girls had, when they wanted an impartial opinion, they asked me.

Because I didn't give a rat's ass.

And they all knew it.

Before filtering through my memories of the night, I paid proper respect to my most recent one. I revisited the sex that began against the wall, moved to the stainless steel counter—yeah, that needed disinfecting—and finished with Amber's screaming orgasm that she muffled into my shoulder as I pulled her straight up against me. I snorted; I could've pulled a back muscle, but it was worth it.

As my thoughts drifted from my party high note, I reflected on the rest of the night. "Barbara Willingham said she was glad she stiffed the Taylors' annual gala to attend our party. And that was before her third vodka tonic.

"I also overheard someone commenting they'd kill to have a party like ours. I think it was Phoebe Trent. Yep." I nodded, remembering. "She went on to say, 'That country club overcharges for its pretentious toothpick affairs. I'd pay double for something new and wild.'"

Kendall chimed in behind the opened refrigerator door as bottles clinked. "Kristen, didn't Missy Thompson ask if she could have our help with a Valentine's Day party?"

Kristen nodded, as if suddenly recalling. "You know, she did."

Upending my second beer, I took the new bottle Kendall offered and pointed it at the three of them in silent accusation until I finished swallowing. "See. You all were so busy worrying about the details of the party, you had no time to enjoy it. Tragedy, really. Everyone else did. We pulled together an incredible event."

Silence filled the room. I wisely kept my mouth shut, predicting the flow, knowing the conclusion before they ever uttered a word. I knew them well. Knowledge was the only way a Y chromosome would survive unscathed in a nest of all these X's.

I took several more long pulls of my beer; I needed to be less sober for this.

Soft words came from Kiki. "I say we form a business."

I wasn't surprised Kiki was the one to speak up. She'd graduated from art school, but although a few of her pieces were displayed in some high-end galleries, none had sold yet. Starving artists grew bolder when hot on the trail of easy money.

I waited.

"I second that." Kendall held her beer in the air.

Kiki followed suit.

Kristen straightened from her former lump on the other end of the couch. She grabbed an uncapped bottle from the refreshers Kendall had brought and lifted it up. "I third it."

Tradition. The element ran thick as blood in a family whose tree hailed from such things. Old money mixed with new throughout our family's history of business endeavors and worthy philanthropic causes. And our generation was no exception.

Bottles brandished from their outstretched arms, like we'd done as kids with wooden swords to defend tree houses. *All for one and one for all.*

I raised my bottle, ready to capitulate.

"I fourth it...*with conditions.*"

Their arms sagged without our common celebratory shout. Kristen eased into her corner of the couch, but remained upright, watching me, waiting.

Luckily, I was in my last year at Wharton. Business wasn't just the focus of my master's, it was my passion. I lived, ate, and breathed all things related to making money.

I glanced at them, one at a time. "We are *not* taking all comers. We do have pride, after all. This isn't about money on the front end. We establish a reputation for only holding events that meet our standards."

"How do we develop standards?" Kiki swished her half-empty bottle, staring into the beer vortex behind the glass as it spun.

"Well, I don't know about you girls, but I have a few rules. Like *no* kids' parties."

Kendall shot upright, thrusting her beer-bottle sword into the air. "I second that!"

Kiki stared at me with narrowed eyes from across the room, sitting uncomfortably in the wingback chair I'd relegated her to. "No parties given by *anyone* you've had sex with."

I shot my bottle up also. "Fuck, I second that." I didn't need to be bossed around by some scorned client on a tear because I hadn't called her back.

Our reserved Kristen added to the list of rules, raising her bottle. "No balloon animals."

"We already said no kids' parties," Kendall replied.

"Oh, no. I'm laying down the law. No balloon animals. Even at an adult party. They freak me out." Kristen shivered while a vibrating "ehhh" came from her.

We busted up, laughing.

"No clowns." Kendall's morbid tone made us choke back our laughter, only to set it free again.

When our amusement faded, we sipped from our beers, each lost in thought.

Kristen set her bottle down on the corner of the table. "We need a name."

"Easy. 'The Party Posse.'" My snarky remark earned me groans and a pillow launched at my head, which I expertly deflected with an arcing forearm, not spilling a drop of beer; then a crumpled cupcake wrapper landed on my chest with a soft thud. "Hmmm." I picked up the chocolate cake crumbs with a licked index finger and stuck them on my tongue.

Other names were tossed around, but nothing stood out.

I sighed. "We need something different. Unforgettable."

Kiki, ever the creative one, sat taller. "What about inspiration from wedding invitations?" Her eyes lit with excitement. "They always begin with 'You've been cordially invited...', and Cade, you said we need to be selective. What about 'By Invitation Only?'"

We fell silent, mulling over the suggestion, which was more than we'd done for any other contender. We were cautious because we all knew the stakes; once a decision had been made by us, it stuck.

One by one, their gazes turned toward me. I nodded slowly, repeating the three words in my mind. "I like it, but it seems off. Doesn't roll off the tongue. What about shortening it? 'Invitation Only.'"

"I love it!" Kiki squealed out.

"Invitation Only!" we shouted simultaneously, creating our new business name.

"Oh, that reminds me. I have one more rule." I sat up from my comatose position on the couch.

Kristen exerted her status as eldest. "You don't get another rule. We each had one."

I shook my head. "This rule is nonnegotiable. You want me in this? I won't budge on one important stipulation."

They looked at one another, considering the idea of giving me an additional condition.

I set my jaw, holding fast. No way in hell would I bend on this point.

"Fine, what is it?" Kristen cast me a put-out expression that matched her tone.

"Do you agree to it?" I crossed my arms, drawing a battle line.

"You want us to agree without knowing what it is?" Kendall chimed in.

"It's a deal breaker. Does it matter what it is?"

One by one they all looked to Kristen, giving slight nods.

Kristen slid a cautious glance toward me. "Fine. We all agree to your mysterious rule. Please tell us, dear brother, what have we agreed to?"

"*No weddings.*"

Raised brows and nods followed. They knew on the surface that weddings with me around spelled disaster. What they didn't know was how deep the damage went.

They moved on from my condition as if it was a nonissue and went into earsplitting screeching from their excitement about the new business. In fact, the drunker they got, the more they warmed to my last rule, citing legendary wedding stories, including my coup at Kristen's wedding.

"But you did her right before the wedding!" Kristen wailed into her beer, still lamenting the fact.

I shrugged. "You're the one who put those sexy friends of yours in *fuck-me heels*."

"And, of course, you had to give her *just-been-fucked hair* to match," she grumbled.

I grinned, recalling how that uptight bridesmaid's hair had become loosened curls. "Of course."

Kiki whispered to me from across the room, her expression conspiratorial. "Didn't you also bang Simone?"

I nodded. "Hey, at least I waited until later that night. Her hair was intact when the reception began."

Kendall laughed. "She was picking grass out of it on the way to the valet."

"See, ladies? I rest my case. You don't want me anywhere near a wedding."

All-seeing Kristen stared hard at me from her corner of the couch. I knew her MO. Behind her calculating stare, she tried to figure out why the "no weddings" thing.

My reasons didn't matter. They were none of their business. And as all three had learned over the years, when I wanted to keep something from them, I succeeded.

I gazed at her coolly.

With reluctance, she looked away, forfeiting the unwinnable battle.

"Ben would be our bar guy," Kendall murmured, scrawling notes on the back of an extra silver paper napkin from tonight's New Year's bash.

"Yep." I swallowed down the rest of my beer and closed my eyes, my buzz helping me relax further into the couch.

"Hannah could do the cakes!" Kiki's high-pitched tone was too animated for 2:00 a.m. But then her tone dropped, heavy. "Oh, and *no* doing the help."

I tilted my head, cracking open my eyes long enough to see the deadpan look from Kiki. "Uptight Ice Queen Hannah Martin? No problem." But the woman did have memorable curves, and oddly, her attitude had drawn me in until she'd shut me down cold.

So if that ice ever thawed, I'd have to watch myself. Because no matter how difficult it was for me to follow rules, keeping my word to my sisters was important to me.

She shook her head. "She's not an Ice Queen."

I snorted. "Says you. When a guy approaches a girl and frost coats his skin from the chilly reception, she is."

Kendall crossed her arms. "Don't blame a girl for being immune to your charms. Not every female wants her skirt blown up to her shoulders when you come near."

I rolled my eyes. "Well, she bakes a great cake; I'll give her that." Fucking awesome cake, actually. And all I'd done with Hannah was appreciate a beautiful woman I'd just met, yet she'd given me the glacial treatment all the same.

Kristen glanced at me. "You need to take that meeting."

I coughed, nearly choking. "What? *Hell* no."

"Yes, Mr. Wharton Business School."

I pointed my bottle toward Kiki. "She's Kiki's friend. She should take the meeting."

Kiki shook her head. "She's not that good of a friend. I just know her from art class. Art. Business. You do the math."

Kristen pursed her lips, staring at me. "You and I will go together."

Knowing my going to the meeting made the most sense, I didn't argue and gave her a curt nod. But the whole idea sounded painful. About as much fun as when my sisters tricked me into sticking my tongue on a frozen light pole when I was four.

Resigned, I mentally prepared to meet the Ice Queen again.

2. ICING ON THE CAKE

Nine days later, I stepped out of the shower, barely awake, when my cell phone's incessant buzzing on the nightstand caught my attention.

Irritated at the world that I had to get up early on the only morning I usually had to sleep in after a punishing week of school and work, I grabbed the damned thing off my nightstand, clicked it on, and shoved it against my ear. "What?" I growled.

"Cade, you need to go to the meeting at Sweet Dreams on your own." Kristen sounded stressed. There was a beeping noise in the background, then a car door slammed and an engine started.

"Tell me you're joking." Gears started to click in my uncaffeinated mind—even she wouldn't pull a stunt with something so important to her. "Wait. Is everything okay?"

"Yeah. Jason's car broke down on the pike. Dead battery. I'm already on my way to rescue him so he can make his investor's meeting."

"Shouldn't we reschedule?" I stared at my bed, thinking I could crawl back in.

"No." she countered, her tone firm. "Today may be our only shot at this. Hannah was leery on the phone about the idea of partnering with us while launching her new bakery. Make sure you're there by 7:00 a.m."

I groaned. "Sis, I know nothing about baked goods. And I'm confident Hannah doesn't like me."

"Learn. And make her." She hung up.

The day was off to a shitty start. *Coffee. I need coffee.* I went straight to the kitchen and poured a cup.

I couldn't be mad at Kristen for rescuing her husband. I liked Jason and didn't want him stranded either. Or late to his business meeting. A trifecta of sibling code, business code, and bro code obliterated the weak hold I had on my grumpy mood.

Waiting for the caffeine to kick in, I put on a pair of jeans, tugged a black T-shirt over my head, shrugged on a jacket, and pulled on my worn boots before grabbing my keys and helmet off the entry table.

I shivered and grumbled under my breath at Jason's damned car battery. It was cold as fuck out so early, even with unseasonably warm temps in January. I eased back onto the cold, worn leather of my custom motorcycle.

A few turns onto the sleepy downtown streets of Glen-haven, and I saw my destination. A sign stating "Sweet Dreams" above a yellow-and-white-striped awning told me I'd found the right place. I parked then walked up to the entrance as I took a deep breath, not looking forward to the meeting.

The sun hadn't risen yet, giving a grayish cast to the abandoned street, but faint light glowed from within the bakery from somewhere in the back.

With care, I knocked on the wood frame that surrounded the glass panes in the top section of the door.

After waiting a minute and getting no response, I tried the knob. It turned, and I pushed in.

"Hello?" I surveyed the clean space while stepping inside. Three stools lined a low counter. Beside them was a large, empty display case.

From somewhere further inside, a metal clap and a ringing sounded out. I followed the noise to the back, into a kitchen sizable enough to accommodate an army of pastry chefs. The lone occupant, however, stood with her back to me, surrounded by hundreds of colorful cupcakes and a few multi-level cakes. The sound came from a metal bowl that spun to a stop a few feet from her, mere inches from a cake half-covered in icing.

Her shoulders slumped in relief.

A ruffled apron had twisted on her body; the bottom sat crooked on her hips. Dried remnants of various frosting colors dotted the tanned skin on her arms, making her look like she'd broken out in rainbow chicken pox. She wore shorts short enough that I could see toned thighs beneath her apron skirt.

A quick glance at my watch: 7:03 a.m.

Oblivious to my presence, she bent over, focused on icing a different cake, armed with some weapon of pastry, a plastic bag with a gleaming metal tip on the end. I kept silent, unwilling to interrupt her flow. Curves in motion reminded me of what I'd admired during the grand opening of Loading Zone, yet the image of the woman in front of me was day and night to the one I remembered.

The master craftsman standing before me proceeded to coat her creation in what looked like shining green scales, each one laid perfectly upon the last. Her speed with the icing tube was such that I barely saw her movements before the entire surface had been coated.

She straightened and eyed her work from several angles before nodding once. She discarded the bag, then pulled off a plastic lid from a glass bowl and picked up a small spatula. After she dipped it down and scraped up, the tip was coated in pink frosting.

I watched, amused that her determined focus made her completely unaware she was late. Another time check: 7:07 a.m.

From my position leaning against the edge of a stainless steel counter covered in rows of cupcakes, I cleared my throat.

She jumped. Pink frosting flew out in an arc as she whirled around, splattering onto everything in its path, including me.

"Whoa! Easy, Maestro." It was an apt nickname, the way she orchestrated creations with the flick of her pastry wand. I dragged my finger along my forearm, scraping frosting off, and then stuck it in my mouth, licking the sweetness while I stared at her.

She dropped her frosting weapon and fully faced me, wiping green-stained hands on her apron. "Oh! Oh my God. I'm so sorry. I...I forgot the time."

Striking greenish-hazel eyes stared back at me, flecks of gold sparking in the bright light. Her cute face had smudged flour on one cheek, her chin, and a long smear across her forehead. Long dark brown hair had been clipped up, but some pieces had fallen loose, brushing her cheeks.

A purple V-neck tee clung to the top of her breasts before the apron hid the very interesting curves from sight.

But out of sight meant on my mind...

Her brow furrowed. "Wait. Are you here about our meeting? Where's Kristen?" Her expression hardened further into something resembling annoyance.

"Yeah, sorry. I didn't mean to startle you or intrude into your private space. I knocked and tried to get your attention, but you didn't hear me. Kristen had an emergency. I'm here to present the proposal."

With a cautious expression, she held out her hand. "I'm Hannah."

My memory flashed to the hand I'd offered and she'd rejected six months ago. Regardless, I shook hers, surprised by her strong grip as it held mine for a brief second. "We've met once. I'm Cade."

Her eyes narrowed for a split second as she released my hand. "Oh, yeah. I remember. The player, Drink List Guy." She turned away and proceeded to use the insides of her outstretched forearms to scoot her cupcakes away from the edges of the counters.

"Player?" Well that answered a question about the ice-queen treatment six months ago.

"Kiki shared your exploits. You sounded like a player to me."

I closed my hand to find it sticky. I flipped it over. Green icing coated my skin. I rubbed my palm clean on my thigh. If the color didn't wash out of my jeans, I'd deal.

By the time she turned around, her "cute and disheveled" vibe disappeared behind a calm, collected demeanor. I smirked. There was a touch of the Ice Queen Hannah I remembered.

I still had to take a deep breath, though. The girl in close proximity to me was beautiful and sensual, even with her false demeanor. I decided it was all a front, because her true identity was the one I'd caught unaware while she lost herself in her craft.

With quick fingers, she untied the apron, pulled it over

her head, then tossed it onto a wheeled chair in the corner by a desk. "Let's go up front so we can sit down."

I nodded and walked to the front area of her store. She passed me, heading toward two chairs stacked upside down on a table. I went beside her and grabbed one as she pulled down the other, righted it, and took a seat.

She regarded me casually, as if she had all the time in the world. An eager potential business partner would show more interest, but I got the impression nothing Hannah did would reveal what lay hidden beneath her now-shellacked expression.

I glanced at her bare forearm that was splattered in frosting, thinking if she had a mirror, she might be less confident about her chances of winning a business negotiation. When I met her gaze, however, her calmness left me uncertain. She looked like she could wrestle an alligator and win.

I almost smiled, but forced a hard expression. Her distracting appearance aside, I focused on the task at hand. Two could play hardball, and I'd been trained by the best.

"As I'm sure Kristen explained, we've formed an event-planning and hosting company. We need a supplier for cakes, and you come highly recommended by Kiki."

Her head tilted, her expression shifting from cold to curious as her gaze searched mine. "Only by Kiki? Didn't you taste the cake I made for your club's opening? What did you think?"

I shrugged. "Yeah, it was good." Fucking amazing, actually. But I wasn't about to tell her that. This was a negotiation.

"Good?" Amusement flashed in her eyes. She glanced out the window, getting a faraway look as a smirk played at the corners of her lips.

Then she shifted back in her seat and regarded me.

And I took a good hard look at her as well. She was nothing like the Hannah Martin I'd expected before I walked into her kitchen. I grew more fascinated by the second with the hard-edged woman across the small tabletop from me. And although she was interested in the business portion of this meeting, instinct told me she was curious about what lay under my outer shell as well.

Well, good luck with that one.

"Since Kristen was supposed to be here, I don't have one of the subcontractor agreements with me, but I'll email it to you later today. Essentially, we need someone as the sole supplier of our events. We're demanding no less than three weeks' notice from our clients, so that's the possible amount of lead time you'll receive as well. At the time of booking, we can ask them if they have a cake preference, but ultimately, most will have no say, as we're trying to keep control of the creative details once they pick a theme."

A spark of interest showed in her eyes. "I'd have total creative control?"

I gave her a nod. "Unless they make a specific demand when they book."

She drummed her fingers on the table. Her nails were perfectly manicured but short and free of any polish. "How many parties are you doing a month?"

"We figure it will be a couple of parties a month to begin with. Our preferred themes center on holidays, but we'll still do the occasional charity event or special occasion."

"What are you paying?"

Those greenish eyes held mine, and I think she stopped breathing. Although I could've drawn out the suspense, I wasn't a masochist. Still, I found it oddly reassuring to see the fracture in Little Miss Calm, Cool, and Collected. Maybe

Kiki had been right—Hannah was *possibly* not an Ice Queen after all. But one had to look past the glacial exterior she tried valiantly to maintain.

I leaned forward, holding her gaze. At closer range, I became consciously aware of her scent. Not one hint of over-drenched, alcohol-based perfume. Instead, a slight sweetness drifted up, different than all the cake makings in her kitchen—something floral.

"We'll pay whatever it costs." I held my tone soft but firm. She hadn't known until now that we weren't negotiating price here. Only her availability. Her commitment.

"Whatever I *charge*?" she clarified. Smart girl.

"Within reason, of course. Decide what your time is worth per hour. Make works of art, and you can charge accordingly. Heavy-hitting names in social circles, both here and from Manhattan, will attend these events."

She blinked. Her gaze fell to the surface of the table, her eyes scanning back and forth in thought. "What's the catch?"

I leaned back with a nod. "You can't ever say no. We need to rely on you without exception. You'll be required not only to create the cake, often solely from your imagination, but it also must be *the perfect* one-of-a-kind cake. You'll be expected to deliver to the function, no matter where it's held, which may be here in the Philly metro area, at a location in Manhattan, or possibly anywhere in between. We'll expect you to remain at the function, serving to the guests when the time comes, and then packaging and disposing of the cake when the party's over."

Sitting now on the edge of her seat, she listened to the list of requirements my sisters and I had created over the last week in a volley of back-and-forth emails. I'd taken no notes then. Hannah took no notes now.

"Is that all?" Her eyes gleamed, even though her tone was smartassed; it was a lot to ask of a baker. But at the same time, when she had the ability to name her price, details became inconsequential.

"No. One last demand. You can't create or cater cakes for any other event-planning company. We'll have your exclusivity during our business relationship and for two years after termination. A noncompete clause is built into the contract."

That rule was mine from the email volley. We weren't creating a business that everyone would crave to be a part of, only to have some copycat edge in as competition. Our suppliers needed to be exclusive. In exchange, they would be a part of something unique and amazing.

"What if one of your guests wants a cake for a birthday party?"

"If the client only wants a cake, and they call you direct, then it's acceptable. But no other party-planning company can hire your services."

She sat back then and looked out the window on to the empty street. We asked a lot. I was about to reveal something else that would likely make her balk. My instincts told me I could convince her to sign with us, but truly, when one didn't know the deeper motivations of the person you bargained with, anything could happen.

"There's one other thing." I waited until she pulled her attention back into the room.

She glanced at me but remained silent.

"We won't be doing any weddings. With you as our exclusive baker, you can't either."

Her eyes narrowed, as if I'd suddenly become the mean kid in the sandbox who'd yanked her favorite toy from her grasp. A loud foot tap began from beneath the table.

I'd dealt my final card then remained silent, stoic. *In the art of business war, he who speaks first, loses.*

"Why?" She leaned back, crossing her arms over her chest.

I kept my gaze locked to hers, unaffected by her coolness, sensing her interest.

I shrugged. "Not your concern at this point. It's the way we've decided to run things."

She scowled. "It *is* my concern. What you're suggesting isn't equitable and may be contractually illegal. If you want me to buy into such a harsh restriction, you need to give me a really good reason."

"It will be equitable and legal if we come to fair terms we both agree to. There are sound reasons from our company's standpoint, but the only one you need to be concerned with is that it exposes Invitation Only to too much risk."

Her eyes narrowed again for a split second. "Being exclusive to your company is one thing. The weddings I'll have to think about. And if I agree, the price will be steep for that kind of sacrifice."

"I'd expect so."

"I'll want to review my contract for a few days before making a decision."

My respect for her heightened as she played her hand with caution, but she'd said "my" contract. The possessive meant she already pictured herself in the role. *Perfect.*

"The contract I'll email gives you until 5:00 p.m. Monday." I leaned back. "I have one more stipulation."

An incredulous laugh burst from her. "Really? How many 'one mores' will there be?"

I smirked. "Just this one 'one more.'"

She arched a brow, waiting. Her lips pressed into a thin line.

"I need to taste test your current product." I didn't, really. But something about this paradox of a girl made me want to stay a little longer than necessary.

Humor gleamed in her eyes. She shook her head and finally gave into the smile threatening to break free. And just like that, her tough exterior melted to reveal a much warmer side beneath all the "prim and proper" of the former Ice Queen. Apparently, I'd been granted exclusive access behind the curtain in Oz.

She stood and nodded. "You can taste to your heart's content."

I followed her back to the kitchen, becoming increasingly aware that Hannah—Off-Limits Hannah—had some very appealing curves. The loose cotton shorts and shirt she wore clung to her body in an understated way, hiding nothing of the beauty beneath.

Gritting my teeth at my ogling her body in those uncontrolled seconds, I forced my attention onto stainless steel appliances and colorful rows of frosted cupcakes.

"Forgive my mess. I get out of control when I bake." She laughed, but this time, it was different, more relaxed. The action lit up her whole face.

Banishing all thoughts of Hannah's physical appearance, I glanced around at the product of what looked to be days and days of baking. "What's all this for?"

"Practice. I'm doing trial runs to see how much I can create in one morning and determine which products I want to sell."

My jaw slackened. "You did all this in one morning? By yourself?"

"Yep. Got here at four."

I whistled, impressed.

She pointed to the counter beside her. "These are chocolate cupcakes. Those are yellow cake with vanilla pudding in the middle. Behind you is red velvet with a dark chocolate cream cheese frosting I'm experimenting with. Will you try one of those?"

I examined the dark frosted cupcakes. They were the least decorated among the bunch, which made me feel slightly less guilty for destroying one.

As I lifted one from the counter, my mouth watered. I quickly peeled the wrapper away and bit off half the cupcake. I closed my eyes and moaned as tart and sweet flavors flooded my mouth. "Oh my God." My words were mumbled through a full mouth.

When I went to inhale the other half, she snatched it from my hand and put it aside. I nearly bit her hand off for the offense but snarled instead.

She grabbed my hand. "Don't gorge on just one. Try these others." Then she stopped suddenly, her running shoes squeaking on the floor. "Oh, wait. You need to cleanse your palate." She detoured to a large refrigerator stocked with cream, butter, and other baking ingredients, and pulled out a large bottle of Pellegrino.

I took a few sips, swished my mouth clean, and swallowed as she grasped my free hand and led me further down the stainless steel counter. Row after frosted row, I enjoyed the impromptu cupcake tasting. In the span of fifteen minutes, I'd sampled one of every kind of cupcake she had made, from carrot cake to crème brulee. On a serious sugar high, I'd officially entered a cupcake coma.

Her eyes sparkled with pride as I moaned for the final time and let a last bite of dark chocolate salted whisky caramel melt in my mouth.

I held my hand over my stomach, groaning. "Done. Do you have a white napkin? I wave it in surrender."

The thought occurred to me that I'd been played. We'd spelled out a list of demands, but Hannah had a secret weapon. No one made cakes like she did. She could call the shots. Demand anything she wanted. And after assaulting me with that kind of ammunition, I'd likely give her everything in my sugar-induced stupor.

When I glanced at her, though, no calculating businesswoman stared back at me. Only the smiling eyes of a young baker pleased with an enormously satisfied customer. Her ice-queen persona continued to perplex me, seeming at times to manifest in flashes during our business dealings, and yet none of it seemed as harsh as I'd remembered half a year ago.

Regardless, clearly she loved what she did. She would do well with her business, whatever her decision with our company was. We'd offered her a rare opportunity in highly influential social circles, but with her talent, she could do anything she set her mind to.

I remembered the empty display cases up front. The barren tables stacked in the corner. The bare, painted walls that made it seem like she'd just moved in. "When do you open to the public?"

"Not for another week."

"What are you planning to do with all of this?"

She shrugged. "Toss it, I guess."

My eyes must've popped out of my head because hers widened. I scanned the room at the hundreds of cupcakes. "No. You can't." The mere thought made my taste buds want to scream in protest. But the always-thinking business side of me hatched a plan.

"Whatever your plans for 10:00 a.m. tomorrow are, cancel them." That would give me enough sleep after closing tonight to function. With a quad espresso.

She scoffed, narrowing her eyes as she dropped her hands on her hips. "Excuse me? Why?"

"Because this—" I gestured around me with a wave of my hands "—is not trash. It's your investment in marketing."

Wide eyes blinked in surprise. She opened her mouth in confusion, but nothing came out before I continued.

"Do you have any business cards?"

She shook her head.

"Make some. Nothing fancy. Just your store name, the address, phone number. Your cupcakes will do all the rest."

I backed out the door before she could say no. I had a shitload of work to do before my shift tonight if I planned to take tomorrow morning off to help her.

And really, was it helping Hannah?

The way I saw it, she didn't see the potential of her business the way I did. And I could easily point her in the right direction. Her gratitude would be boundless. So actually, a donation of a few hours of my time on a Saturday morning helped with Invitation Only's goal.

Because after I gave her a glimpse of what smart business marketing could do, she'd want more. She'd want the full tour.

And that...would only come after she signed on the dotted line.

3. ADDICTION

"**Y**ou're a drug dealer."

"What?" Hannah gave an imperceptible scowl.

Those hints of her ice-queen demeanor—a brief flash of her furrowed brow and narrowed eyes—became more and more intriguing after experiencing her free-spirited Maestro side. I forced my gaze away from her face and onto the platter of cupcakes she held.

Dressed in what she called a "vintage" apron, which resembled a ruffled dress, she wore a basic black shirt beneath—but per my instructions, the top was low-cut, offering a peek at a tasteful amount of cleavage.

"Great top. Where's the skirt?" I'd asked her to wear a short skirt, but she wore tight jeans.

She dropped me a deadpan look. "I'm a cupcake peddler, not some Betty Crocker role-playing streetwalker."

It was all I could do not to burst out laughing. But she had a point. The jeans were a good choice.

I whispered as we walked, giving her last-minute instructions before we reached the large group of people standing in line at Curio, the most popular bistro in this quaint town. "Instead of throwing these delicious cupcakes away as experimental trash, you're giving potential customers a taste of heaven for free, and then a business card so they can pay the next time they need a hit of your drug."

Understanding dawned in her expression. "Instantly addicted."

I nodded. "Like me." I'd devoured three of the red velvet numbers before leaving her store this morning. Just because I helped her, which actually helped me, didn't mean I had to do it for free. Or on an empty stomach.

She gripped the edges of the platter, her knuckles turning white, as she gaped at the line of nearly two dozen people.

"Don't be nervous. You're going to be a sensation." *I hoped.*

No matter how incredible those little cupcakes were, it would still be a tough sell. They were waiting to go into a dining establishment for a lunch that, unless you had a reservation, you had to wait in line for, hoping to get a table. Zagat's rating had put them on the map. The kitchen's world-class-chef-turned-fashionable-bistro-owner didn't hurt.

We were up against gastronomic brilliance, and we risked alienating a neighbor business, but we could do this. The best marketing spin turned any challenge into a business opportunity. And if we handled it with a delicate touch, the restaurateur would be all the better for it.

I pressed a firm hand into the small of her back for reassurance but looped a finger through her apron tie, slowing us down. We strolled down the sidewalk until we hit the beginning of the line.

"Follow my lead," I whispered, tilting my head down for

her ears only. I turned to the first customer in line. "Would you like an *exclusive* first tasting of a cupcake sent from heaven?"

The woman wore a smart business suit. She shook her head but looked the platter over anyway.

I gently put pressure on Hannah's back, urging her forward. She leaned in, holding the tempting tray within scenting distance.

The woman licked her lips. "Well, maybe just one." She picked up the most extravagantly iced one on the platter. She peeled back a portion of the wrapper and took a small bite with bared teeth. A second and a half later, her moan caught the attention of three people behind her, and they all leaned to the side, trying to see what we were about.

I winked down at Hannah and urged her on to the next victim. And while her first instant, loyal customer took a second, much larger bite, she held out a hand to take the business card I offered. Hannah had done a tasteful job with the business cards. Ivory stationery. Black script. Nothing more on it than I'd suggested. Simple. Impactful. Perfect.

Next was a graying man who stood with a folded *Wall Street Journal* under his arm. Definitely not the cupcake type.

Only a few seconds ticked by before Hannah jumped right in, assessing the cool customer and seizing on the best angle to gain his interest. She leaned forward ever so slightly, making maximum use of the two stunning assets God had given her.

Smart girl.

"Would you mind trying one of my cupcakes?" She made it sound like a plea for his help.

"Of course." He cleared his throat after his voice cracked. And seconds later, after he made his choice, he sounded his approval. Even stuffy old men were not immune to her charms, or her cupcakes.

And so it went. Not one of Curio's customers passed on the rare opportunity we offered to have an initial taste for free. And all of them made sounds of ecstasy, like they'd been marooned in a cupcake-free world their entire lives and had been given their very first morsel.

With an empty platter tucked under her arm, and enough cupcakes passed out to feed the entire line plus three passersby, Hannah smiled wide, nearly vibrating with excitement.

I grinned—couldn't help it. Her happiness was contagious. "Well, what do you think?"

In a startling flash of movement, she grabbed my hand and lunged down the sidewalk toward her shop, yanking me alongside her at a jogging pace.

Unable to stop myself, I laughed, letting her drag me along. She'd discovered what good marketing could accomplish, and *she'd* become addicted with her very first hit.

When we reached her door, she slammed into it, and with my hand attached to her death grip, I crashed into her. Breaking free of her hold, I tempered my impact by shooting my arms up onto the doorframe.

She stilled, her key halfway into the lock.

We were pressed against each other in a compromising position, and it struck us both.

I dropped my head down, resting my head against the windowpane, unable to move—only able to breathe. And her delicate scent wafted up. Tropical. Enticing. I closed my eyes, fighting the urge to stay. And losing.

She swallowed. I heard it.

I felt her turn around and drop the platter to her side as

it brushed my hip. I opened my eyes to find hers closed as she pressed her soft body up against me.

She inhaled deeply, and her body shuddered.

"Cade, I..." She opened her greenish eyes with those little flecks of gold in them. Uncertainty washed across her expression.

I exhaled but didn't move. This was so off-limits. But the fact that I couldn't have her suddenly made me want her all the more. "*Fuck.*" I pulled away. Shook my head.

Cold air flooded between us, breaking the spell we'd both fallen under when we hadn't been paying attention. Hannah looked surprised, like she couldn't believe I'd rejected her like that.

"I can't, Hannah."

She nodded furiously, like she agreed. But I could tell as her expression hardened and she turned to slide the key into the lock with a shaking hand that she struggled with her emotions.

I put my hands on her shoulders, stopping her from pushing in through the now-open door. "Hannah, it's not you. Trust me, it's not. I'm..."

Fighting my attraction had been difficult enough. Knowing she also felt the pull made our working together dangerous. I needed her help to keep our dealings purely professional.

Her voice trembled. "You want me? You feel it too? I..."

Ah, fuck. Hearing her repeat my thoughts made this excruciating. *Figures.* The first girl who challenged my mind, in addition to physically attracting me, would be the one I couldn't pursue. Damned "no doing the help" rule.

I exhaled, counting to five. "Yeah, but I...we...can't. Not only would it be a really bad idea, based on past experience, I promised my sisters. It's as good as a sworn blood oath." I ground out the words, shocked I could form coherent sentences with my blood flooding much farther south from my brain cells.

I clenched my fists, digging my nails into my palms while I eased back, putting a good couple of feet between us. In desperation, I vowed to maintain said safe minimum distance at all times.

Slowly, she turned to face me again. Confident, proud, a woman now in charge of herself, body and mind, Hannah nodded. "I promise too. No matter our attraction, we keep it strictly business."

I blew out a fast breath through tight lips. "Good. With you and me both working on that, it'll be a lot easier."

A slow smile crept onto her face, a devilish gleam sparking in her eyes. "Oh? You mean if I didn't play along, things could get difficult for you?"

My face fell. She wouldn't. Would she?

She placed a palm on my chest, smiling sweetly. "It's okay, Cade. I promise not to tease you...too much."

Dammit. Just when I thought I had my shit together, something (or someone) proved me wrong. I silently cursed fate for throwing me into this situation. But I was unable to do anything but suck it up and deal, so I followed her inside and back into her kitchen.

She pulled a second, larger silver platter up from a shelf beneath one of her long counters and began loading the first tray with a balanced assortment of cupcakes. "Well, don't just stand there—help me stock up. You're carrying one this time. That was amazing, by the way. You're a genius. They all wanted a card."

I blindly obeyed her, lining cupcakes onto the platter, giving my body time to rush blood back into my brain so I could think rationally. *Business. Focus on her business.* "And those people are your walk-in customers. Pennies. You want the big bucks? Solicit backdoor business: hotels and restaurants. They could be your biggest regular customers and might mean the difference between your survival and failure."

Pausing with a cupcake in midtransfer, she gave me one of those world-class scowls again. "I thought you wanted my exclusivity."

"We do. As the team member of an event-planning company. But you can still supply cakes and cupcakes as menu items for restaurants and hotels who don't have a pastry chef and want to outsource."

"Oh." She blinked, processing my suggestion as she returned to loading her tray.

While making sure to load two of each kind, I glanced beyond her at the enormous cake with green icing that I'd watched her finish yesterday. "What's that one for?"

She looked up as I pointed. A blush spread along her cheeks. "For me."

Confused, I cocked my head.

"I wanted to create a dragon. That's part of the body."

All I saw was a rectangle. "Where's the rest of it?"

"In my head. It's so intricate that I wanted to get the scales right before moving on to the detail in the tail, the claws on the arms and legs, the webbing in the wings, and finally the head, complete with horns and flames coming from its flaring nostrils."

"Wow." Based on the beautiful scales she'd done on the body, I imagined the final cake. "Where will you serve it?"

She tilted her head to the side, her gaze unfocused. "Not sure. If I accept your offer, I won't have a chance for anyone to see it unless one of your clients requests a dragon."

My attention focused on only one of her words. "*If* you accept our offer?"

"I haven't even read the contract yet."

I lifted her loaded platter, shoving it in front of her, forcing her to take it with her hands. "Well, hurry up, Ms. Martin. We have more unwitting customers to ensnare in our cupcake trap. And I have to make you feel so indebted to me for my brilliant assistance that you have no choice but to say yes."

"*You're* indebted to *me*, smartass. You've eaten how many cupcakes?"

Unable to think of a quick retort to her valid point, I blinked. Then my thoughts clarified, and I dropped a bomb. "I expect you to read that contract the moment you return home today. I've moved our deadline for your response up to tomorrow noon."

Her tone was instantly glacial. "If that's your decision, then it's a no."

While walking out of her kitchen, I stumbled as my mind processed her words. I spun back around and leaned my filled tray back toward her. "I'm sorry. Did you want the invaluable marketing and business advice to stop?"

Her eyes narrowed. "No."

I arched a brow. "Then that's a yes?"

"No." She took a deep breath and sighed, nodding toward the front of the shop. "That's a yes for you helping me now. A maybe for me helping you later."

"Sunday. Noon," I pushed.

She gave me a steady stare. "We'll see."

I exhaled a breath, relieved we were back on track again. Note to self: Hardball tactics bring out the Ice Queen.

4. NIGHT SHIFT

The rain had dissipated by the time my wheels hit the pavement that night for my shift at Loading Zone. Shiny reflections lit up Philly's revived Old City Arts District where I called home four nights a week, for at least the next few months anyway.

Fifteen minutes from my house wasn't bad. The ride was twenty to Kristen's. Ninety to Mom and Dad's on Fifth. Twelve to Sweet Dreams. Yeah, my head constantly spat out numbers. No surprise, the last was a hot little number I hadn't been able to stop thinking about all day.

I shook my head, clearing it of all things Hannah. Random thoughts had never skewed my focus before, and I refused to let an unexpected reaction to a girl I barely knew send it haywire. My world needed to remain exactly the way it was.

By the time I turned my bike down the back alley and eased between Ben's Escalade and our bartender Lisa's Smart Car—yeah, we got the irony, figuring the two cancelled each other out in Energy Karma Points—my head had cleared. The cool night air after a steady drizzle for the better part of the day helped too. Something about that heavy mineral tang in the air made me inhale deeply and feel reset again.

I parked my bike. Two wide-angle security cameras and three floodlights bathed the space. We wanted it bright as daylight to keep the vehicles parked in our six spaces as secure as possible. Barbacks coming and going with empties to recycle and trash to toss, not to mention rotations of our security staff, also kept the perimeter of our building secure.

My gaze fell on the rusty, disintegrating sign that had inspired Loading Zone's name. At Kiki's insistence, we'd had the thing sprayed with some kind of matte-finish coating to prevent further decay. But all the red lettering was intact on the white backdrop. I grinned, remembering how too many beers and lack of inspiration had us all sitting on crates out back tossing rocks at the sign in target practice before our name epiphany struck.

My smile faded when I noticed the back door was ajar. Again. I strode over and yanked it open, kicked the rock aside, and let it slam shut behind me.

"Ben, the back door was wide open again!" My shout bounced along the polished concrete floors and steel paneling to reach Ben's office and his all-hearing ears, even over the loud music pulsing from up front.

Ben glanced up from the scattered paperwork on his desk. "Yeah, yeah, I know. Tracy's been in and out stocking and told me she'd secure it when she's done."

It was well past nine. Stocking should've been done hours ago. "Well, either she forgot, or she's the slowest worker in the world and needs to be fired. I'm a bad guy. I have a gun. I just emptied your safe and shot you 'cause I got sloppy and you saw my face." I dropped a finger gun his direction and fired it with a snap of my wrist. "Bang. You're dead."

He gave me a dramatic eye roll. "Fine. I'll have another talk with her."

"Good idea," I said over my shoulder as I left, heading into the employee area.

It took me exactly ninety seconds to change into the black, tight T-shirt we all wore, stash my stuff in the locker, and be behind the bar, filling my first order.

Lisa was a blur of motion, filling the orders of people already packed into the club. And without skipping a beat, I entered my Zen Zone—my private domain of Loading Zone —thinking about nothing but the next drink. This wasn't work for me—it was stress relief.

I didn't let pressure get to me here; I had plenty of that kind of demand at school. No drama made it into my ears, nor rumors past my lips. I tried my damnedest to remain a personable Switzerland, and everyone knew and respected me for it.

I filled my first tickets, which were electronically delivered on tablet screens mounted to the bar, as I rattled off beautiful numbers in my head. *Two Silver Bullets: buck a piece. Vodka Tonic: two. Strawberry Daiquiri, Cosmo, and Screaming Orgasm shooters: three each.*

No, I wasn't counting points. Sure as shit wasn't calculating drink prices. Each pretty calculation was our take per drink in dollars. I owned a piece of this cash cow, and whenever I made drinks, I saw dollar signs flowing into our pockets. For simplicity, we created our prices from how much net we could make off of a sale. And I rounded things up or down in my head.

It was a game I played to pass the time, but it made every night I worked fly by. And we raked in the dough like nobody's business. Seriously. No one else in our vicinity made as much money as we did. Because we didn't get greedy with our prices, we ran a clean bar, and made the patrons happy.

And as it turned out, the rusted-metal industrial look happened to be eco-chic. Who knew? Kiki, apparently. Rather than throw out decaying twisted sheets of metal in the small warehouse, she repurposed it all. It covered the bar top, the walls in several places (but let the worn red brick show through in others), and even lined the walls up three feet from the floor in the bathrooms.

And don't get me started on the bathrooms. Troughs of molded steel sprayed with a protective coating *to protect the rust*—works of art according to Kiki—formed the sinks, with motion-sensor faucets made to look like spigots pouring from the wall.

Maple-wood accents and concrete floors that had been roughed up to prevent slipping, along with all of the rest of her suggested décor, made the place just the right amount of "shabby" according to Kiki. The customers, and all their flowing money, resoundingly agreed. So did *Architectural Digest*, *Design Magazine*, and *Coco Eco Magazine*, who'd clamored to do feature articles before and around our opening.

That was almost seven months ago. Things flowed seamlessly now. My role remained as mostly a silent partner and part-time bartender. I'd fronted a larger monetary investment to be out of the spotlight and work when I wanted, with the luxury to stop working anytime I decided. Ben put in less money and ran the place as he saw fit, taking the more visible role. Our third partner, my dad, stayed relatively undisclosed and uninvolved. The amount of money we made kept him a very silent and an extremely satisfied investor.

"Hey, Cade."

Flirty and sexy Jillian walked up to the bar, displaying her pushed-up rack for my approval. Which she didn't in any way need, but it was our thing.

"Lookin' fine, Jill Baby." The same words were exchanged every night. But it made her beam with happiness, which made me smile, cementing the positive ritual between us.

Her T-shirt was a black, ultrathin baby tee, standard-issue ripped like all the girls' shirts to reveal a glimpse of the hot-pink pushup lace that cupped her perky C's. No, I'd never personally verified that fact. Yes, my eyes, hands, and mouth could nail with accuracy the cup size of any woman. But in this case, she was an employee.

And Ben and I had taken our hiring process very seriously. First, we established written guidelines, then agreed not to vary from them. All the waitresses had to be C, D, or DD cups. Not smaller or larger. Then, among those candidates, they needed letters of recommendation from a former employer but couldn't have worked for more than two of our competitors. They also had to have a great personality that never slipped during their shift, be honest and loyal to a fault, and serve drinks to a customer's satisfaction like their life depended on it.

Not too much to ask, really. We demanded a lot from those we employed. We also paid them handsomely for it. Not many bar owners gave their employees—every last one of them, from the bartenders to the janitors—a percentage of the take.

But we did.

It had always seemed a sound theory of mine, one I'd tossed around to my dad on our occasional talks. He seemed impressed with the notion every time I'd brought it up but had never heard it in practice before. Now he was a part of the test run in action.

Our experimental gamble paid off. We didn't earn less by giving away more. We made more. *Hand-over-fist more.* Amazing how motivated every cog in the machine became when a portion of every dollar flowed into their pockets just like it did ours, in an appropriate percentage to their level of contribution and ranking, of course. But it didn't matter how much one received compared to others in our company. Even the barbacks and janitors made way more than any competitor offered.

Happy employees equaled happy customers which, in turn again, equaled happy employees. The sound business theory had proven itself in practice.

Damn. 10:30 p.m. The time seemed to drag tonight. *Kamikaze shooter: three bucks. A dozen Sex on the Beach shots: thirty-six bucks?*

I glanced up at April, another one of our waitresses, then pointedly at the drinks, opening my hands up in question. She grinned. "Bachelorette party."

"Niiice. Keep 'em happy, my friend."

She winked. "Always do."

April picked up the tray, and I watched her tight ass weave through the crowd in those low-cut jeans. No, I didn't want to tap that fine body. It was pure common sense from an owner's perspective that we did not fraternize with the employees. It also fell under the no-drama, no-gossip personal clauses I had. I'd even inserted the rule into our business plan, and Ben had agreed, adopting the standard as well.

I'd never once thought about breaking that rule. And nothing in the world would ever make me. I enjoyed the bar too much. Was proud of what we'd accomplished, taking it from a figment of our drunken imaginations one night into a larger-than-life reality.

All of a sudden, one of the five members of our security team blurred by, sprinting through the crowd, using his big hands to safely move unsuspecting patrons out of his way. I scanned ahead and saw his target. A group of rowdy college-aged guys had their hands on Mandy. She struggled to break free, but the stronger men overpowered her, tossing her around like their personal plaything.

It took every ounce of willpower I had to remain behind the bar. Any occurrence like that always did. With a clenched jaw and my hands gripped around the steel rail below the counter, I watched as Trey expertly diffused the situation.

Our security teams had been trained by the best in the industry. Trey knew the key was to calmly address the belligerent customers and remind them of the consequences, or *deliver* them, depending on the circumstances. Sometimes they listened. Sometimes their egos got ahead of their common sense.

A punch was thrown. Trey grabbed Mandy, shoved her to safety behind his back, and took the punch but turned slightly, allowing the blow to glance off his cheekbone. Then he locked both hands around the guy's wrist while it still shot through the air and twisted his arm around.

Trey leaned his face into the guy's ear, no doubt listing out the next requirements of his continued ability to breathe. The cavalry arrived seconds later, each covering a rowdy friend, subduing them before a full fight broke out. Only customers within a ten-foot radius were aware of the skirmish, just the way we liked to keep it. Dance music still thumped, drinks still flowed, and everyone still had a great time. Well, everyone except for those four idiots who were now being escorted out the door.

We'd established rules for the hiring of our security too. Level heads and experience in handling people with a minimal amount of force were a must, but they each had another valuable talent: excellent memories. Two of them had near-photographic retention. All knew not to ever rely on that talent, however. Identifications were documented, names and descriptions of crowd disrupters added to the list. If you ever got kicked out? You never got back in.

Respect. Simple. Not everyone understood the concept. You either had it, or you didn't. We had plenty of other customers to protect and refused to allow rude assholes to affect their good time.

Over the next hours, I lost myself in pouring drinks, making small talk to those occupying the ten stools at the bar, and observing the crowd at large like I always did. The night finally ended at 2:00 a.m., and I cut out right on time, more tired than usual.

Rubbing the back of my neck as I made my way to my bike, I remembered why I was so tired. I'd gotten up early. Even earlier the day before.

And the reason why I got up early on both days? Hannah.

Fuck. There goes my Zen.

5. THE LIST

Sunday night, play-by-play action flashed brightly on the big screen across my living room, but I didn't care. I dropped my forearm over my eyes to block out the light and did my best to ignore the noise.

Carmen made her presence known for the umpteenth time, sidling her ass between my body and the edge of the couch, carving a space for herself in inches that hadn't been left for her. Irritated, I growled and scooted back, giving her enough room to sit where she hadn't been invited, propping my body at an angle on my hip, wedging my ass into the crack of the couch.

She claimed my bicep as a pillow, and I lost my arm (and the last quarter of the beer, in the now-useless hand attached to it).

At the soft sound of clinking glass getting louder, I shot my free arm up from my eyes, knowing my roommate Mason brought in refills. "Mase, beer me."

A cold wet bottle filled my palm seconds later, and I leaned my head up, bringing the rim to my lips to take several swallows. I shifted the bottle's neck between my fingers and dropped my arm over my eyes again, blocking out the rest of the world as best I could without moving off the couch.

"What's got him so broody?" A sweet voice rose above a blaring insurance commercial, belonging to Stacy, a girl Ben had started seeing.

A snort came from Ben. "That's not broody. He's grumpy."

Right he was. I didn't brood.

"What are you now, the three dwarfs?" Laura, Mase's girlfriend, added the snarky comment two seconds before her squeal pierced the room.

I cracked open an eye, tilting my head to see right as she tried to dodge Mason, who was already airborne in a lunge. He nailed her, and she rolled helplessly before he pinned her to the rug. "You know there's nothing dwarf about me." He growled into her neck. "Do you need a repeat demonstration during halftime?"

Ben shouted at the TV, "Aw, come on!"

Sighing, I tuned out the racket. I wasn't in the mood. Hannah had defined me as a player. A more accurate definition would be a man who'd been fractured—and was attempting to cope. And yet, mind-numbing sex with Carmen, my version of therapy, hadn't pulled me out of the shitty day I'd had. Although God and Carmen both knew I'd valiantly tried.

My only other distraction was the football game, but it sucked ass in the first quarter, which only heated my temper further.

The cascade started earlier when the noon deadline passed. No contract had been faxed. My email box sat empty. No missed calls or voicemail. When I rode my bike over to Hannah's store, the lights were out, the shop locked up tight. My half dozen calls and two voicemails had gone unanswered.

Had Hannah and I crossed that fine line between business and personal? Barely. More like the line got blurred. But then we'd forced it into clear business focus. Or so I'd thought.

In hindsight, Hannah had always been the Ice Queen, even if the persona was only a mask. Why had I expected anything different? The fact that I had and got blindsided meant I'd been played. And lost.

And I didn't like losing.

Kristen expected me to deliver her a team player. They all had. And even though I'd moved the deadline up a day, it had become crystal clear that instead of spending tomorrow doing intensive research for a school paper due that afternoon, I would be scrambling to find a last-minute replacement for Invitation Only's baker.

Nothing I could do about it on a Sunday night, though. I blew out another lungful of stagnant air, downed the rest of my beer before dropping it against the cushions, and sank deeper into the couch, hoping to numb out with sleep.

Sometime later, Carmen moved off my arm and I fell forward. I stretched out onto my stomach, claiming the rest of the couch in a face-plant.

"I wouldn't do that, Carmen," Ben said, his voice low.

The warning in his tone made me crack open my eyes, but Carmen had propped up against the couch, and I couldn't see anything beyond her wavy red hair.

"Shut it. He has full access to my pants. It's a given." Carmen's feisty retort made no sense.

"Your funeral," Ben replied, louder.

Alarm bells rang inside my head, starting to penetrate the grogginess of my brain.

"*What the fuck?*" Carmen's screech sliced through the haze.

I shoved against the couch, pushing upright. "What the fuck's goin' on?"

My snarl silenced the room, game announcers giving play-by-plays the only sound amid the tension. Carmen made a show of standing and turning to face me. She held my opened wallet in one hand and a yellow, three-inch sticky note square in the other.

"Your room. Now." Her brows furrowed over sparking blue eyes.

"No." My irritation escalated. She knew what frame of mind I was in, and yet she still poked a waking bear.

"You don't want to do this out here." Her feistiness flared into rare form.

My lips curled into a sneer. "Yes, I do."

"Fine. Want to tell me what this is?" She held up the slip of paper, like she'd found incriminating evidence.

"You know what it is." She'd always known. All my girls did. That was the deal. If they wanted some of me, they agreed to be one of a handful of girls who I had a good time with. No commitments. No attachments. Only fun. To play, they had to understand and subscribe to the rules.

"There are nine names with numbers on this list." She held the thing high in the air, then flipped it over with a flick of her wrist for the silent jury of four in the room to see.

I didn't glance up at her stolen prize. I glared at her as I held her eyes. "Eight."

She tossed the thing at me. It hit my chest and fell into my lap. "Nine. I counted. Twice."

"There *were* nine." My voice remained calm, lowered. "Now there are eight."

With a heavy blink, recognition wiped the smug look off

her face. In an instant, tears welled in her eyes. "You don't mean that."

"I do. Now, get out. You should've heeded Ben's warning."

Trust didn't come easy to me. Not one of those nine knew the depths of betrayal I'd survived. The list existed for a reason. When I needed reliable therapy, they provided. Every one of them knew the score, and all had agreed to it. In fact, they didn't make the cut in the first place unless they'd expressed a need for the same, unprompted by me.

But when things changed, smart people rolled with the punches. Women, the more sensitive of our species, let their emotions overrule their brains. There was enough blame to go around though; maybe I'd been asleep at the wheel and hadn't noticed subtle changes, possessive warning signs.

Enraged, Carmen tore my shirt off her body and threw it across the living room, growling in frustration. Naked from the waist up, she made a bouncing spectacle of herself as she ran off. I heard several thuds, imagining objects being tossed around in my bedroom while she found her scattered pieces of clothing.

My gaze fell to the list in my lap. I picked it up, examining it. Four on one side, five on the other. Nine reliable (and quite spectacular) fuck buddies who'd agreed to a good time with no strings attached. Now there were eight.

A flash of movement blurred by, followed by the slam of our front door.

As pictures rattled on the walls of our entry hall, I stood. "Yeah, I'm done. Hope I didn't ruin game night." Walking out of the room, I sighed.

Mase called out from behind me, "Nah, man. It's all good."

On a detour through the kitchen, I grabbed two more

bottles and headed back to my room. My mind felt smothered. I slowly closed my door, unable to feel anything more than tired, the anger somehow dissipating out of me.

Chugging down half of one bottle, I placed the other on my nightstand. I held the list between two fingers and swiped my cell phone off my desk before falling back onto the bed.

Apathy hadn't created the list. Indifference hadn't been at play then—self-preservation had. Superficial pleasure helped bury the pain. Had the rules of the game changed? Maybe. Perhaps enough time had passed for me to reassess what the fuck I'd been doing with my life.

For a couple of years, I'd been going through the motions, but I hadn't been living. Hadn't wanted to. Stay busy enough and reality doesn't look as dark. Focus on all the shiny so you don't see the grime underneath.

In a sudden cleansing moment, I needed to find out where the rest of the girls stood. I wasn't ready to ditch the list altogether, but I didn't want a repeat of tonight's unnecessary drama. If the girls wanted physical release when the occasion warranted, we were still on the same page, or rather, they were still on the yellow sticky note. Otherwise, a culling of the list would begin.

Decided, I clicked the control button on my phone. Nothing happened. I furrowed my brow as I held the power button down to reboot. I vaguely remembered hitting random buttons hours earlier, trying to mute texts chirping in from Ben while Carmen and I were finding our mutual release.

When the phone flared back to life, I entered my passcode and stared at the apps. Yeah, I saw the irony right there in my hand; I could've hidden those girls behind a locked screen in my phone.

Maybe on paper, the list had served as a booby trap for the untrustworthy girl. Carmen certainly failed that test. Or maybe, on a subconscious level, I'd wanted to sabotage my happy, shallow escape.

Before I gave more ammunition to my self-deprecation, my focus got stuck on my phone app. A number three appeared in the red alert circle. When I touched the app, it showed two missed calls from a number I didn't recognize and one voicemail, none of which had been there when I'd last checked hours ago.

Unthinking, I clicked on the voicemail.

"Hello, Cade. I read your agreements. The terms aren't equitable to both parties. Expect a counter offer. It will be delivered by 5:00 p.m. tomorrow, per the deadline still in writing in your contract."

After the second replay of Hannah's message, I grinned. The Ice Queen was back, but the ball was still in play.

And the list?

Long forgotten.

6. BLURRED LINES

Monday afternoon, I left campus at 3:50 p.m. and had plenty of time to grab a bite at home before heading over to Sweet Dreams, and yet, I ate nothing. For some stupid reason, I was nervous before our business meeting. Although Invitation Only's concept had been Kristen's idea after the renovation of her barn, and therefore her baby to take the lead on, I made it clear to her that the follow-up meeting was mine once Hannah had agreed to negotiate. Kristen agreed, wisely leaving the negotiations in my capable hands.

Extreme punctuality had always calmed me in an oh-so-OCD way, so I grabbed my laptop and the printed copies of the agreements and shoved them into my messenger bag before heading over to Hannah's.

Pre-rush-hour traffic was so light, I slipped into the end space in front of Hannah's shop inside of ten minutes. I glanced at my watch: 4:15 p.m. Undaunted by what she might think of my encroaching on her time, I stepped through the front door of Sweet Dreams.

The empty display case and stacked chairs all remained

the same, with the bistro set remaining exactly as we'd left it, ready and waiting for our meeting. I took a seat, pulled out my laptop, and set the bag on the floor.

"You're early," a disembodied voice called out from the kitchen, tone flat.

"Got Wi-Fi?"

Unintelligible words were mumbled from the back, but I flipped open my laptop and it fired up, hooking into Hannah's Wi-Fi like a charm.

Calm washed over me as I typed away on a business theory paper.

Yes, business theory.

Actually, it was a subtopic I'd requested in my Entrepreneurship and Venture Initiation class. The instructor was cool and gave me some leeway off syllabus as long as I met the core requirements of the class. Considering myself a budding entrepreneurial philosopher, business theory had become a hobby of mine, and I was interested in further exploring the subject for feedback.

Hannah appeared from the back at exactly 5:00 p.m.

I glanced up after I finished typing out a thought.

Holy shit.

She wore black, thigh-high stiletto boots, a black mini skirt, and a corset-style top. Her hair was down, long brunette waves flowing down her shoulders. I forced my gaze up to her face. Her expression was all business—hardened, actually—as if she was testing me.

Nice move.

But I'd been negotiating since I'd learned how to talk, thanks to my dad's unorthodox father–son lessons. Tearing my attention away from her, I took a head-clearing breath, saved my business theory paper, and pulled up electronic copies of the agreements. I would've pulled out my printed versions, but I noticed she'd brought sets of her own.

When she sat down, she held a pair of folded glasses in one hand and two clipped packets in the other. She pulled her chair closer to the table and leaned toward me, sliding one of the packets over.

She put on the glasses, and I had to stop myself from entertaining a sexy librarian fantasy. "On top is the agreement I've signed—with revisions I won't waver from. I also added in my fees. Although it seemed sensible to charge by the hour for my time, I took an estimation of the hours and materials in various scenarios and gave you a range depending on the circumstances. There will be a flat rate charged for each event, and it will be quoted within forty-eight hours of notice."

I nodded, listening and understanding. All reasonable. I scanned through her revised contract, noting every word change. I knew, because I'd created it. "You got anything to drink?"

Her eyes widened, likely because I hadn't balked yet. "Sure." She got up and went to the back.

Business required a calm mind and tough negotiations, when warranted. It also required plenty of hydration to keep the brain cells firing.

She brought me a chilled Pellegrino in the bottle then took her seat again. I took a few swallows while flipping to the second page.

Hannah crossed her legs but sat there in silence, waiting.

When I'd identified a third talking point, I reached down and grabbed my yellow lined notepad, unclipped the pen attached to it, and flipped to a fresh page. I wrote down my thoughts, then continued.

About fifteen minutes later, I finished reading the four-page counterproposal. I folded the pages back into their order and glanced at the Confidentiality and Noncompete Agreement she'd included in the packet before looking up at her.

"I didn't alter that agreement," she said before I could ask.

"Good." I picked it up from the table, flipped through the pages to confirm she'd initialed and signed in all the appropriate places, then slid it into my bag.

I leaned back in my chair, shifting my gaze back to hers. "You have valid points. I'm agreeable to all your terms—except for one."

She looked at me without emotion. Her demeanor suggested it didn't matter which one was unacceptable, either because she didn't care a great deal about any single one, or they were all important enough to be deal breakers.

Knowing how to read the signals in any negotiation was paramount to winning one. It was like the perfect game of poker. Anyone could play decent hands and bluff. A good player had to study their opponents' body language and make their next move accordingly.

I took her tells into consideration before speaking my next words, countering the one sticking point we were predictably going to butt heads on. "No weddings."

Yeah, I didn't give a fuck. That was a deal breaker for me. She would accept it, or we would find another cake maker. Was it personal? Yes. Were there sound business reasons? Absolutely.

Her head cocked slightly to the right, but her gaze never left mine. She focused on reading me too. "Why would you care whether or not I make wedding cakes?"

I shrugged, easing back into the chair which creaked under the pressure. "I don't. You can make cakes for whomever you choose. But if you want to be a part of Invitation Only, you'll work with us exclusively with regard to events. A wedding is an event."

"It doesn't have to be me 'working' for them or with them. I could just be the cake supplier. They order, I supply."

"No."

She narrowed those darkened hazel eyes at me, hiding them behind thick black lashes. I understood her irritation over the point. Weddings were the stuff of girls' dreams. She named her store Sweet Dreams for Christ's sake. Like all women, she got caught up in the fantasy painted into their minds by commercialism—manipulated by the billions-of-dollars-a-year industry.

Kudos to the wedding industry.

But not from me. I wasn't ensnared by the hype. Nothing pretty went on there. The entire pretense was only to provide momentary escape from the guests' lives onto the shoulders of one couple's stress and dollars under the guise of a "celebration."

I waited while she regarded me under that scrutinizing gaze.

Her move. Nothing on Earth would make me speak first. Or budge on the one point.

"I will provide cakes to hotels."

I blinked. The left-field comment lost me. "What?"

"Hotels and resorts. I will provide cakes to them. They're my backdoor business, as you so aptly pointed out. You were the one who argued I couldn't ignore my biggest money-maker. If I have to give up working with all other event companies to remain exclusive to Invitation Only, including those that throw lucrative weddings, then I claim any and all business directly from a hotel and resort as fair game."

I cocked my head.

She leaned forward.

Her meaning registered a split second before my protest hit my lips.

In calm confidence, she clarified her point. "Even if it's for a wedding."

I shook my head. "No."

An empty laugh. "Is that the only word you know?"

I smirked. "No."

She crossed her arms, pressing them into the pert breasts already spilling over the corset. Really? Who the hell wears that shit to a business meeting? *Clearly a female angling to win*, I thought as I tore my eyes away from her absent neckline and met her eyes.

Now she smirked. "My contact will only be the hotel staff. No communications with any event planners. You said yourself it would be business suicide not to solicit the resort industry."

Cunning. Using my own words against me. I didn't make a habit of arguing with myself, even if someone else spouted off the quoted material.

"Fine."

"Fine?" She pulled her arms away, surprise widening her eyes.

I chuckled. "Don't get used to it, Maestro. And you cannot attend those events. You want to be a supplier to the resorts? You supply the cake. Nothing else. No deliveries by you in person, and no attending any of the events."

She leaned back in her chair, shaking her head. "No. You obviously don't understand what I do. I create works of art. I deliver and set up. You agree to that, or we have no deal."

I took a deep breath. "I can't agree to that." The whole point of keeping her interactions away from other event-planning companies was to minimize the risk of her forming any kind of relationship with another company. That's how business ideas and clients got stolen.

Her eyes narrowed. "Can't or won't?"

I smiled. She was still in the game. She just didn't realize it. And the next words out of my mouth could make the difference between her continued interest or her withdrawing entirely. "What if we don't sign the contract yet? How about we do a trial run with our first party?"

She tilted her head to the side, gaze holding mine. "Why would we do that?"

"Consider it a good-faith act on both our parts. We'll get to see how each other operates. I'm hoping you'll come around to our side of the fence. And I don't have the authority on my own to alter such an important contract point."

I knew the whole thing sounded harsh, but this wasn't coming from just me. The Founding Foursome of Invitation Only had pounded these additional rules and details out over a fierce game of Monopoly. And that shit was set in stone.

"I'll agree to that."

"Good. Why don't I make the changes we've agreed upon and destroy the ones you've already signed?"

She nodded. "That sounds okay."

I took the contracts back out and tore them in half. Deal sealed. Well, almost. But I felt confident her signature on the new dotted line was only a technicality.

After a solid handshake, I typed furiously on my laptop, making the revisions to the contract with our agreed-upon amendments. I tried not to notice the generous amount of toned thigh Hannah revealed between the tops of her boots and the bottom of her skirt every time she shifted her legs, recrossing them.

By the third time, I stopped typing midsentence and raised a brow, not bothering to take my eyes off the screen. "I noticed. A man would have to be blind not to." Then I leaned back, removing the laptop that obstructed a full view, and glanced over, taking a good long look, deciding two could play at her game.

She sucked in a breath as my gaze lingered at the juncture of where those thighs met.

I imagined what she had on underneath there, probably some lacy black thong. I let my thoughts drift over what treasure lay waiting beneath the thong and licked my lips. Slowly scanning up from there, I made plans of how I would take my time working my tongue up her body until I reached those gorgeous tits before setting them free from that confining material.

On a deep inhale, I thought about the deep pink tips hardening for my touch and raised my gaze further, to those matching full lips that would be parted on a moan. By the time my gaze met hers, those beautiful green eyes had darkened, dilated.

Oh, fuck yeah. No line had been crossed. The off-limits zone hadn't even blurred. The damn thing had been obliterated.

Ignoring the hardening demand behind my fly, I focused my thoughts and calmed my hammering pulse. Now all Hannah could see was a collected exterior, which was all she needed to know.

Her lips pursed, and she let out a slow breath.

I chuckled and returned to the matter at hand, lifting my laptop screen and finishing the amendments. Business first.

But the rest?
Game. On.

7. BEER AND CAKE

"That is *not* a holiday." Kiki stood in the center of the room, hands on her hips, standing behind an imaginary line she'd drawn in Kristen's antique looped rug. Anti-sports Kiki.

My Seahawks had won, and we were going to the Super Bowl. It was *so* a holiday.

"All in favor of the event?" I didn't pull punches. On my side of the line were die-hard football fans. In my peripheral vision, I saw Kristen's and Kendall's arms shoot up in the air.

"The 'ayes' have it. You, my dear artistic soul, are overruled."

Kiki rolled her eyes in the cute way she always did and stormed to my favorite corner of the couch. I almost let her have it, but then I casually walked over and sat on her.

She became a spider beneath a boulder, arms flailing. It was only when I fell over, grunting from an elbow jab in the ribs, that she settled down, relishing her small victory with a grin while huffing to catch her breath.

Giving Kiki a moment to bask in the glory of her territory nab, I grabbed my Fat Tire from the table and flopped into the other corner. The cushion wasn't near as flattened on this end. Maybe I needed to break in a new side.

I grinned, sighing. For as much trouble as my sisters had been growing up, I truly relaxed being here with them among family. More than mere blood ties, they were true friends and protectors and had my back no matter what.

Even if I did keep secrets from them.

Hannah was developing into a big one.

Guys didn't share feelings. Not with other guys. Definitely not with sisters. It's why we invented locker-room talk. If we couldn't share our inner touchy-feely, you're damn right we'd share the conquests. Without an outlet, guys might burst out crying in random places, like walking down the sidewalk during rush hour, from the pressure of being bottled up.

And that embarrassing shit ain't right.

"You seal the deal with Hannah?" Kristen's calm voice interrupted my thoughts.

I coughed, choking on the beer that had decided to make a run for my lungs. After a dozen coughs, I looked at Kristen through tears in my eyes. "What?"

She glanced at me with concern. "You okay? Drink much?" She spoke slower and moved her fingers in fake sign language at me. "I said, did you seal the deal with Hannah?" She slumped back from the effort at harassing me, as if it was too much, and sighed. "Do we have our cake supplier or not?"

I snorted, shaking my head, then nodded. "Yes. And no."

Kristen's brow furrowed. "What the hell does that mean?" She got up and went into the kitchen.

"Hannah wants to supply to restaurants and resorts, even if it's for weddings. I'm sticking firm on the point of her not interacting with other event planners. It's too risky for

Invitation Only. But I could tell she wanted to be a part of things, so I offered her a trial run on our first party."

Kendall turned toward me. "And she agreed?"

"Yep."

"And will she sign?" Kiki asked.

"Yeah. She explained the importance of her setting up the cakes on location, and I get that. We'll have to cave on that point and trust that she'll protect us when she does."

Kristen called out from the kitchen. "Perfect. Call her and set it up. We've got less than two weeks before the event." She came back into the room with a platter of club sandwiches right as Kendall finished setting up the Monopoly board on Kristen's coffee table. Playing had become a ritual while we hashed out our business plans. Competitiveness flushed out the best ideas.

I was always the dog. Imagine that.

SWEET DREAMS WAS quiet before eight in the morning. Feet up on a chair opposite me, I typed like a madman. Outside, pedestrians occasionally walked by the large plate glass window next to me. Every now and then, one would stop to admire my bike, rotating around her to take in all the custom chrome details, turning her into a one-bike show.

I shouted out to the empty front room, "You know, you really should think about getting a couple of overstuffed leather chairs up here, maybe a couch."

On that comment, my tenth random statement in the last hour, Little Miss Baker finally graced me with her presence from the back. "Why? So you could make yourself *more* comfortable?"

Under steady brows, I dropped my head to the side,

sending her a deadpan look. "You know you want me here. Who else would give you invaluable business tips? Oh, and speaking of business, our first event has a Super Bowl theme. And is *at* the Super Bowl."

Dressed in one of those little tees she liked to wear, she crossed her arms over her chest. "Invaluable? Wait, what? At the Super Bowl?" Her eyes widened.

I nodded.

"Nice." She got this faraway look like she'd already begun planning out the cake.

Pulling my feet down, I straightened in the hard chair, glancing left and right. "And yes, I'm giving you invaluable advice. Do you see customers beating down your door? I don't."

Glaring with narrowed eyes, she strode over and took the seat where my feet had just been. "Okay, Mr. Hotshot Business Man, what would you do if you were me?"

I made a show of scanning the room, pretending to take in the place through a fresh set of eyes as if I'd just walked in. And even though I had plenty of ideas without having to take another look, I ran through what came to mind anyway.

The display case was perfectly arranged with a rainbow of cupcakes decorated in unique themes. She had classic black-and-white photographs on the walls in tasteful, matted frames. Large potted plants occupied two corners. An open credenza along the far wall held a few perfectly stacked books. The place *looked* nice but didn't invite you to sit down and stay awhile.

"Who's your target market?"

A blank look on her face told me she hadn't done her homework.

"Who are you baking all of this for?" I clarified in layman's speak.

She shrugged. "People who like cakes and cupcakes."

"And you're just waiting for them to show up?"

A confident nod.

While I liked her rose-colored-glass enthusiasm, it was misplaced. She'd been open for an entire week, and I'd been there at different times in between classes. Not because I'd had nowhere else to be, but because I found something calming in her store that I didn't find anywhere else. It had become my own personal study library of sorts. Hannah popped up front every hour or so to keep me stocked in free Pellegrino, and she gave good Wi-Fi.

An occasional stray customer would wander in, and after seeing her assorted temptations, would always buy at least one. One customer ordered a dozen. But I'd never seen more than one or two people an hour walk through her door.

"Do you want to cater to an adult clientele or to children?" *Please say adults.* I cringed to think what might happen if my study sanctum transformed into a sticky playground.

"Adults, I think. I don't mind kids, but I need calm up here to be able to create in back."

Thank fuck.

On a deep breath, I let my mind race. "Okay. Here's what you do. Make this a haven for those looking to escape. Like me. Make it like a home library. You've started along that vibe, but you have all this empty space up front. Utilize it. Get rid of the plants and put in a few more comfortable furniture pieces."

She leaned forward, absorbing my rapid-fire suggestions.

"Think about serving coffee. Maybe not everything a coffee bar offers, but a gourmet choice or two. Are you considering hiring help anytime soon?"

"Yes, but with this amount of business it hasn't made sense yet."

"Put an ad out and start interviewing while you beef up your marketing efforts. Our sidewalk attack might've been a good initial blast, but you need to keep up the momentum. People can't buy your cakes if they don't know about you. The location is good for pedestrian traffic, but you can't rely on it."

I tapped my chin. "Oh, and think about serving wine."

She furrowed her brow. "What?"

"Don't you girls ever go out for each other's birthday parties? Imagine fifteen women in here all eating cupcakes and drinking wine. You need to get some board games. Plenty of room on the bottom shelf of that wall unit over there."

"Won't I need a license for the wine?"

"Yeah. I've got a contact down at the liquor licensing department." I furrowed my brow, trying to remember the rules for establishments other than bars. "I'm not sure if you can get one for just wine. Maybe it's a beer license I'm thinking of. Oh, hell. There's an idea. Serve beer."

Her face screwed into an indignant scowl. "With cupcakes?"

I leaned back, crossing my arms over my chest, thinking. "Bacon. Make a rich chocolate cupcake with bacon. There's a cigar lounge I know not far from here. Team up with them and serve cupcakes laden with bacon and whatever else tastes good. Ask for Roy. Tell him I sent you. He's the manager, a friend of mine, and an old friend of my father's."

A sudden spark in her eyes caught my attention and I

paused. Those luscious pink lips curved into a lazy smile. Her intriguing demeanor made it seem like she had a secret.

Whatever thoughts I'd had in my head fell away as I leaned forward, sliding my forearms onto the table. My gaze held hers. In casual jeans and that little tee, her hair clipped up off her long neck, she looked like the best thing in her shop to eat.

Without breaking our eye contact, she slowly rose off her chair. After she stood for long seconds, her smile widened.

"Thanks for the 'invaluable' business tips, Cade."

She turned and broke the spell I'd fallen under. Then I got a long look at her fine ass in jeans that gripped her hips like they were painted on.

With a quick glance over her shoulder, she caught me staring at that glorious asset. Her smile twisted into a smirk. "Oh, and Cade, who exactly is your target market?"

I blinked.

She disappeared.

Oh, yeah. Hannah was in a league of her own. And my target had just narrowed to a singular quarry.

DAYS LATER, I stumbled into the front area of Sweet Dreams with coffee, as usual. Only the room was crowded. Eight strange faces greeted me, a couple of them bright-eyed and cheery. The rest had traveled from the sort of place I hailed from: groggy and a little slow on the uptake. The ones without coffee stared at my Starbucks tray. I turned, shielding my coffees from them in case any got the inadvisable idea of tackling me.

Uncertain what provoked the mass exodus of college-aged brethren to show up before store hours, I made my way back to the kitchen. Hannah was intently focused, poring over a stack of papers at her desk.

Understanding finally hit me. "You're hiring."

Blinking, she glanced over her shoulder and smiled when she saw me. "Ooo, coffee." She abandoned her stack and grabbed the cup I held out. "I'm bleary-eyed from reading all those resumes."

"Any potentials?"

She nodded. "Two really stand out above the others. I've already had ten-minute interviews with each of them. Daniel is a little edgy—has a Mohawk, piercings, and tattoos —but I love his fun personality. Chloe's more reserved but has been baking since she was twelve. Both are qualified with great references, and they're smart enough to learn quickly."

"Which one's Chloe?" I edged toward the doorway. Conversations between the applicants had erupted, everyone talking and laughing. A group of five congregated around the couch. Mohawked Daniel leaned forward in the center of the larger group, telling a story that pulled the others to the edge of their seats.

"The one with red hair pulled into a fluffy ponytail," Hannah whispered, pressing beside me.

Chloe sat in the remaining group of three, oblivious to Daniel. She was calm in a welcoming way and engaged with the other two girls about a topic so funny, they all burst out laughing.

You could tell a lot from watching people interact with others: the expression on their face, body language. Both top candidates seemed honest and didn't carry baggage on the outside—critical qualities in employees.

"I like them too. I say hire them on the spot."

GAME DAY ARRIVED. Our first event.

For the occasion, Hannah didn't bake a cake of the football field. And she didn't do a lame football-shaped cake. Nope.

She built the whole damned stadium.

Complete with green-iced trees on the outer edge, lit paneling along the sides, and tiny spectator heads in the stands that angled down to the turf in the center, the cake looked like an architect's model. As if the stadium itself wasn't enough, she replicated a life-sized Vince Lombardi Trophy in silver frosting as an entirely separate cake.

They were works of art.

I couldn't stop staring at the massive creation. Twisted tubes of white chocolate formed the goal posts on either side. She even had tiny sideline benches with water coolers.

The good thing about my absorbing every little detail of her masterpiece was that, for a short time anyway, I could focus on something other than her. Setting up the final touches on the VIP suite right before the guests showed, we'd each been busy with our list of tasks, and the cake had been one of the last items to arrive. In fact, guests had already started to trickle in, several entering right behind the cake caravan.

Rolled in on several carts by the two new staff members Hannah had hired, the cake's slow approach through the entry doors drew everyone's attention. Hannah followed behind, guarding the corners of the cake with a scrutinizing eye to be sure they successfully made the turn with their wide load.

I couldn't have been more proud as I finally pulled back.

I moved closer to her, feeling her palpable excitement. "You did good, Maestro."

Hannah looked up at me, her expression hardened into a seriousness that surpassed any I'd seen before. After a pause of several beats, she smiled.

And she went from gorgeous to stunning.

Wearing simple jeans dressed up with a black, long-sleeved collared top with French cuffs, she pulled off care-free professional with class. The dark color was a change for her, and it turned her hazel eyes a vivid green.

They held mine.

I swallowed. "You look great, by the way."

Her smile warmed further, if that was even possible. "Thanks." Tilting her head, she regarded me a moment. "Why do you call me Maestro? When you used it during our business negotiations, you seemed flippant. But just now, it seemed friendlier."

I smiled. "It is friendlier. The day we met in your kitchen, you'd orchestrated masterpieces with the wave of your spatula like a conductor, and then you inadvertently flicked frosting onto me."

Eyes widening, remorse flashed across her face. "Sorry."

I shook my head. "Don't be. When I'd met you at my bar's grand opening, you were an Ice Queen. But in your kitchen, you revealed this whole other side when you thought no one was looking. The Maestro nickname reminds me of your free-spirited side. Does it bother you?"

Her brows furrowed. "Ice Queen?"

My lips twitched as I fought a smile. "Seriously? The chilling reception you gave was effective and memorable. But I like calling you Maestro. It reminds me that there's so much more to you than meets the eye."

She exhaled a slow breath as her expression grew serious. She searched my face, as if deciding whether or not she liked me thinking of her in that way. "No. I like it."

And yet, traces of the cold Ice Queen were written in the hard lines of her face. Almost like a part of her trusted me with the nickname, but another part of her warned me off.

Her gaze suddenly zeroed in on the other side of the room, and she breezed past me to mingle with the crowd gathering around the cake. The Ice Queen had vanished. In her stead, warmth radiated from a woman I'd never seen before, as if she'd been born a socialite.

Intrigued by the new development, I intermittently glanced her way from the edges of the room in between conversations with guests. By the time I made it to the bar, I was completely stumped.

Ben laughed when I sat down. "You look confused."

"I am."

"Care to share?" He grinned, his attention shifting to the commotion in the vicinity of the cake where the *ooo*'s and *ahhh*'s continued.

"No. Hit me." That was code for scotch. We had top shelf here for the host and his guests, and our cost included our own partaking during the festivities. It was part of our full-service event package.

I swirled the amber liquid in my glass, then sipped it, letting the rich peat flavor roll over my tongue while I tried to get into the excitement of being at the Super Bowl, a first for me and every kid's dream. But no matter how I tried to let my awe of the surroundings sink in, something more distracting buzzed nearby, gaining my attention despite any evasion tactics I employed. And today, the newest facet of an already interesting woman had thrown me.

My one-on-one exposure to Hannah had been minimal during the last two weeks. She'd been focused on building her business, and I'd been busy with papers at school and working four nights a week. Plus, Ben and I had spent time interviewing and hiring another bartender. We now had four others on rotating shifts, enough to cover for my increasing absence as my priorities slid away from tending the bar, just like we'd planned when we'd first opened.

More guests filled the room, family and friends of several star players. Confidentiality prohibited me from disclosing our clientele to outsiders, but suffice it to say, I was one happy boy. I finished my scotch, then rotated through the crowd, ensuring everyone who wanted a drink had one as I laughed at jokes and listened to stories.

A familiar man with dark blond hair turned, eyes wide and blinking like a lone kid who'd wandered into a wall-to-wall candy store.

Grinning, I clapped him on the shoulder. "Jason. Glad you could make it."

"Hey, Cade. Are you kidding? When Kristen told me the news, I rescheduled a business trip to be here. Not every day a man gets to attend the Super Bowl."

"Can I get you a drink?" I glanced over at Ben behind the bar, who gave Jason a chin up in greeting from across the room.

Jason shook his head. "Kristen's getting me a beer, and I need to find her. We made a deal. I got to come as long as I spent the game sitting with her, giving her the play-by-play action."

I snorted. "Good luck with that, man. I hope you enjoy the game."

He smirked. "Oh, I intend to educate the hell out of her. Maybe even some halftime lessons in one of the private bathrooms. With continued play-by-play commentary."

Scowling, I shook my head. "No talking about sex with my sister. Have it, just don't tell me about it."

Jason barked out laughter before heading off to look for said sister. I pinched the bridge of my nose, attempting to scour my brain clean. And made a mental note to use the bathroom well before halftime.

Right after kickoff, I worked my way to an empty barstool off to the side of the large suite and caught Hannah standing by herself, watching me.

I winked.

She smiled.

Damn, I loved being at the receiving end of those smiles. She held them tight to her chest, so I knew when she flashed one, it was real and I'd earned it.

She crossed the room and sat on the only other free stool, beside me. Now that the game had begun, everyone had settled into their chosen seats inside the large suite, watching the action on the field through the glass or on one of the dozen large monitors positioned around the room.

"You did good too," she whispered.

"Thanks." I'd been on fire setting up for this event, in my element from the large-scale organization down to the minor details. "Don't hold out on me, though. You can tell me I look awesome too."

She laughed hard. "Ego much?"

I shrugged, holding back a smile. "Only stating the facts."

Without pulling my attention from the field, I saw her twist, pulling back a bit, assessing me from head to toe. I hadn't worn anything special. Black, lizard-skin cowboy boots, dark jeans, black button-down shirt. My usual.

"Yeah, you clean up okay." Humor edged her voice.

I glanced over, catching the glint in her eyes. "So, I noticed something as I watched you work the room."

"Yeah? What's that?" She turned her upper body more toward me.

She'd mingled with guests for a polite few minutes, but she'd given the same standoffish conversations to my sisters. "You don't seem to be that close with my sisters, not even with Kiki. Aren't you two friends?" I remembered Kiki had said something about it, but wasn't sure.

Turning forward again, she gazed out at the football stadium. "Kiki and I aren't close, not really. We took an art class together and got along well but never became friends per se. I met your other two sisters at your bar opening."

I smiled, wondering how much of the ice-queen treatment she gave everyone else. Every instinct I had screamed it was a barrier of protection. Against what, I hadn't a clue.

"Well, they like you. So do I."

She shot a sidelong glance at me. "Yeah? Well, I like them too."

When she said nothing further, I almost laughed at the omission, glancing at her. "And me?"

She shrugged. "You're not so bad."

I snorted while her shoulders shook with silent laughter.

After that, in companionable silence, we watched the game. I couldn't remember the last time I'd sat next to a woman as attractive as her without needing to do anything other than be beside one another to be content. The relaxed atmosphere between us was nice. Even better, in spite of the wild attraction we felt and the occasional games we played, it was nice to know we could call a truce when it came to business.

"So, what do you think? Do you want to be a part of the Invitation Only team?"

Hannah glanced at me. "My terms?"

"Well, let's talk about those terms again."

"I get to deliver cakes to *any* customer as long as I'm not working with an event-planning company. Even if it's for a wedding."

I stared at her. Something had to give, and I knew it. And really, the "no weddings" stipulation was more of a personal rule of mine with Invitation Only. Hannah doing cakes for weddings would be great for her business and okay for Invitation Only as long as we were protected. I gave a curt nod. "And have *no* contact with any event-planning company."

"What if I'm delivering a cake to a hotel, and I accidentally have contact because an event planner directs me on where to set up?"

I sighed. "*Fine*. Minimal contact. We're going to be extending a large amount of trust to you with this, so please respect the risk for what it is. Look, Hannah, let me explain it in terms of your business. Say you hire an employee and train them to the point where they know a lot about what you know. Then all of a sudden, they become your competition."

"Well, I'll have them sign contracts and non-compete clauses just like you are."

"But what if they work around them, Hannah? What if they develop relationships with your clients? Contracts exist because people breach agreements and then everyone ends up in court. Do you see how it's still a risk? And the greater the contact, the greater the risk?"

Her expression softened, and she nodded. "Okay, I understand where you're coming from. I'll be sure to protect our relationship by disclosing our exclusivity with any event-planning company that approaches me. And I'll be sure to keep any possible exposure to a minimum. But I need you to understand where I'm coming from. A wedding does not always have an event-planning company connected to it. See my point?"

I did. And to not look like a total single-focused ass, I gave her a reasonable explanation. "I get it. With my upbringing, I kept imagining weddings and event planners going hand in hand."

She tilted her head. "I thought you were being oddly unreasonable about the 'no weddings' thing."

If only she knew. "Great. Looks like we've come to an understanding. Ready to sign on the dotted line?"

She nodded again. "Sure. Bring me the revised contract next time you're at the bakery."

"Not necessary." I stepped over to the end of the bar and reached behind the counter to grab my bag. I pulled out the already prepared contracts with a pen clipped to them.

When I glanced up, I saw her stunned expression for a beat before she narrowed her eyes. "Cade Michaelson. You knew I'd agree?"

I smirked. "Helps to know your target market. I had a good feeling you'd agree on the major points. Just give me a second to write in our compromise."

Right as I handed Hannah a pen, Kiki burst in between us. "Oh. My. God. Cade! I *love* football."

Staring at her, I blinked. "Why the sudden change?"

"Have you *seen* their asses in those tight uniforms? So much better in person than on TV."

I shook my head. "Never in the way you mean."

Hannah handed back my copy of the signed contract and pen.

"Well, Kiki, congratulate Hannah. She's now officially a team member of Invitation Only."

Kiki turned with one of her trademark squeals and

crushed Hannah in hug. "That's so awesome, Hannah. Congratulations."

I grinned at Hannah's surprised expression over Kiki's shoulder.

When Hannah pulled away, Kiki darted off toward Kristen and Kendall, presumably to share the great news.

Fairly certain a hug from me would be pushing it, I held out a hand. "Congratulations, Maestro. Welcome to the team."

Beyond us, everyone rotated back toward that phenomenal cake, and I realized halftime had already started. A couple of people held empty plates in their hands.

I nudged her off the stool. "You're on."

"What?" She laughed but then turned and gasped. "Oh!"

Nearly launching off her stool, she hustled over and saved the day.

Still within earshot, I overheard the discussions by the cake.

"I can't cut into it." The woman had a stricken look on her face.

Hannah grabbed the long knife lying along the side of the platform that held the cake. "No worries. That's what I'm here for. I made it, I can destroy it."

Resolved not to interfere, I remained seated, watching from across the room. The cake part was Hannah's gig, and she beamed brightly in her element.

Admiring this new composed yet outgoing facet of her I hadn't expected, I kept my distance, studying her. All wrapped up into one, she was an excited artist, occasional Ice Queen, and a smooth businesswoman. And who could forget the tempting seductress.

The woman continued revealing pieces to an ever-growing puzzle.

8. FOOD FOR THOUGHTS

How did I *not* say *no Valentine's Day*?

If there was any single holiday worse than a wedding, it was Valentine's Day. But worse than the entire Western World's commercialism of a day sprung from Christian saints and courtly love, worse than all the cutesy hearts and obligatory bouquets, worse than even the professions of love and *proposals*, were all the suckers that bought into that shit.

My stomach soured.

I'd been staring at the blinking cursor on my screen for longer than was visually healthy when I sighed and decided to just buck up and deal. They didn't have therapy for what ailed me, but maybe if I drowned myself in little pink hearts and boxes of chocolate, all the sap-filled overload would shove me into a sugar coma—or off a cliff.

Resigning myself to the fact that the event Kristen had booked was happening—whether or not I wanted to stab myself in the eye with a fork over it—I drafted the email, providing the pertinent details to Hannah, and hit send. There. Done. Moving on.

The blender or mixer, or whatever had been whirring in the background on and off in steady rotation for the last hour, stopped. I closed my laptop and settled further back into the corner of a fairly comfortable couch.

Hannah appeared suddenly, stalking toward me with the lit screen of her sparkle-coated cell phone held up by her face. Her hair was a tousled mess, trying to escape a pink hair clip. Her eyebrows were raised. She was goddamn adorable with that incredulous look on her face—kind of made a guy want to keep putting it there.

"Did you just email me from twenty feet away?"

I looked past her, gauging the size of the front room. "No. More like thirty-five." I leaned back, bouncing into the cushion, rocking my thighs forward and back. "This couch is perfect."

Her eyes narrowed, hiding their icy green color behind thick black lashes. "Glad you approve. Couldn't you have just *told* me we have a new gig?"

"Why would I do that? This method was much more effective in getting your attention."

Yes. I was the kid who pulled on girls' pigtails just to make them squeal.

"Urgh!" She clenched her hands into fists and then exploded them out in midair toward me. Her phone went flying into the back of the couch, bounced off the middle seat cushion, and flew onto the floor before skidding to a halt next to her bright yellow tennis shoe. She glared at it, as if bending over and picking it up would lessen her frustrated display.

She stormed off, abandoning the innocent phone.

I scooped it up and chased after her into the bakery war zone. "Awww, c'mon. Don't be like that. I'm kidding."

Ignoring me, except for a cute little snort she made, she

measured off dry ingredients into various sizes of clear bowls. While she pretended I wasn't there, I watched as she visibly unwound with every measure and pour. By the time she dumped them all into a larger mixing bowl, her breathing had calmed, her expression relaxed.

Work was her therapy; it dissipated stress. Very much like bartending did for me. Familiar tasks that required your attention pulled you out of your head and into the present moment. Kendall, all into yoga and meditation, once told me the practice was called "mindfulness." I got it—what I called my Zen Zone.

I walked over to her desk and placed her phone on the center of the surface, in between a fax machine and a neatly stacked pile of mail. "Besides, now you have a written record of the event, time, place, and cake request."

Hannah glanced over her shoulder, her expression softening further. "Yeah, I guess. Thanks."

Leaning back on the edge of the desk, I regarded her while she lost herself in her craft as she poured measuring cups of liquid into the bowl before turning the mixer on again. And, privileged as I was to be ignored, yet at the same time allowed to be here while her guard was down, I saw right through the ice-queen façade. That wasn't her—never had been. She excelled at constructing monstrous walls, then hiding behind them. Compartmentalized like no one I'd ever met before.

Well, besides me.

She turned the mixer off and pulled a bowl of batter out from under it before lifting it with both hands over to a worktable. She glanced up at me before pouring the mixture into a dark-gray rectangular mold, amusement glinting in her eyes. "Were you joking in your email about the cake theme being 'Love is a Battlefield?'"

"No joke. The client didn't have a preference, but I did. So that's the theme."

"Seriously?" She smiled.

"Seriously. It is. Might as well have fun with it." There was no doubt in my mind she'd do something awesome with the idea. And it helped soothe my inner devil. Cupid and I would duke it out till the end if I had to be involved in this nightmare.

She held my gaze, cocking her head. "Hey, I've been meaning to pick your brain about something."

I crossed my arms. "Sure, go ahe—" My stomach growled loudly, and I paused, blinking. "Wait, hold up a second."

Rapid-fire thoughts flowed in. I needed a distraction. She wanted help. My thesis needed attention. Her business needed a shot of adrenaline and a direction in which to run. And I needed to eat...

"You need to feed me."

She gaped, then her eyes narrowed as her mouth closed. "Excuse me?"

My gaze lingered on her full lips while my mind stuck on the split-second image of her wide-open mouth, and I totally blanked, guttering my thoughts. I swallowed, my throat bone-dry.

Her brow furrowed as I looked at her, likely as if I wanted to eat her. I shook my head, closing my eyes, banishing thoughts of burying my face between her bare legs, because I did want to. Shamelessly. Like a starving man.

I crossed my arms over my chest, sighing heavily while I tried valiantly to stay on topic. "You do cook, don't you? Meals? Something other than desserts?"

She scoffed. "What do you think? I'm a graduate of the

Culinary Institute of America." As if that was supposed to mean something to those of us who didn't speak cooking-Greek.

"I think if you want help with your business, it will start costing you." I scrubbed a hand over my chin, thinking this through.

She stared at me as if I'd gone insane.

"You cook a meal and feed me in exchange for one hour of my time. After dinner."

Her hands flew out, that pretty jaw dropping again, before she pointed toward the front. "What do you think you've been doing up there all this time? Using my Wi-Fi, using my space as your own personal library? Now *you're* charging *me*?"

I shrugged. "I don't recall seeing a 'no trespassing' sign up there, and it wasn't being utilized by any other customer while I offered you free advice. Plus, you had the added bonus of me breaking in your new couch."

She blinked, looking dazed.

I snapped my fingers. "Now, focus, woman. Stop distracting me with nonessential information. We're negotiating here."

Her delicate brows arched higher over wide eyes. Then those shards of ice green were hidden behind narrowed lashes. "Two."

"What?" I stood taller.

She came closer, exerting her confidence in our game. "Two. For every dinner I cook you, you will provide two hours of business advice."

Now we were getting somewhere. I took a step closer, causing our bodies to almost touch.

Her face tilted up with my movement, holding my gaze, fearless.

I wanted to kiss her so badly in that moment, but I held fast, keeping my eye on the prize. Which definitely did *not* include kissing a baking Ice Queen. Not tonight, anyway.

"Two. For every dinner you cook me—a five-star, restaurant-worthy meal—I will give you two hours of my time afterward. One will be nothing but business, the other can be about any topic I choose, business or personal."

"P-personal?" She shook her head.

I nodded mine. "Oh, yes. As personal as I want it to get."

Her slender throat worked down a swallow. I knew I had her. She wanted my help too badly not to invest some time into getting more of what I had to offer.

"Fine." She gave a single nod. A wisp of hair that had been falling down broke free, caressing her cheek. "Once a week for a few weeks should do it."

"Three times a week. Sundays, Mondays, and Wednesdays. We'll do it for two months. More if you need it."

She gaped again. My gaze dropped to those delectable lips once more.

Her tropical scent drifted up between us. My mind hazed, barely holding on to the details she and I worked out. Her soft body leaned into mine, heat scorching through the fabric of our clothes. Gauging by her nonreaction, she'd been so blown by my last counterproposal, she had no idea how close we'd become, how dangerous an edge we teetered on.

The desire to kiss her became undeniable, but I balked. The entire suggestion I'd made was ridiculous in light of the fact she was off-limits in so many ways, and yet, I couldn't help myself.

I waited.

Her heated breath puffed little scorches through the cotton of my shirt.

"Okay."

"Okay?"

She nodded, closing her eyes while she backed up a step. Then another. "Don't ask me again, because I might change my mind."

I grinned. "Wouldn't dream of it. Oh, and, Hannah? I'll be using your business as a part of my thesis project. So, thanks for that." Didn't want her to know I got something more out of it than she realized until the die had been cast.

Without waiting for her reply, I turned and strode to the front.

A cupcake thudded into the wall beside me, barely missing my head. I paused, staring at a purple icing imprint on the white paint. I grinned wide.

Oh, yeah. This was going to be fun.

"Good night, Hannah. See you tomorrow night."

A low growl sounded out from the back.

So much fun.

9. ENTERTAINING A FOURSOME

I scrolled through my phone contacts, grinning like an idiot. Couldn't help it, really. I'd gone into full-blown stupid mode.

Clicking on Hannah's number, I hit the text box and typed.

> We doing your place or mine?

I waited, watching two kids on scooters race by on the sidewalk.

Her reply came through seconds later.

> Are you up front on my couch?

I grinned and replied.

> Nope. Breaking in your new chair.

> Spun it around a quarter turn.

Better angle . . .

Her message bubble popped up while she typed her reply.

Did you just make that dirty?

I laughed.

Is that what three little dots does to you? I'll have to do it more often . . .

A minute passed. Then another. No whirring noises happened. I began to wonder if Little Miss Ice Queen had frosted over, or melted down.

Finally, her message bubble showed her typing again.

Your place.

I nodded.

My roommate might be there . . .

The sigh I heard was so loud, she had to be standing right inside the kitchen doorway.

I am NOT interpreting those three dots to be anything sexual.

I don't do threesomes . . .

I choked, coughing like I'd inhaled a gallon of water. My mind blanked—zero thoughts between my ears.

She saved it, compensating for my total wipeout.

> Does he bite . . . ?

I stared at those three naughty little dots. My cock twitched, and I adjusted in the seat. On a deep breath, I shook my head, taking control.

> Only 5-star food.

> Do you do threesomes . . .

> for dinner . . . ?

She appeared in the doorway, smiling.

Damn, I loved that smile. I grabbed my messenger bag from the table and joined her. "Ready?"

She nodded once. "Sure. We need to go shopping first."

"No we don't. I went shopping already."

She pulled her head back, surprised. "How did you know what we'd need? Or that I'd say 'your place?'"

"I assumed one out of our three days you would. And you're a gourmet chef, right? I bought every ingredient imaginable, according to the sales person who assisted me. I figured you'd improvise."

Her eyes narrowed imperceptibly, but then she fought a smile. "Improvising in a kitchen is one of my greatest talents."

My mind spun at the loaded tone in her voice, and I tilted my head as she headed out the door. "One of them?"

She turned around to face me again, walking backward as I stepped through the doorway. "Shouldn't you be focusing on the first part of the sentence instead of the last?" Her eyes sparkled with humor.

I blinked, speechless about the huge innuendo she'd left thick in the air between us.

Her head fell back and she laughed—a deep, rich sound. She'd let her hair down, and it fell in shiny, dark waves around her face. A few strands on the right touched her slender chin. Without thinking, I reached up and tucked them behind her ear.

She gasped at the contact, shuddering. Big trusting eyes looked up at me. I saw deeper than that, though. Fear and hurt were barely masked by the brave and reckless front she put on. They were the same emotions barricaded behind her icy walls.

I stared down into her eyes, but decided not to attempt to break through her carefully constructed shields. She deserved better than that kind of rough handling. I figured she would let down her guard when she was ready.

"C'mon, Maestro. Let's see what you can cook us up."

The spell broken, she nodded rapidly, pulling her small purse from her shoulder.

I stepped outside, waiting as she turned off the lights, activated the alarm, and closed the door. She fished a bundle of keys from her purse and locked it.

When she turned, I pressed a hand to her lower back. "Let me drive."

She stopped cold, pointing. "That thing? No way."

I laughed at her horrified expression. "Ever ridden on a bike?"

She shook her head, hard.

"Live a little, Hannah. Slide something wide between your legs and hold on tight to me. You might like it." I smirked.

Her eyes narrowed, but the corners of her lips twitched.

Yep. I didn't need a text box for sexual innuendo.

When she hesitated, I shattered her ice. "It *vibrates*..."

She burst out laughing. I took advantage of the crumbling walls to grab her hand, tugging her forward. "I promise it's safe. I get here in one piece often enough. That should tell you something."

She let out an undignified grunt.

I handed her the extra helmet I'd brought—yeah, I was that confident—and helped her fasten the chin strap. She looked adorable: pinked cheeks, dark waves of hair flowing out.

I straddled my bike and held out my arm, thankful she'd worn jeans. She took it and expertly swung her leg over, with that little purse snug over her shoulder.

Before I backed us up, Hannah adjusted, tightening her thighs around my hips, sliding her hands around my waist, and tucking them up in front of my chest. Her body pressed into my back. "This okay?" she asked.

"Yeah." It was more than okay. This was the most body contact we'd had, and although the rational part of my mind worked out that there was no other way she could've ridden on the back of my bike, I hadn't actually prepared for having her wrapped around me.

I decided right then and there, I wanted her on my bike. A lot.

Like a champ, Hannah remained calm during the short ride to my place, holding on tight, but not clamping on for dear life at every turn. I looked at my street with fresh eyes, seeing what she would see as we approached. It wasn't great wealth by any stretch of the imagination, but it was an established neighborhood close enough to Loading Zone and school to make it a worthwhile investment. The house wasn't huge, but it was comfortable. Although I could afford to live there alone, I chose not to, taking on a friend whom I trusted enough to live with as a roommate.

Wordlessly, she followed me up the walk to the front

door. The silence between us was comfortable, maybe because I'd been lost in my own thoughts or possibly because I felt connected to her in a loose friendship way I found hard to define. It definitely wasn't due to my not caring about what she thought of the place. I was honest enough with myself to admit that I cared about her opinion of me, and where I lived was, in many ways, a reflection of me.

I dropped the keys in the entry table bowl. "Feel free to poke around. Be nosy, open drawers and cabinets as if it was your place. Rest assured, I intend to at yours."

That earned me a shove and an easy laugh. I chuckled.

"Mase? Ya' home?" With the garage closed and the house quiet, I wasn't sure.

"Yeah." A grunt from his bedroom.

"Well put some pants on, dude. We got company."

As we made our way down the hall, Mase popped his head out sideways, then grinned. The sandy blond mop on his head was its usual shaggy mess.

Hannah stopped short of Mase's bedroom. He was shirtless.

He eased the rest of the way into the hall in low-slung tattered jeans and bare feet. "Don't worry, I got pants."

Hannah grinned. "Awesome."

"Mase, Hannah. Hannah, Mase."

They shook hands, but I pressed mine to her lower back and glared at Mase. He dropped her hand and backed up, holding spread palms up in innocence.

"That's obviously Mase's room." I nodded into the hurricane-devastation zone as we passed. At the end of the hall, I opened a closed door. "This is mine."

She stood in the doorway, scanning the room but not going inside. In between classes earlier, I'd done a five-minute whirlwind clean job, which consisted of shoving things in drawers and under the bed, to be sorted out at a later time.

When she turned back around, I kept it casual, returning down the hall. Mase had vanished behind his closed door. I continued the two-minute tour, pointing as she followed. "Living room, kitchen, breakfast nook, back porch. Out there is a bricked patio and barbecue. Around that corner are the stairs down to a finished basement with laundry and game tables." I turned to face her. "Want to see the basement?"

Hannah stood in the kitchen I'd renovated, spinning in a circle to take in the culinary terrain. When her gaze landed back on me, she shook her head. "No, I'm good."

"Seriously? You don't want to see my basement? The very best part's down there..."

Her eyes sparkled, then her gaze drifted down, lingering below my beltline. "No, I don't want to see your basement. Maybe later..."

I blinked. "Shit. Are we talking about square footage in my house or my pants?"

"You tell me." She held a dead-serious expression for a few heavy heartbeats, then her hand flew to her mouth and she burst into laughter.

I snorted, shaking my head. "Woman, you intrigue me more and more."

Through the entire house tour, Hannah showed no interest in exploring the place further, but in the kitchen, she investigated every drawer and cabinet before standing in front of the stainless steel refrigerator, studying its contents. A quick nod was the only indication I got that she was satisfied.

Pulling half of the new items from the refrigerator onto

the butcher-block island, she reopened cabinets and drawers, grabbing a skillet, a saucepan, and various bowls and utensils. Not wanting to get in the way, I stayed off to the side, leaning against the counter, watching.

She finally relinquished her tiny purse to the end of the counter after pulling a hair clip out from inside. With a quick twist, she spun those sexy, unruly locks into submission, clipping them to the back of her head. I stared at her, fascinated.

She glanced at me. "You helping?"

"Absolutely." I pushed off and stood beside her. "What do you need?"

She grabbed a metal colander and pointed at the leafy greens and root vegetables. "All of this washed and rinsed, then chopped into large pieces."

I nodded.

As I went about my assigned task at the smaller sink in the island, she rinsed the chicken breasts in the larger sink, skinned them, and then cut them into strips with efficient slices of our razor-sharp butcher's knife. She dumped the pieces into a bowl of raw scrambled eggs, tossed them onto a platter of flour, rolling them to dust all the surfaces, then laid them in the sizzling oil inside a pan on the stove. She placed a splatter screen over the top of it. Once she cleaned her preparation surfaces and the knife, she joined me, grabbing a turnip, a parsnip, and a bunch of carrots in unusual colors: white, purple, and orange.

Her soft voice held a tone of respect. "This is a beautiful kitchen—a dream kitchen, really. Do you cook?" As I cut the leafy greens, she nudged up next to me. "Here, let me. You're using the wrong knife. And the wrong angle to cut."

Maintaining contact, her hip against mine, she used that same butcher knife and balanced the point onto the cutting board, raising and dropping her forearm in a blur, each time moving a half inch over. Then she turned the strips and made four fast chops the other direction.

"See, it's all in the wrist."

I had no idea what she was talking about, but loved watching her work. This was her domain, and she ruled it well.

"So, do you?" She arched a brow, staring at me.

What was the question? Oh, did I cook. I shrugged. "Enough to get by, I guess. If I had the time, I'd experiment more. I insisted on a gourmet kitchen in the remodel, and the designer took charge with her vision, down to every last detail." I held up the vegetable peeler.

"She did a great job. Here, put that detail to good use." She handed me the washed carrots.

Dinner took about thirty minutes to make. By the time we'd filled the house with a mouthwatering aroma of fried chicken and steamed vegetables, Mase made an appearance and stayed, like a stray dog wanting a home. At least he'd put on a T-shirt.

"Here, make yourself useful." I handed him napkins and plates.

We sat down right as the front door opened and slammed shut. "Holy shit! What happened in here?"

Ben appeared from nowhere, as was his MO.

Confused, I lowered the tongs onto the platter of chicken. "I thought you were working tonight."

He shook his head. "Lisa wanted an extra shift, and the new bartender needed training, so I took off." His eyes widened as he came closer. "Wow. What's for dinner?" He grabbed a plate from the cabinet and sat down.

Hannah glanced at me. "I don't do foursomes."

Mase dropped his fork onto his plate. It clattered in the middle of the sudden silence.

Her mischievous gaze met mine. *Naughty.* And just like that, I got more intrigued.

"I've never entertained three men at once," she clarified, glancing at the other two.

The poor guys stared at her, blinking. I couldn't blame them. She was gorgeous. And she could cook. And with that wicked mind and her naughty implications, the combination was deadly.

"Food! I'm talking about food!" She grabbed her water glass and took a sip.

Ben burst out laughing.

Mase picked up his dropped fork. "Good, because we were about to kick you the hell out." He winked at her.

"This is Ben, by the way, my best friend since kindergarten. Ben, Hannah."

Hannah leaned over the table, holding her hand out. But Ben scraped his chair back, went behind me, and lifted Hannah out of her chair and into a bear hug. "Thank you for cooking for us."

I would've gotten jealous at Ben taking from her something I hadn't yet had—a hug—but I let it slide. Funny how a home-cooked meal civilized the savageness out of a man.

Plus, I would have her all to myself soon enough. "She cooked for *me*." I loaded a pile of fried chicken strips onto my plate beside all the vegetables. It had been a long time since I'd eaten this well. "Consider yourselves lucky you're included."

"Lucky indeed," Mase said.

Ben moaned, his mouth full of chicken.

Hannah laughed, shaking her head. "I like your friends."

"Trust me. They like you too. I'm pretty sure they've bonded with you for life."

Not one scrap was left on anyone's plate by the time we finished. Had Hannah not been there, I'm certain the plates would've been licked clean; I saw Mase eyeing his, debating just that.

"You guys good to clean up?" I asked, pulling Hannah up from her chair by the hand.

Mase stacked the plates and brought them to the sink. "Gladly. Come over anytime you want, Hannah. Please, Cade. Bring that woman back over."

Ben collected the bigger platters off the table. "I second that."

I glanced down to catch her grinning so wide, her cheeks looked ready to burst. "We'll see." Her tone was teasing.

Part of me was thrilled that the guys had instantly taken to her, which was a rare occurrence among my friends given my field-playing history.

But a larger part of me wanted Hannah all to myself. For a while, anyway.

10. TO STUDY WITH PLEASURE

W here Hannah had been reserved in the rest of my house, she turned inquisitive once I'd shut the door to my bedroom. My guess was that she was nervous in such close quarters with my bed mere feet away, but she delved into my stuff with such enthusiasm, I wondered if she just wanted to throw me off-balance. Which is exactly what she did.

"Curious much?" Amused, I folded my arms and leaned a shoulder against the closed door.

She paused while she pulled a drawer open and arched a brow. "You did say every drawer, every cabinet."

I chuckled. "That I did. Along with fair warning of my free-for-all pass at your place in return."

She smirked, but continued exploring. "You have quite the CD collection." Her finger glided along the top edge of one of the rows. "How are they sorted?"

"By genre. Then alphabetically."

Her eyes narrowed a fraction, and she looked at me, as if she could see more of me by my OCD music-organization tendencies.

I shrugged.

She turned and kept investigating as she moved toward the head of my bed.

Nothing much else to see. I didn't keep many personal items. Most of the stuff on my desk was school or work related. Her hand paused when she turned toward my nightstand, and she glanced at me.

I arched a brow. "What? The brave explorer grows afraid of what might be behind drawer number three?"

"No. I'm just not sure I need to go there. I'm good with imagining."

I laughed hard. "Condoms. Nothing frightening in there, only condoms."

"Depends on your definition of frightening."

I ran my tongue across my teeth, then smiled, slow and easy. Undaunted by her uninformed judgment, I shrugged. If she knew the quantity of condoms and the number of girls, she might actually be frightened. But I was who I was, a product of circumstances beyond my control, and I'd done my best to cope. If she ever grew brave enough to open my nightstand drawer, she would deal.

When she turned, a baseball cap that I'd left on the corner of the nightstand fell on the floor. She bent down to pick it up. "What's this?" Crouching further, she picked up the yellow sticky note.

That yellow sticky note.

I shrugged. "A list of girls." Looked like Hannah would get a glimpse after all.

"Friends?" Her eyebrows arched.

"In a manner of speaking."

"Friends with benefits." She gave a curt nod, as if she understood without confirmation.

"Closer," I hedged.

She cocked her head and flipped it over, examining it. I sat down in my desk chair, watching her. There was nothing I could do about her discovery, so I let it play out. No point in making an effort to hide what it was.

She put the list on my nightstand. "That's a lot of friends."

I shrugged. "I'm a friendly guy."

Kicking off her shoes, she put her purse beside the list, above the drawer with the condoms. I tried not to smile at how her actions had staked a subconscious claim—well, in my deluded mind, anyway. She sat on the bed, then pushed back until she'd moved to the center of it.

"So, that's like a small harem."

I huffed out a laugh. "What does that make me, an Arabian prince?"

Her eyes gleamed with humor. "I doubt that."

"You'd be right. I'm no prince." I leaned forward, bracing my forearms on my thighs, curious to see her reaction to the truth of me. "It makes me a sexually satisfied and very lucky man."

A glance at the list, then back to me. "Those women would have to be very satisfied to agree to be in a harem."

I smirked. "One might think that."

Our gazes held, locked. The temperature in the room started to escalate.

I had no idea what she was thinking, but with all the talk of my being sexually satisfied, I was already undressing Hannah in my mind and coaxing her into a number of sexual positions. But then my primal thoughts faded away as I got lost in those vivid eyes of hers.

Behind her sensuality, the girl sitting in the center of my

bed held a large amount of vulnerability she couldn't hide from me. I'd seen it before in her, but not to this magnitude. Both brave and scared at the same time, she didn't know quite what to think of me.

Hell, I didn't know what to think of me.

Sitting here with someone I actually cared about beyond a physical attraction was new territory since the devastating fiasco nearly two years ago, which had pushed me over the edge. And now that I'd climbed to the top of the abyss I'd fallen into—had been lost in for so long—I wondered if my salvation lie buried somewhere deep behind those greenish eyes.

"How about we not talk about my harem tonight. The only girl I want to focus on is you." I leaned forward, swiped up the list, and dropped it into my top desk drawer.

Her eyes widened.

I clarified immediately, remaining three feet away from the sexiest temptation ever to grace my bed, keeping my ass firmly planted in my desk chair. "Business. The next two hours you wrangled out of me will be *strictly* business."

Excitement lit up her face as she realized all of the time tonight would focus on helping her, and she moved to touch one of my pillows. Her hand hovered over the pillowcase, but she hesitated, and her brows drew together. Instead, she turned around on the comforter and eased down onto her stomach, facing me.

Her hesitation in touching something of mine, where I laid my head down at night, felt like a gut punch. I frowned and made a mental note to fix that shit ASAP with new pillowcases that no other woman had touched. I wanted her completely comfortable here. With everything.

She'd moved on, however, dropping her chin onto her

raised hands and kicking her feet up behind her, crossing them. She smiled at me, looking eager to learn.

My throat went dry as I stared at her, blinking.

That was one position I hadn't put her in.

Innocent, trusting, comfortable.

And that position had now become my favorite one of all.

11. LOVE IS A BATTLEFIELD

The Valentine's Doomsday had arrived. Activity buzzed around me at the event, but all of it seemed light years away. My gaze was lost, unfocused.

My unsteady hands slipped into the side pockets of charcoal dress pants. They hadn't been worn for exactly two years to this day. Since then, they'd hung in my closet, ignored, but not forgotten. The tailored wool had been brought out today as a cleansing of sorts. I decided who I was beneath it all, not others. Lasting healing came from within.

And so I stood silently, hands in my pockets, staring down at the ultimate catharsis in cake form. When I'd told Hannah the theme was "love is a battlefield," she hadn't disagreed.

But she'd expressed an entirely different perspective.

At first glance, the cake looked like a long table, like one would imagine existed inside the dining hall of a stately English manor, where the lord sat at one end, the lady at the other.

But instead of chair backs tucked beneath the table, they

were gray headstones. And instead of a tablecloth, there was a sea of grass that stretched from one end of the eight-foot table to the other. Tufts of the vibrant green poked up through a littered mess of papers which were covered in a scrawled handwriting.

Most of the papers were torn letters that had words running down them, like tears had streaked the print. Bits of hearts in crimson red had been shattered, their pieces scattered like shrapnel.

The destruction was, at once, all consuming and inconsequential. Devastating and uplifting.

Because it told a gut-wrenching story.

As I took in all of the heartache depicted, understanding dawned. The two grave markers on the far ends were empty, devoid of any engraving, any marking of life. The two headstones in the center, however, told something else entirely. They were positioned so closely together, I almost thought they were one, but there was the barest light shining through them. At their feet, an abundant mound of grass sprang forth, bright green and healthy. Between them, in that indistinguishable space that hardly existed, was a pure white whole heart.

And inscribed on those two headstones, in bold letters, were matching his-and-hers epitaphs.

LOVED

The sounds of the party grew louder and more distinct. I felt a quiet presence beside me. Had no idea how long she had been there.

We stood in comfortable silence for a while, two people appreciating a work of art. Patron and artist. After absorbing the enormity of detail and emotion reflected in modest baked flour coated in sugar, I finally asked, "How can you create such beauty in impermanence?"

We remained facing forward, but I could see she'd shrugged. "It's my medium."

"It should be in a museum."

"Thank you." Soft-spoken, hidden emotion edged her voice.

"Cade! There you are." Kristen sounded frantic. "I've been looking everywhere for you. There's a disaster happening in the sound booth."

She probably didn't yet realize the disaster was my sense of humor. Or therapy. Like the pants. And the cake.

I glanced down at Hannah. Her eyes met mine.

A connection flared stronger there. Some unnamable bond, fragile and new, had begun to form between us, and it had flickered to life long before she'd created a mural of every tattered heart's emotions exploded into a million pieces. Only now, I realized something very important—she knew devastating heartache too.

"I've got to go."

A tender smile brightened, her face full of understanding. "I know."

In a rush, I was assaulted by three female linebackers and bulldozed away. My last view before I had to become a businessman and fix technical problems was of Hannah laughing.

Oingo Boingo's "Dead Man's Party" played. No, it hadn't been on the original soundtrack for tonight, but it was crucial for levity. The playlist was highlighted, of course, by the great Pat Benatar's "Love is a Battlefield." Connected on a wavelength with depth I didn't yet understand, I realized Hannah had created her graveyard art, and without knowing it in advance, my music choices paid homage to her masterpiece.

By the time I returned, several members of the local press, one arts magazine, and one foodie magazine were taking photographs of Hannah standing beside her amazing work of art, posing with the first slice on her silver cake server. Although the PR had initially been intended to highlight our new business, and it would, all the photos and interest centered around Hannah's unconventional creation.

Throughout the evening, glares came my direction from my sisters. They began when they caught sight of the morbidly themed cake. And their freak-out continued when every song that played would've been perfect for a Halloween party.

Each time they objected, I insisted they trust me with a tired, deadpan stare. Anyone could throw a boring, sappy Valentine's Day party. What was happening here tonight caused the entire place to buzz with energy.

We'd knocked the ostentatious world of high-society events off its axis.

And if we had anything to say about it in the years to come, it would never be righted again.

Hours later, ribbon streamers patterned the wood floors in pinks, reds, and silver. The music had ceased. The lights, dimmed.

The cemetery cake? Demolished. But unforgettable.

"Well?" Hands in my pockets, I walked toward the Michaelson Three as they hovered by the same sliding barn door as they had on New Year's Eve, waiting to pounce.

Only this time, no anger or frustration marred their expressions. One by one, they broke into huge smiles. Kiki began bouncing in excitement.

Kristen closed the three-foot distance, tackling me in a hug that nearly knocked me over. "Everyone loved it!"

Her high pitch made me wince.

After her crushing embrace, she pulled back. The rest of them crowded in until we'd hunched over, whispering, like one of our huddles from childhood.

Kendall nudged my shoulder with hers. "Not one person left tonight without praising us for throwing the best party they'd attended in years."

Kiki added, "The party of the century."

"We have five new orders. I had to start taking notes on my phone." Kristen brimmed with excitement. "Several said they'd call or text to get more information. And everyone gushed about the music."

I nodded, smug. "Told you we needed to go edgier."

Kristen looped her arm around my neck, rubbing her knuckles on the top of my head. "You were right, baby brother. We'll stop giving you so much shit about your decisions."

I stood, breaking our huddle. "Good. 'Cause the next soundtrack? Gonna be brutal."

Panic flickered over Kristen's face. Worry transformed all three of their expressions.

I smirked. "Pink Floyd. And...Led Zeppelin."

"No." They stalked me, shaking their heads, horror reflected in their eyes.

I continued the torture. "Lynyrd Skynyrd."

Their mouths fell open.

I bit my lower lip hard to keep from laughing, then raised my hands high and wide, a prophet in my element. "Gotta give the people what they want."

Backing through the doorway into the cold night air, I burst out laughing.

Hannah had left a while ago. I figured she'd gone home, but as I walked to Kristen's house, movement down by the pond caught my eye.

A nearly full moon cast everything in a white glow, silhouetting the girl who sat alone on the edge of the dock. Wrapped in a puffy coat, mittens on her hands, and a knit hat on her head, she resembled a kid who'd been dressed to play in the snow.

"Warm enough?"

She glanced up and smiled. "Yeah."

"Room for me on that dock?"

Although there was plenty of space, she scooted over, as if she'd been reserving a spot just for me.

I crouched down, planting my ass on the aged wood. "Nice. You warmed my seat." I shivered. I'd left my jacket inside Kristen's house.

Hannah began to unzip her coat.

I furrowed my brows. "What are you doing? It's freezing out."

"Sharing my warmth."

Shocked by her offer, and a bit confused as to what she planned to do with that tiny coat of hers, I sat there, waiting.

She fully unzipped, then turned her upper body toward me, wrapping the open sides over part of my front and back as she pressed into me. "There. Now you don't have to be cold."

I looked down at the light blue knit material on the top of her head as she turned her face toward the pond again. Simple as that: I needed warmth; she provided.

Unthinking, I wrapped an arm around her. Didn't mean anything deep or committal. It was more comfortable that way—the two of us leaning into one another on the edge of a dock.

So many thoughts jumbled into my head, yet none came into focus with everything happening on this one night. A night that had once been a bull's-eye on a calendar had become something altogether different.

And that had everything to do with the person who had opened her coat and offered me warmth when I needed it most.

She didn't pry. Neither did I.

We each had scars on that battlefield. I knew that now, after tonight. Evident, and yet hidden behind beauty, it took someone who'd been there to recognize it.

Instead of asking about her scars, I offered up mine. "It happened two years ago. On this fucking holiday. I opened my heart and offered her the world. Like a dumbass, on bended knee, with the perfect ring in hand, I promised to love her for the rest of my life. Turned out, I wasn't enough for her."

I stopped, a cramp locking up my throat as I shared what I'd told no other soul. But I couldn't tell her everything. Some would have to do for now.

Strong arms squeezed me beneath the coat. "I got that promise. And accepted it from the man of my dreams. Standing there in a gown of white, before friends and family, mine and his, he decided not to show up for the rest of our lives. He decided he didn't want me."

My heart lurched at words so lacking in emotion, they sounded dead. I turned more toward her, wrapping my other arm around her, holding her tight. I dropped my cheek onto her hat-covered head. "He was an idiot, Hannah."

"Yeah, he was." She snorted.

I chuckled. I got it. Trashing them helped us deal. I'd done plenty of dealing.

"So explain the cake, then." A dramatic picture, revealing heartache and destruction, there was more under the icing. I saw it, but tonight, I needed to hear it from a survivor.

She shrugged a little. "When you gave me the hilarious inspiration, a dead part inside me flickered to life. I don't even know how to explain it, but a fresh viewpoint helped me make that cake. Love is a complete and utter disaster. But even with all the heartache, we have to believe there is joy. I need to believe there is one person somewhere out there, meant for us, who will bring us some kind of happiness.

"Of course, I also think it's not all pretty ponies and fairy tales. Real love is messy. It's fights, but more about the making up. It's pulling apart to find our own paths, but running together and holding on tight, refusing to let go. Love is the calm in the middle of the storm."

Hannah painted the world beautiful in a way I hadn't expected. In a way I related to. Casting a jumble of pieces into complete disarray, she reassembled it into a whole new perspective. Life didn't have to be good or bad. We didn't have only one predestined road to follow. Life existed not in the black and white, but in the gray.

The realist in me knew that. My business mind had embraced the notion without ever giving it a second thought. Failure in business was not an option, it was only a learning point—a means to succeed, part of living in the gray.

Why was I so black and white when it came to my heart?

As I sat there, held by someone who had been there and survived, I remembered why. And accepted it. I'd buried my emotions behind a wall of steel because I hadn't been ready. I didn't want to trust that it would never happen again.

And...it had hurt like a motherfucking bitch.

12. TWO IN TANGO

Dinner at my place had turned into something *more* than just dinner at my place.

Ever dance with someone without touching?

Neither had I.

Until Hannah.

Nothing more of any emotional importance had been said on the dock that night. We'd been tapped out and retreated to our separate mental corners.

Our dinner and business-study arrangement had continued at my house the next few times, a comfortable routine that I'd begun to look forward to. I liked having her in my house, in my kitchen that she seemed to come alive in, that she commanded with expert grace.

The guys grilled me for the dinner schedule, rearranging plans if anything conflicted. They wanted to make sure they were present for any meal she cooked. And it wasn't only about the food. Her clever wit and jibes kept us on our toes. What I'd once thought was her ice-queen demeanor seemed to be transforming, in part, into a wicked sense of humor.

"I don't know, Mase. What's wrong with your hair?" She peered over her glass of the chardonnay she'd brought to pair with the fish, an entrée she'd prepared and we'd decimated.

I glanced at Mase. His mop had grown to a whole new level of ragged, hanging past his brows, spiked ends shadowing his eyes. Laura hated it and kept harping at him about it.

Which made the defiant guy only want to grow it longer. "Laura seems to like it just fine when fisting her hands into it." He smirked.

"That why you're growing it out? Giving her handlebars to hold on to for the ride?" Hannah arched a brow, fighting a smile.

Mase blinked and his focus fuzzed out, like he imagined Laura riding him in pornographic detail. I tossed a dinner roll at him, and we all busted up, laughing.

No other girls were allowed at these sacred dinners. We hadn't outright discussed the subject, but in unwritten guy code, we wanted Hannah all to ourselves. She'd become one of us with her raunchy banter and fearlessness. She was ours. And we didn't want to share.

When dinner wound down, Ben and Mase happily cleaned up the mess. We went back to my room, which had slowly gotten cleaner as her visits continued. Each time, her attention strayed to the new details, but she never said anything. And although I hadn't felt the need to become a total neat freak (my OCD tendencies didn't go *that* far), a little tidying seemed the least I could do for her caving and coming to my place all the time.

And just like the first time, and the handful of nights since then, I took the chair by the desk, giving her space on my bed. It had become her territory.

The bedding had also been completely redone. I never wanted her to hesitate with touching my pillow, or anything else of mine, again.

A complete one-eighty from the stark black sheets and comforter that had once covered the bed, I'd had the sales girl pick something less "sex god" and more "safe study zone" while emphasizing no flowers or patterns of any kind. I had no idea how people relaxed with all that blaring visual noise surrounding them, eyes closed or not.

Hannah threw her body into the center of the organic, beige duvet cover (the sales girl had raked me over the coals, insisting it was the safest fabric to cover my new down duvet). Yep, I now own something called a duvet. Four new organic pillows rested against the headboard, covered in pillowcases that were a pale green—"celery," if I remembered the sales girl correctly.

None of the sales pitch had made any difference to me, though. All that mattered was Hannah had made herself comfortable there. Sure, upon discovering the bedding makeover on her second visit, she'd cocked a questioning brow at me. But I'd simply shrugged and cited a long overdue need to replace threadbare sheets, which had been true, even if not the sole reason.

She glanced up at me, waiting, with a huge smile on a face that had grown more beautiful every time I saw it.

Since that night on the dock, we'd gone back to our old routine: my teasing her from her front lobby, her catching me off guard with a heated stare, even if she was speckled with bits of frosting. She'd stopped going through the effort of wearing high heels and skirts, which was fine with me, because it didn't matter what she wore—the girl beneath the clothing made my pulse catch fire.

"What?" She cocked her head, gazing at me from the bed.

We'd been holding back around each other, not quite breaching the distance to get closer. No further serious talks had occurred, only an occasional contemplative glance, like we kept gauging the probability of success if we finally connected on a deeper level.

Well acquainted with the risk-versus-reward model, I understood the wise hesitation on both our parts. The reward didn't hold us back; in fact, it beckoned me in a way nothing else had in the last two years. We both knew we risked a great deal in going for more.

In my twenty-four years of life, I'd never once had a platonic female friend outside of my sisters. No woman had ever had the depth or capacity to want a friendship with me.

Until now.

In the company of the guys and privately on a dock on a cold, bitter night, a girl I'd never seen coming, one I'd never thought existed beneath her ice-queen mask, had breached my outer defenses. Unaware of the danger, I'd let someone unexpected into my heart. And it scared the fuck out of me to lose the ground we'd gained, but the temptation of an even greater possibility kept gnawing at me.

"Let's do your place tomorrow." I leaned forward, holding my breath.

I didn't know where it came from. Probably, I knew something had to change, and maybe throwing the ball into her territory would shake things up, but I could no longer remain Switzerland here. I knew she might hesitate. The heaviness of privacy would shift everything for us.

No longer on neutral ground at her cupcake shop, and no longer in the mixed company of the guys, our dance would finally escalate.

"Okay." Her voice was quiet, but sure.

"Yeah?"

Her smile appeared. "Yeah. You can do my place tomorrow..."

I swallowed hard.

Her tone had gone soft, sultry. I didn't need my phone and the text box to know three little dots were there. I'd heard them, as if she'd typed them oh so slowly: *dot, dot, dot.*

"Fuck, yeah!" I launched from the chair and jumped on the bed beside her, causing her body to bounce high before settling.

She burst out laughing.

No, I'd been wrong.

Before, we hadn't been dancing with one another without touching; we'd been circling, hesitating, not quite flowing into the same rhythm.

I leaned over, brushing the hair off her face, noticing that the gold flecks in her hazel eyes sparkled more brilliantly. "I have something very serious to ask you."

She stared up at me, implicitly trusting.

I waited a beat. "What's your business forecast?"

With a shove, she pushed me over, laughing. I shifted the conversation to true business, planning to strategize a personal plan later.

In deciding to take the next step and spend more intimate time together, *now* we danced *with* each other. And my partner deserved my undivided attention.

13. HER PLACE

When you watch the glassy surface of a lake, pay closer attention. Much more happens beneath that calm than meets the eye. Having buried secrets deep beneath a collected exterior myself, I should've known the phenomenon better than anyone, and yet, I'd been blindsided by the depth of Hannah's.

Although it was still early to understand all that made her tick, knowing she was a fellow casualty on love's battlefield with deep wounds under her scars, I understood enough. The details of her trauma weren't important at this stage.

Hannah lived on a manicured street in an older part of town. Pride of ownership from people who'd lived there for decades showed in personal touches, like potted plants lining brick walkways and park benches beneath oak trees. But many also lived behind stone walls and down long driveways, which lent the neighborhood a feel that was, at once, both welcoming and private.

I rode into her driveway through a gate she'd left open in the middle of a classic white picket fence. Snowflakes fell from a darkening sky onto the gray cobblestones of her single driveway.

Her ivory house was more of a cottage, dark green shutters banking two small windows on either side of a natural wood front door. A red brick chimney rose above a gray-shingled roof, its spiraling column of smoke mixing into the clouds above.

Grabbing the now-damp brown paper bag that I'd secured to the seat behind me with a bungee cord, I glanced down the street. Lights were on in almost all of the windows. Three houses down, a four-door BMW turned, pulling into a leaf-littered driveway. The house across the street still had colored Christmas lights glowing from the eaves.

Knowing where Hannah came home to every night after she closed up shop filled me with a sense of peace, calming an unease I hadn't known was there until that very moment. She lived in the middle of a sedate suburban neighborhood. Absent an alarm system, barking dogs, and a two-man security detail armed with semiautomatic weapons to protect her, I couldn't imagine Hannah in a better place.

I climbed the two brick steps to her square landing and knocked on the door. It opened seconds later to her beaming smile and a blast of scents that made my mouth instantly water.

"Hey, Cade!" Before I was able to step inside, she embraced me in a full hug—our first. I held her tight, inhaling her tropical scent as I relished the full-body contact.

Although the hug didn't mean much on the outside—it was a common way of greeting, after all—and it paled in comparison to our embrace that night on Kristen's dock, it still meant a great deal to me for Hannah to offer.

Another deep breath brought in the incredible scents of

her kitchen. "Damn, woman." I searched over her shoulder when she broke our contact and ushered me inside. "What're you cooking in there? I've died right here on your doorstep and gone to heaven."

She laughed, crossing her arms over her chest. She wore a green sweater, its V-neck teasing forward a nice amount of cleavage with her stance. "You think you've earned heaven?"

I snorted. "*Hell* no. But a man can hope."

She grinned, eyes glinting with humor. "You better earn it, Cade. Good things only come to those who deserve it."

"Are we talking about food?" I had a strong feeling we weren't. And I was *so* on board with the earning thing. Food and otherwise.

Hannah's game was in full force, though. She simply licked her lips, regarding me, then smirked and disappeared around the corner.

I stood there holding the bag. Literally.

Exhaling, I studied the furnishings of the small living room. One floor lamp in the far corner and two table lamps were lit. The bright space was comfortable; two worn chairs in pale yellow fabric sat by the window, angled toward each other with a small maple table in between. A chess set carved of semiprecious stones, one side appearing to be obsidian and the other jade, sat on the square tabletop. A built-in bookshelf filled with well-worn but clearly loved books lined the wall. Across from the chairs was a matching sofa with two colorful pillows.

"I'm opening every cabinet and drawer now..." I called out, smiling as I lifted a silver picture frame. A teenaged version of Hannah stood in an elderly woman's embrace. A frame beside it held a younger woman and a little girl.

"I'd expect nothing less," she replied from behind white painted shutters that had been closed, screening what would have been an open window area between the rooms.

A metal bang sounded out, and I imagined it was the oven door. Fresh scents bombarded me. Feeling like a peeping tom who'd trespassed inside, I abandoned my investigating. I'd rather do my snooping under her watchful gaze. When I could tease her mercilessly.

Following the sounds and smells, I rounded the corner and entered a decent-sized kitchen. "My God. What is all this?"

Hannah stood by a small table for two in front of a bay window. She put down a platter between two place settings. "Duck à l'orange, braised parsnips and golden beets with shallots, and sautéed sugar snap peas." She came toward me, picking up a dark wine bottle with two hands, angling the label forward for my approval. "And an Argentinian malbec."

"Did you make dessert?" I glanced back over to the table. Three small candles flickered in squat glass holders.

A delicate brow arched. "What do you think?"

I smirked. "I think you're trying to impress me." I smiled at her soft laugh.

"Do I need to impress you?"

I shook my head. "No. Not even a little."

When I set the brown paper bag down on the marble surface of her small rolling kitchen island, her gaze shifted to it. "What's that?"

"Ah, ah, ah, that is for after dinner." I grasped her shoulders, turning her back toward the table as she grabbed the neck of the wine bottle. I swiped the bottle opener from her counter and took the bottle from her.

After I poured us each a glass, I glanced up and out through the largest of the three windows to the view behind her house. Garden lights edged a large deck and a walkway that led to a wide body of water. Across the way, the lighting of another house shimmered off the waves.

"Nice view." I sat across from her, holding my glass up.

"Thanks." She raised hers.

Normally we toasted silly things. Once, Ben toasted Mase's left shoe—that it always be next to his right.

I tilted my head. "Why don't you give the toast tonight?" This was her house, and she'd never been given a turn. Overrun by three hungry overbearing men, she'd hardly had the chance.

Her expression softened as she glanced down to the table in thought. When her gaze met mine, her eyes blazed with passion. "To business partners and friends."

And so much more. She didn't voice the thought, maybe she wasn't ready. But I saw the desire in her eyes.

"I'll drink to that." Friends for now, so much more would come in time.

As we dug into the delicious meal she'd made, she grew quiet. Although the silence was comfortable, my curiosity won out. "Do you own this house?"

She nodded, swallowing down a sip of wine. "It was Gran's. She raised me through high school and died just last year."

"Something happened to your parents?"

Her expression fell, sadness shadowing her eyes. "Parent. My mom was a single parent. She'd never been sick a day in her life. Then she got food poisoning and died in the hospital."

"Oh, God, I'm so sorry, Hannah."

"It's okay. Gran and I had already been close."

"No brothers or sisters?"

"Nope." She leaned over and whispered, "No dog or cat either."

I laughed. "Is that an important item to take note of? Are you allergic? Do I have to take back the kitten in the paper bag?"

She gaped, turning to stare at the bag on the island. "There is *not* an animal in that bag."

I snorted. "No, there isn't."

Regardless, she held a dubious expression and stared at the bag for several more seconds before shifting her attention back to me.

I put down my fork, wiping my mouth with my napkin. "I don't have any pets either. We did growing up, but I haven't since I bought the house. Mason keeps hounding me to get a dog. I told him no dog. No cat. No bird. No turtle. A goldfish would be doable, but only because we could flush it when it dies. That's how anti-commitment I've become."

She gasped. "You would not flush a goldfish!"

I arched my brows. "Only after it *died*. I'm not a goldfish murderer."

Laughing, she shook her head, like she couldn't quite figure me out.

Well, that made two of us, because in the next breath after saying how noncommittal I was, I felt drawn toward her in a way I hadn't with anyone in a long time. And it scared the shit out of me. But even knowing how I could be hurt again, betrayed to my core, I still couldn't fight how I felt about Hannah.

Unthinking, I blurted, "I think we need to go out."

Her brow furrowed. "Go out where?"

"On a date."

She blinked. "What about your rule? What about your sisters?"

I blew out a hard breath. A twinge of guilt tripped through me, but I banished it as quickly as it appeared. The Cade who my sisters made promise not to fuck the clients or the help wasn't sitting here with Hannah. And Hannah was not "the help" to me.

And as much as I advocated no fraternizing in the workplace, something had shifted inside me, knocking me off-kilter. In fact, the ongoing shift kept unbalancing me every time I was around her.

Hannah had become the exception to every rule.

"Forget what I said. Clearly, the rule was made to be broken with us. I know you feel a magnetic pull between us just as strongly as I do."

Her brow furrowed. "But you just said you've become noncommittal."

I gave her a hard stare. "You make me want to reform."

She tilted her head a fraction, eyes narrowing. "I think the first step would involve burning one yellow sticky-note list."

I leaned toward her. "Hannah, from the moment I realized you were more than a business partner, that list ceased to exist for me. I will *torch* the damn thing."

Her expression darkened, her hands clasped tightly together on the table. "Because I could never be a girl you would ever put on a list."

I put my hands over hers. "Look, I know the idea of that list is intimidating. Don't let it be. They were just girls. It was just sex. Some guys turn to alcohol or drugs. Others get professional therapy. That list was my therapy."

Her gaze fell to the table, her voice quiet. "I could never have 'just sex.'"

I lifted my hand and, with a gentle finger beneath her chin, lifted her face until her big eyes met mine. "You will never have 'just sex' with me. When we decide we're ready, it will be a mind-blowing heart and body experience."

She fought a smile. "That good, huh?"

I smirked. "Yeah. That good."

Her expression turned serious again. "How long do we have to wait for that?"

I coughed out a laugh, leaning back in my chair.

Her look grew pensive. *She* is *serious.*

My smile faded. "Do you want it to be tonight?"

She stared at me, giving the matter thought, then shook her head.

I tilted my head, holding her gaze. Now that she'd brought it up, I wanted the topic to play out. "Why?"

She smiled shyly, turning away from me, staring out at the water beyond the windows. "I'm not sure." She shrugged. "I guess I'm not ready yet."

I'd thought as much. Hannah was a date kind of girl. She wasn't a girl you got only physical with. She was a girl you got *everything* with.

"How long has it been since..." I didn't know what to call it. The Ultimate No-Show? The Jilting?

Her gaze shifted to meet mine. The sparkle in those beautiful eyes went flat. "Since I was stood up at my wedding? Nineteen months."

I leaned forward, taking her hands in mine. "And have you seen anyone since then?"

A slow shake of her head.

"Not even one date? Coffee?"

"No. Nothing."

I suddenly understood the ice-queen demeanor. It only appeared as a protective mechanism, showing itself when potential suitors were in the vicinity. The shield had been activated like a blinding neon sign when I'd first met her at the grand opening of Loading Zone, warding off any and all men. The cold, hard mask was an effective deterrent. Men didn't want to try that hard to see beneath a woman's armor.

But it wasn't Hannah's true self. This was.

She hadn't put on her armor for Ben and Mase because, in her mind, they would never bother trying. And she was right. That was my territory, and guys had an unwritten man code: you don't poach another man's girl, no matter the reason for her being there—friends, cooking, or otherwise.

I nodded. "And now? Do you think you're ready to try coffee? Or maybe a date?"

Her answer didn't matter. She would be going out on a date with me. This didn't count. Our dinners were only glorified prearranged business meetings and fell into the safe zone.

A date was a risk. Hopes were thrown out there and leaps of faith were taken, no matter how small the steps were, even if safety line calls had been staged with friends as an exit strategy.

No, I didn't want Hannah in the safe zone. She would take that risk and make that death-defying decision with me, heart racing, fears and all.

Hopeful eyes that sparkled rose, meeting mine. Her small smile widened. "Yes."

I arched a brow, my heart nearly bursting from my chest. "Yes, what?"

"Yes, Cade. I will go out on a date with you."

"Excellent." I blew out a held breath, grinning wide and leaning back.

Her expression grew serious again. "Now, what's in the bag?"

14. SECRET OF SUCCESS

Hannah didn't have a television in the front room. She didn't have a back room. The cottage-style home had a smaller room adjacent to the living room filled with drawings, paintings, books, and photo boxes. And off the kitchen was a bedroom suite, equally as large, with another bay window and an amazing view of reflected lights on the water beyond.

A loveseat faced the only TV in the house, a 32-inch. So did a queen-sized bed. With the focus of Hercules, I gave the bed only a brief, uninterested glance. But I was very interested.

Her entire home was decorated in white or ivory with splashes of bright colors in accent pillows, a vase or treasure here and there, and one blooming orchid in practically every window. The space was cozy, and it fit her perfectly.

And although I had free reign to search every square inch of hidden real estate, per our tongue-in-cheek agreement, I passed. The adventure would be finding out what lay beneath all the layers of Hannah *with* her. I didn't want to tarnish the impression with superficial clues.

Her bedside clock displayed the time to be just after 6:00 p.m., perfect for the surprise in the bag.

We stood beside the bay window in her bedroom, gazing out into the night through the large center pane, which had a ledge beneath it with a cushion. Through a cracked-open side window, an owl hooted.

"Ready to see what's in the bag?"

She let out a soft giggle. "No."

Surprised, I looked down at her. "You've been wanting to all night. Now you don't?"

Amusement lit her eyes and the side of her face was illuminated by the light in her hall. "Now that I can, I'm not sure. I'm kind of scared."

I laughed. "Wait here. It won't be bad. Well, at least not 'scary' bad."

Her brow wrinkled.

I winked.

As I returned to her bedroom, I made great fanfare of crinkling the brown wrapper by rippling my fingers over both sides.

She crossed her arms. "I'll decide for myself whether it's 'scary' bad."

"Now, this is not for pleasure. It is strictly for business. Keep that in mind before passing judgment. We have—" I reached into the bag and pulled out its contents "—*The Secret of My Success* or *Chocolat*."

A broad smile lit up her face, and she clapped her hands together. "Movies?"

Happy she was delighted, I forced my expression back to a serious one. "Studying. Have you seen either?"

She shook her head, closing the distance between us and taking both DVDs from me. I snatched them back when she flipped them over and started to read about one of them.

"Nope. No reading. Watching." Waving the cases at her, I shooed her toward the remotes until she scrunched her adorable face and obeyed. "I had limited options at home. We can delve into other titles, but both of these classics are studies in hope, perseverance, and creativity in business. One is a fun *very-eighties* romp in the corporate world. The other's an artsy story of a woman and her small business, and how she wins over the town on her terms."

"Can we watch both?" She raised her brows, clasping her hands together.

With her hopeful expression, it took great effort to remain serious. "It goes over our agreed-upon two hours to watch both."

She scowled, snatching both cases with lightning speed. "It's my house. You are my guest, but I get to make the rules. And we are watching both."

In a blur of dark brown hair and sexy green sweater, she turned and leaned down before her electronics, pushing buttons. And damn, how that woman inadvertently pushed mine. Suddenly, it was all about the jeans from my perspective—that denim may have been painted on her tight ass and hips, but with her bent over before me, it melted away, my mind guttering.

At the aching twitch in my jeans, I forced myself to turn away and stand closer to the coolness of an open window. It was no cold shower, but it would have to do for now.

Not five seconds later, and way too soon to calm my raging blood, she called out, "Ready?"

I turned to find her sitting in the middle of that pillow-filled bed. In the past, I had always hated the idea of putting a ton of throw pillows on a bed. Why? So you had to remove a million pillows to sleep in it, only to toss them all back on during daylight hours?

Kiki called it fashion. I'd only ever seen it as a waste of time.

Now? I was so damn thankful for pillows. Because sitting on top of the bed, amid all of her colorful pillows—some with lace, others tubular with tassels on either end—Hannah was happy. And when she patted the space beside her with all the confidence in the world of her safety, I was ecstatic.

Not needing to be asked twice, I kicked my shoes off and joined her on the bed.

Our thighs touched through our jeans, warmth radiating between us. I raised an arm above her and propped an elbow on the mass of pillows before wrapping my hand around her shoulder. Uncertain how she'd take the bold move, I waited, breathing deeply as the intro to *Chocolat* flared to life on the screen. Her only response was to press closer against my body.

I smiled. "Good choice for our first. This one is closer to your situation: a small shop. She uses creative displays and innovative marketing to entice customers. The story is a little quirky, but that's what makes the movie different."

She shifted, glancing up at me. "Are you planning to give commentary throughout the entire movie?"

"Would you like me to?"

Settling back down against me as the narrator began telling the ancient legend behind the story, Hannah replied with a softness to her voice. "Yeah, it's nice. You're like my business and movie tour guide."

I scooted lower, getting more comfortable. "I like being your tour guide."

Almost halfway into the movie, Hannah squealed. "Johnny Depp!"

I laughed. "You got a thing for Johnny Depp?"

"Nooo…" She elbowed me in the ribs for my infraction.

Another twenty minutes later, she pushed away from me and grabbed the remote, pausing the movie. "This is so wrong. We need popcorn."

When she disappeared without a backward glance, I followed her into the kitchen, slowly drawing out my words. "I don't knowww…popcorn implies a more casual atmosphere. Almost date-like."

Her eyes narrowed for a split second as she pulled out a large pan with two hands. "This is not even close to a date. What would you suggest instead, a notepad and pen?"

I leaned a hip on the far counter, watching her light the stove and drop a large tablespoon of solidified coconut oil into the pan. "Would you be wearing those sexy librarian glasses?"

She raised her brows. "You think my glasses are sexy?"

Leaning up on her tiptoes, she reached for and pulled down a glass container full of popcorn kernels from a cabinet beside the stove. A few hundred kernels pinged into the pan before she replaced the lid. With both hands, she lifted the pan a few inches above the gas burner and gave it a good shake before resting it back down.

The response to her question demanded her full attention, so I waited. She turned, leaning back on her counter edge. We faced each other, her island between us. The few feet may as well have been inches with the way the air was charged between us.

I gave her a heated stare.

Her breath caught, her chest expanding.

Which caused my cock to twitch. I began to feel like one of Pavlov's dogs.

"*You* are sexy." I held her gaze captive. "Therefore, anything you wear becomes sexy."

She smirked. The power she knew she had over me emboldened her. "Even my apron?"

I inhaled, remembering that ruffled apron, her thin T-shirt and short shorts hiding underneath. "Sexy as fuck."

A kernel popped.

She swallowed. "'As fuck?'"

I nodded. "Doesn't get any sexier than that."

A slight tilt of her head, and Hannah began to play. "What if I wore a potato sack?"

I snorted. "Do you own a potato sack?"

She crossed her arms, shaking her head.

My eyes were drawn down to that tempting cleavage. I took my sweet time dropping my gaze down her body, imagining her in a potato sack.

Pops sounded out. One after another. Faster and faster, like my pulse going out of control. Hannah began shallow breathing under the intensity of my stare.

"I would love to see you in a potato sack. Just like I'd love to see you in lingerie. To me, they're both the same."

She laughed, then turned quickly, grabbing the heavy pan with both hands and giving it another hard shake. When she turned around again, she resumed her stance in the same place, back to the counter.

This was another dance—a different location, a more enticing rhythm, but a dance all the same. Two partners circled each other, deciding how long to draw out the beginning steps before pulling each other even closer.

"How can they both be the same? You'd find me equally sexy in either?"

A deep inhale was the only thing I could do to clear my mind, keep me sane. That, and the white-knuckled grip I had on the edge of her counter, holding me immobile, keeping me from launching at her and *showing* her just how sexy I found her.

I tilted my face down, holding her gaze beneath my lowered brows. "Hannah, you have no idea. Whatever you think you do to me, magnify it. I don't see you *in* anything. I just see you. And if you're ever brave enough to wear a potato sack for me, wear nothing else underneath."

The popping slowed. Her attention was needed at the stove at that critical point.

She didn't move. "Why?"

"Because I'll shred it and have you naked in three seconds flat. Might as well save the lingerie."

Her eyes widened.

At the first scent of smoke, she gasped and flew to the stove, grabbing the pan off the flame and turning the knob off. "Damn."

"Wait." I rushed to her side. "Grab some bowls. All the stuff on top is still good."

And just like that, we let all the sexual tension fade away into a teamwork project of sifting out good popcorn from the burnt. We managed to salvage over half of it. She liberally salted the contents of the large glass bowl.

By the time Michael J. Fox began instructing Hannah on the finer points of business with boardroom-to-bedroom antics, she had grown quiet. The popcorn had been demolished long ago, and she'd nestled deeper into my side, her cheek resting on my chest, one of her socked feet thrown over my shin.

Were it not for her occasional questions, I'd have thought she'd fallen asleep. As the onscreen company-retreat deceptions escalated, Hannah shivered. Without disturbing her, I reached over to the arm of the loveseat and lifted the blanket.

After shifting it to my other arm, I swept it over her body. She pulled the edge over as far as it would go, covering part of me too.

"This music is great." She yawned.

"Classic eighties soundtrack. I would've brought *Pretty Woman*, except for there was no lesson to be learned there. You're no hooker."

She snorted, her body shaking against my side. "Gee, thanks."

Her intoxicating scent drifted up again, barely noticeable. I dropped my nose into the hair above her ear, inhaling. "What is that fragrance you wear?"

"I don't wear perfume. My shampoo? Maybe my body wash. It's coconut mango, I think."

"Well, I like it." I could bury myself in that scent. Intended to, actually. Which reminded me of our unfinished business—or pleasure, to be more accurate. "So, about that date."

She turned her face into my chest further, but didn't look up. It was like she didn't want to break the spell we had going, and I didn't want her to.

"What about it?"

Snuggled together on her bed, under her blanket, in her house, we'd crossed the line. We hadn't had sex, hadn't even kissed, but the line had definitely been crossed. DVDs that were "business lessons" were really more than that, and Hannah and I both knew it.

Kristen and the girls would flay me alive if they knew what was happening, but they weren't here. It went against every tenet I'd created in my business dealings, because mixing emotions into the business world created the risk of volatility; the situation alone clouded judgment.

I didn't give a shit about any of that, though. Businesses were built, and they fell. And from the rubble of one failed business, another would rise. My business code of conduct had been amended as of tonight with a bolded, underlined exception for Hannah. Because women like Hannah didn't come along every day.

"How's next Friday night?"

She pushed away, propping herself on an elbow, looking at me with a furrowed brow. "Why not this Friday night?"

"Because this Saturday night is the benefit dinner at the country club, and I don't want you distracted."

She grinned. "What makes you think *I'd* be the one distracted?"

15. SPREADING THE WEALTH

Tonight was the first event Invitation Only held at a stodgy country club—*our* stodgy country club. Actually, the old-money set was trying to form a revitalized image, and embracing a brand-new event company started by the children of two of its most respected and generous members was their valiant attempt.

We didn't want to let them down.

For weeks, we'd been arguing over how far we could push tradition. I wanted to buck convention entirely, and free-spirited Kiki had been right there by my side. Kristen and Kendall, however, vehemently opposed our radical, trial-by-fire approach and insisted on going strictly conventional with just a touch of edgy.

How the hell do you do that? My playbook was only written in go-big-or-go-home language.

In the end, Mom overruled us wild ones, siding with Kristen and Kendall. Mom was on the charity committee, and her reputation was on the line.

So instead of a string quartet, we hired a three-piece jazz ensemble to shake things up. And rather than holding the event inside the bland ballroom, we braved the cold March nights with plenty of those artsy, column heat lamps.

And a healthy dose of denial.

Because the philanthropic set never wore a coat over an evening gown. Well, unless it was an inherited fur. But that was considered tacky, unless you were coming or going from a Rolls or a Bentley.

Thousands of white lights snaked up the trunks and branches of the evergreen trees in the garden. Colorful lanterns swayed in the wind. In the pond next to the walkway, dozens of lily pads held tea light candles, making the black water sparkle.

Hannah stood by my side in a shadowed alcove, admiring all the decorations. "You look really handsome tonight."

"I'm in a tux." I tugged at the choking collar. Only for my mom.

She laughed. "You say that as if it's in argument to my compliment."

"It is," I grumbled. I glanced down at her. "Now, *you* look amazing. Watching you move in that dress is the only thing keeping me sane." Though I spoke the words, I forced my gaze outward to the horizon line of party guests. I was a mere mortal man, and Hannah had turned into a goddess.

"Oh, you mean this old thing?" she teased, stalking forward into my line of sight, showing me the backless silver silk as it fell in a "V" just below her waist. There was nothing on underneath, which I noticed every time she turned her back to me.

I growled low as she turned slowly. "Be careful, Hannah. A man can only take so much."

A wicked smile appeared on her angelic face. The temptress had returned.

She dropped her hands to her hips. Beautiful didn't even begin to cover it. Dark waves of hair framed her face, swept down on one side below her shoulder. Those hazel eyes had become dark, glistening in the shadows.

A smirk lit up her face. "I've no idea what you're talking about."

"You know exactly what I'm talking about." I stepped forward and brushed my hands over hers, where they were still propped on her hips, then slid mine over her ass. Proprietary, I know. But I laid claim just the same. She didn't stop me.

Her eyes simply flared wide. She bit her lower lip, then slowly released it.

I stared long and hard at the luscious lip that I wanted to bite, suck on, taste in long, slow licks until she surrendered to more. My gaze rose upward to meet her eyes. Dilated. For me.

"All I see is a potato sack, about to be shredded."

A slow smile curved her lips. "You mean, you think I'm sexy."

"Devastatingly so."

"Cade! Hannah!" Kristen's voice sounded close.

Two seconds away from being caught in each other's arms, I couldn't break the hold. I moved my hand up from her ass just in time for Kristen to nearly run us over.

"We need you two! The cake is being wheeled out!" Kristen gripped my forearm, yanking me away.

I grabbed Hannah's hand, and she held it as we hurried behind a frantic Kristen. When I gave Hannah a conspiratorial glance, she winked. We'd escaped discovery by the skin of our teeth, and Kristen was so busy micromanaging the event, she'd failed to see the bigger behind-the-scenes picture. Which was just fine with me. Kristen could lead, staying all business through the night from beginning to end. I would play my part when needed, an arrangement that suited both of our natures.

The cake was rolled out onto the patio. Without any theme to go off of, Hannah had only wanted to know the charity.

And in the end, the subject was a serious one. My rowdy, rule-breaking tendencies aside, I had no desire to make light of the cause this event was raising money for.

Victims of human trafficking.

So how do you make that edgy? It already is.

No music would ease such a heavy topic. No cake ever could.

But tonight was about coming together for a common cause. Any celebration was in raising more awareness and dollars to fight the perpetrators and set the victims free.

Shocking or not, there were people in this world who had obscene amounts of wealth, more money than they would ever know what to do with. And although the benefit dinners spent lavish amounts of money on food, drink, and cake, plus the jewels and clothing on its attendees, all the window dressing at the events were mere pennies compared to the billions of dollars represented among the hundreds of guests who mingled around us.

Kristen approached the podium near the doors of the veranda, but stopped short and waved her hand, beckoning Hannah to follow her up there. I squeezed Hannah's hand, then released it.

She glanced up at me with bright eyes, brows raised, as she puffed a lungful of air through pursed lips. "Wish me luck."

I smiled. "You don't need luck. These people are here in support. You're already fabulous."

She grinned, one of those heart-stopping flashes of pure happiness. Then she disappeared through the guests.

I spread my stance wider, crossing my arms over my chest as I watched the crowd that gathered from my vantage point on the side. In silence, I dared anyone in attendance to act up. Although no one paid me any direct attention, I pushed a powerful "play nice" vibe out there anyway.

The podium stood only twenty feet away, but the patio stretched wide, and guests slowly pushed their way forward as the music stopped and additional lights came on under the eaves. Everyone seemed well behaved. Kendall had become point man for Caroline Evans, a notorious drinker and troublemaker at these refined events. Kristen was in charge of Mr. and Mrs. Fulsom, whose marriage had been on the rocks and whose public fights had been escalating, but the Fulsoms were actually on the far edge, holding hands.

Kristen adjusted the microphone. "Thank you for coming here tonight to bring awareness and support to a very worthy cause. I would like to introduce the coordinator of this event and the chair of The Unity Foundation charity committee, my mother, Victoria Michaelson."

You heard right.

No "K" name on the mother hen of our flock.

I scanned the crowd once more, and then watched respectfully as my graceful mother approached the podium. Like all of us, she was dark haired and light eyed, but when she moved, the woman held an incomparable regal grace.

Victoria Georgette Michaelson had grown up in a wealthy family that spanned generations. It was Dad, Garrett Michaelson, who'd come from a marginal family of new money, earning his way and reputation into the accepting fold of higher society.

However, the four of us had grown up in a family that didn't give one single fuck about the money or the society. Mom didn't. Dad sure as hell didn't. And we kids had all been raised to value money, but none of the excesses and vices that inevitably came with it.

Why were we even here then? Because there was a fine line between buying into the mechanism and using its methods to the best advantage.

With this level of wealth came power and responsibility. The money, if well managed, grew exponentially. And because we didn't believe in squandering, we needed the ideal conduit to have that money flow where it was needed the most—which meant mingling with the social elite, networking on golf courses, and an occasional tennis match.

Them. Not me. I did *not* play tennis.

But I got the idea. I'd swing a club every now and then for a good cause. And I'd put on a tux when the situation warranted. Not that I ever enjoyed it, but it's what we Michaelsons did for the greater good.

My mother addressed the crowd. "Hello, everyone. Thank you all for coming tonight with generous hearts and open pocketbooks. This cause has become one near and dear to us and affects adults and children worldwide. I'm talking about human trafficking. Don't think it's not happening in your neighborhood, because it is."

Murmurs and gasps rippled through the crowd at Mom's strategic pause—the woman delivered a speech with flair.

"Remember when one of our own—Felicity Williams— ran away from home as a teenager? Luckily, the police found her in time, but she'd been abducted within twelve hours of wandering the streets by some very bad men. A ring of predators are waiting for the right opportunity to 'help' innocent children who are temporarily lost and looking for anyone to believe in them. *Our children.*

"And for all of you who have housekeepers and gardeners from other countries, imagine if they'd never made it to your home. Many struggling immigrants hand over thousands of dollars on the promise of a better life, only to be whisked away into slave labor under the threat of harm to them or their loved ones, money stolen, promises broken.

"And the Super Bowl we had a few weeks ago? It is the largest event worldwide for human trafficking, with criminal rings flying girls in from around the world to service clientele willing to pay, thereby creating demand. Human trafficking is a horrific tragedy, and we need to use our money and influence to stop it. The Unity Foundation is a parent foundation, funneling income down to underlying charities doing hard work on the ground where their efforts are needed the most, helping to capture perpetrators and to rescue and rehabilitate victims. A list of charities supported with all funds collected by The Unity Foundation is on the billboard on the easel beside me. The event tonight is only the first of many to bring attention to the cause and to help gain your involvement. I hope you join us with your generosity."

A round of applause roared. When it died down, she gestured to the side. "This evening we've been lucky enough to have our event thrown by a new company that my children have formed, Invitation Only. And they've been blessed to have a talented artist on their team whose creations are causing a stir in the media. In fact, the press is here tonight, not only to support the charities, but also to witness and share in the unveiling of the baker's latest work of art. I would like her to say a few words. My friends, it is my pleasure to introduce to you Hannah Martin."

Polite applause followed. The crowd always held back their approval of outsiders. They rendered judgment on their own set of rules, some biased by class beliefs, others by ego. The phenomenon was a psychoanalytical study in human behavior.

Hannah stood behind the podium, her shoulders back, head held high. If she was nervous, she hid it well. Her gaze scanned over to me and held for an instant. I smiled and nodded. She beamed a megawatt grin at me. *Oh yeah, she's got this.*

"Thank you, Victoria, and thank you all for inviting us here tonight. I can think of no greater cause than showing kindness to those souls who are lost in this world, who have been trapped against their will, who may have lost hope.

"*We* are their hope. We are one, worldwide."

At the last words, Hannah stepped back, the lights on the crowd and podium went off. Special halogen lights beneath the eves illuminated, casting bright spotlights on the table that held the cake behind an ivory curtained wall.

Hannah stepped to the corner of the cake and pulled the curtain away.

Gasps followed.

Rainbows shot everywhere, refracted from unseen crystals. The crowd pressed in closer to get a better look.

A four-foot-tall globe rose up from the table, pure white and sparkling. This time, Hannah had run the entire idea by me before she'd begun the undertaking. She'd wanted to know my opinion. I'd thought it was brilliant. And it was, literally.

The entire world, frosted in white, spun slowly on a mechanism beneath the base. Sugar crystals formed the continents done to scale and with such detail, Rand McNally would be proud. White cream frosting painted the oceans, with tiny waves peaking in their centers. And where the globe ended at the bottom and the base began, ever-widening pedestals of white were coated in Swarovski crystals, catching the beams of light.

Hannah wound her way through the crowd toward me, but her path was lost to a crush of new fans wanting to know more about our baking prodigy. Through the sea of heads, she cast me a helpless glance.

I laughed, watching her. Unless Derek Johnson tripped on Sophie Madsen's trailing hemline as they jockeyed for position to speak to her, Hannah would be safe. Regardless, I worked my way through the guests between Hannah and me, shaking hands and sharing in the praise of both the cake and the event.

Mrs. Hopkins, an elderly widow, pulled me down to her four-foot-ten height to whisper, "That Hannah is a stunning woman." She pursed her lips together, tilting her head toward her topic.

I chuckled. "Yes, she is."

My humor disappeared as Mrs. Hopkins glared at me. "You'd do well to land a beautiful, talented, and intelligent woman like that."

Although being schooled by the upper-class entitled didn't ever sit well with me, I forgave her the slight. Because she was absolutely right. "Yes, I would. The man who 'lands' Hannah Martin will be a lucky man indeed." I winked at the old bird.

Her eyes went wide, but I left her to her thoughts as I finally wound my way behind Hannah.

A young Susan Warner, just graduating high school in a few months and allowed to attend her first adult social function by her parents, admired the cake. "It's a work of art, Ms. Martin."

Hannah smiled, tipping her head to the girl. "Thank you."

A member of the press edged closer, taking several snapshots. When she dropped the camera down, letting the strap hold its weight, she pulled out a small notepad and unclipped a pen from it. "What do you call this piece?"

Hannah cocked her head. She hadn't thought to name her pieces before the Valentine's Day party, and when asked that night, she'd copped out and used the theme as the title: Love is a Battlefield.

She glanced at the reporter, then to me. "This one is called United Hope."

A nod, followed by a scribble.

"Kincade Michaelson. Wherever did you find this gem?" A familiar voice, a hidden agenda.

I turned toward Stuart Simms. We'd grown up together, only we didn't play very well in the sandbox. Always out for the new angle, or intent on acquiring the next shiny toy, Stuart had become a human embodiment of everything I loathed in the country-club circles.

He'd also inherited tens of millions, and in cutthroat corporate raiding, had multiplied his wealth. Ego radiated off the man. And the way he looked at Hannah just now, so did blatant lust.

"Don't bother, Stuart. She's out of your league."

The fool arched a brow, turning toward me. "Is there such a thing?"

I shook my head, leaving the shark in my wake. "In regard to that woman? Yes."

Other admirers had filled in the space between us, but I worked my way against the current until I stood beside

Hannah again. She smiled up at me, but looked a bit shell-shocked.

I pressed a hand to her lower back. "Want to get out of here?"

Her eyes grew wide. "Can we?"

"Do you have the cake covered?"

She bit her lower lip, frowning at the towering confection. With a serious expression, she glanced back. "Give me ten minutes."

"What if I helped?" I picked up a plate.

A small smile touched her lips. "I would love that."

While Hannah carved into the globe, starting in the vicinity of a glittering iced Greenland, I dutifully held up fine china for the slices of white cake to rest on. In ten minutes, we'd destroyed half the world.

A waiter joined us, and Hannah handed the cake server over to him. "Just be sure to serve only from the top tier of the base and up. The bottom portions are not edible. We don't want anyone choking on a crystal."

"Or breaking a tooth," he added.

"Exactly." Hannah looked around, making certain nothing remained that needed her attention.

I spotted Kristen in the center of the wooden dance floor, looking calmer than usual. "I'll be right back."

Hannah nodded, stepping off to the side, under the veranda.

Kristen turned toward me and raised the beveled crystal glass in her hand. It was filled with an amber liquid. "To a successful country-club event."

Absent a drink, I nodded and gave her a half hug. "Very successful, thanks to you."

"Pfft. I only did my part. We all pulled together." Her words slurred a bit.

"You gonna be okay the rest of the night? Hannah and I are taking off."

Perceptive eyes narrowed. Kristen was a sharp one, even if she had ventured from buzzed to drunk. "'Hannah and I'? Didn't I see you two in the garden earlier?"

I chuckled, kissing the top of her head. "You saw nothing."

Yet.

16. AFTER PARTY

W hen we left the fundraiser, I removed my tux jacket and draped it over Hannah's shoulders. Initially, she shook her head and backed up. But with a hard look from me, she relented. I then made certain her arms went into the sleeves.

"I look ridiculous in this." The hem of the jacket went almost to her knees.

I ignored her protest, wrapping the lapels, one over the other, trying not to smile. "You look adorable." And she did. She belonged in more of my clothes.

She rolled her eyes. "Great, adorable was the look I was going for."

"It suits you. Besides, I like you in my jacket."

"Don't take it as a claim on me, mister. It isn't a letterman jacket. It is warm, though." She pulled it tighter around her.

We made a detour through the kitchen, where I grabbed a bottle of Champagne. "After you." I gestured toward the back door.

We emerged on the other side of the building. Stray guests wandered across the sprawling lawn in the dark, but all the glowing lights from the party were hidden by the massive building.

Since Hannah wore a sexy pair of high heels, I kept to the paved areas, following the sidewalk down to the winding pathway I remembered playing on as a child. When the wider path broke into stepping stones and Hannah slowed, hopping from one to the other, I stopped. "Hold this."

She raised her arms in her oversized coat, exposing her small hands. She took the Champagne bottle from me with one hand on the neck and the other cradling the bottom.

I stepped behind her, squatted, and hooked my arms behind her knees and back, lifting her into my arms.

She let out a squeal. "Put me down!" Squirming, she began to fight my hold.

I tightened my grip. "Nope. No twisting an ankle on my watch."

After a moment, she accepted my reasoning and settled. "Where are you taking me?"

Her weight was slight in my arms, but I lifted her higher. It enabled me to lean to the side every few steps to be certain I didn't trip on the stepping stones. They began to disappear the further we went, overgrown lawn around their edges fighting to swallow them whole.

"To a secret place where we used to play as children."

She quieted as we wound through manicured hedges that fully screened us from the party now. Distant strains of jazz music drifted toward us. A glow from the lights and the half moon rising above the tree line provided enough light to navigate.

Landscapers might have ignored the path to a forgotten area of the garden, but when we finally broke into the clearing in the far corner of the property, the structure still stood exactly as I remembered it. As we approached the steps, Hannah shifted in my arms, facing it.

I placed her onto the wooden entrance steps, and she gasped, gazing up.

Overrun with the dormant stems of wisteria vines, the gazebo's white bones still held strong. Shaped into a giant octagon, the structure held vivid memories of bored children seeking to escape into a fantasy land.

With a shoulder propped onto the pillar at the entrance, I watched Hannah explore. She placed the Champagne bottle on the end of the nearest built-in bench, then walked along the inner perimeter before standing in the center and looking out at me. Then she twirled, laughing.

Yeah, the place had that kind of magical effect on people.

"We used to come here and enact the scene from *The Sound of Music*. Of course, I was Rolfe, and the girls took turns playing Liesl."

Hannah laughed, crossing her arms in my flappy sleeves. "They must've worn you out."

"Nah." I stepped inside.

The protection of the cover and the mass of trees surrounding us made the chill in the air disappear. Hannah remained in her spot, watching me as I approached in measured steps.

"You really don't need this anymore." I moved behind her, pulling my jacket from her shoulders.

"No, I guess I don't." Her voice softened.

I folded the jacket and laid it over an open section of wooden railing.

"Wait! It's so dirty." Her face fell when she realized her warning came too late.

"It's okay. I've got a great dry cleaner."

On a deep exhalation, she smiled, but then cast her face down, her shyness coming forth.

A burning sensation filled my chest, an ache I hadn't felt in a long time. "Hannah, look at me."

Slowly, she raised her face.

"You're not nervous, are you?"

Her head began to shake, but then turned into a nod.

"There's nothing to be nervous about. We are two people in an ancient gazebo that I played in as a boy. And all the boy is asking for is a dance." I extended an arm toward her.

A smile lit her face in the shadows, and she came to me, stepping into my arms. "I am *not* leaping between the benches like in the movie."

I pulled her close, and she molded her body into mine, pressing her cheek into my chest. "Never. I wouldn't dream of it." Full body contact was all I wanted.

"Too bad it isn't raining like in the movie." Her absent-minded comment was toned with innocence.

"Yeah, too bad." Mine was breathy, tinged with under-tones of meaning. Imagining Hannah with her flimsy silk ball gown plastered to her body—her lack of *underthings* body—did things to me.

I pressed us closer together with my arms, wanting her to *know* what she did to me. No inhibiting denim held me restrained tonight. And I didn't wear underthings either.

"You're..." Her voice had dropped to a breathy whisper.

"Hard."

She nodded.

"You started it." Yeah. I was twelve. I blamed the gazebo.

Hannah laughed softly. "I'd say I'm sorry, but I'm not."

The slow jazzy song ended. Silence followed. We continued swaying around to our own rhythm. I felt like I could dance with her forever, hidden in our private garden, mixing great memories of my past and present.

My gaze fell on the bottle. In spite of my not wanting an intimate moment to end, the band had taken leave, and there was only so much close proximity a man in need could handle.

"Let's make a toast to tonight." On a deep, determined breath, I broke away, striding over to the bottle.

With a few quick twists, I pulled off the wiring and wrapper. Hannah joined me, but eyed the frayed wood on the bench.

I grabbed my jacket from the railing and spread it on the splintering surface. I bowed deeply. "A gentleman covers a puddle for the lady."

"Most obliged." She dipped her head and spun around. And although she could've sat in the center, she chose to sit closest to me, her silk-covered thigh pressing into my mine.

She looked beautiful. Dark eyes sparkling. Waves of hair tumbling down one shoulder. The barest fabric teasing across a body meant to be...

I took another cleansing breath. Then I gripped the cork steady in my left hand, grabbed the base of the bottle with my right, and slowly twisted the bottle. The cork gave way with a *pop!* and frothy foam poured out as I tilted it away.

She smiled.

I swallowed hard.

On another breath, I wiped my mind clear and focused on the beautiful woman looking up at me expectantly. I raised the bottle. "To a Julie Andrews musical and child-hood memories."

She reached up, placing her hands over mine. "To new memories. And musicals."

I pulled the bottle down. "Oh, no. I don't do musicals."

She bit her lip, then smiled wide. "Oh, yes. You do."

I shook my head. "No."

She nodded, grinning wider. "Yes. It's a nonnegotiable point."

I sighed, lowering the Champagne bottle. "One."

"I can live with that. One."

I angled my head, glaring at her. "But not on the first date."

She burst out laughing. "Seriously? Okay. We should make a rule, though."

"Date rules? Like how far we can go without seeing a musical? Fine. Fifth." If I had to attend a cheesy musical, it would be at the last possible moment.

"Fourth. And since we're paralleling date rules? I also mean sex."

Fuck. "Third."

"Done." Her eyes gleamed with humor.

In the history of dating, I'd be willing to bet no man has ever made an appointment for sex and a musical on the third date. I raised the bottle and took a healthy swig, then passed it to her, casting her a sidelong glance. "Shrewd. I'm impressed."

Then she wrapped those full lips around the bottle opening.

I blinked.

The third date? I didn't know how I would make it that long.

17. BEST LAID PLANS

The day had finally arrived for our first official date.

After another week of dinners at my place that Hannah had insisted upon, and with her teasing me mercilessly at every stolen opportunity, my nerves were fried. I'd become one snarling, horny bastard.

However, Ben stood in the entrance to my bedroom and had dropped the worst possible bomb. "Sorry, man. I know you had plans with Hannah tonight, but I can't get out of this."

"It's a *wedding*." I cringed as the word left my lips. Leave it to another celebration of the death of two more singletons to ruin the lives of the rest of us.

Ben glared at me. "It's my brother's wedding. I'm the best man. Don't be an idiot. Reschedule Hannah. She'll understand."

I sighed, unable to tell him why *I* didn't understand. The guys knew I had plans with Hannah, but they didn't know the extent of my feelings for her, nor did they know tonight was supposed to be our first date. Hannah and I kept things completely cool in front of the guys. But if they knew, I think they'd each give their left nut to trade places with me. This was Hannah. Their Hannah too.

I scrubbed a hand over my face. "Seriously, the flu?"

"No shit. Cherise *and* Kyle. Scott is on vacation. We only have Lisa. And you know the bar can't run on one bartender on a Friday night."

"Tell those two to stop swapping spit. And licking shopping carts." I sighed. "Fuck."

"I know, man. Listen, I gotta go. We're flying down in two hours. I'll be back Sunday."

I groaned as he closed my bedroom door. Face-planted on the bed, I reached for my phone, sliding my hand blindly on the nightstand. When I pulled it under the covers, the light glared painfully bright under the sheets.

I squinted until I found Hannah's number. "Hey."

A pause stretched on the other end, then a soft, "Hey."

"Sorry to bother you so early."

"It's almost noon, Cade."

"Mmm-hmm. Early."

"Get out of bed, lazy ass. You've got a date to take me on tonight."

"Yeah, about that. I've got to reschedule."

At her silence, I wasted no time in explaining. Including blaming Ben. And spit swapping. And shopping carts.

She laughed. "It's okay. We'll make it for next weekend."

"Can't. That night is McGinty's." We had an event for St. Patrick's Day at a local bar.

"Oh, I forgot."

I stared at the ceiling, thinking about my calendar. "How about the following Friday night?"

"Not Saturday?"

I groaned. "Can't wait that long."

A soft laugh. "Not one more day to Saturday?"

"No. I *will* die if it's not Friday night."

I should cancel one of the weekday dinners; it would serve Ben right for having his family's wedding be the reason my sex life got postponed. Mase would get over it. But Hannah looked forward to dinners at my place. I'd begun to think she needed the adoptive family contact. And with three siblings of my own, I related.

"Well, okay. I wouldn't want you to die. I'm going to miss you, though."

I sighed. This day sucked ass already. "I'm going to miss you too."

"I bought a killer dress."

"Yeah? So I was fated to die anyway?"

She giggled. "Death by dress."

"Potato sack, baby. Remember, it's the woman under the dress."

"So the low-cut number skimming my breasts, just for you, should be discarded?"

I swallowed hard.

"It has a super-short hemline."

I inhaled deeply. "How short?"

Her voice lowered. "Like you can't tear your eyes away, hoping-for-a-peek short."

"Damn. Keep the dress on ice."

"I also have a pair of matching strappy black stilettos..."

"Stop. I'm already dying. And I'm now hanging up the phone before you tell me what's underneath it."

Laughter chimed out as I disconnected.

Okay, maybe waiting wasn't the end of the world. Hannah made waiting worthwhile.

WALL-TO-WALL PEOPLE FILLED the dance floor. We were bursting at the seams and threatened to risk the wrath of the fire marshal if we weren't careful. Bar glasses clinked as we restocked to keep up with the demand. The night broke sales records after another "polar vortex" deep-freeze for days on end had given the entire Eastern Seaboard cabin fever.

"It's stretching back about a block." Mark, our floor manager and, at the moment, lead doorman, informed me regularly on the hour how long the line was.

"And our VIP sections?"

"Packed to the maximum. Trey took care of that already."

I nodded, pouring another tray of drinks, trying to keep up with orders. "Perfect. And tell the guys to stay on their toes. Anyone even looks the wrong way, they're out in favor of waiting patrons."

"Got it, boss. I mean, Cade." He laughed, honoring my request at discretion. When I was on shift, except for when decisions needed to be made, I was one of the team.

A quick nod at the best security money could buy, and he was out, keeping the club running at its optimum and protecting the patrons.

Although it made sense for me or Ben to take a floor manager role, we didn't want to be tied down to the club. The idea was to create a business that could run on its own, and we followed a formula we'd created to accomplish that goal. Our hands-on involvement in the last year had been as efficiency experts, examining and streamlining every process. And with the hiring of extra bartenders, we'd been able to pull back quite a bit, letting the rest of the employees take the reins.

I glanced over at Lisa, who was a blur pouring drinks at the other end of the bar. A hard worker and ethical beyond question, she'd become an invaluable asset.

"So, Cherise and Kyle? They been hooking up?" Not that it was any of my business who the employees dated, and due to Pennsylvania law, we didn't prohibit workplace romance. But it helped to know what was going on to be able to properly manage the situation—for short-staffing issues just like this.

Lisa shrugged. "Not sure. Don't know if it was mouth-to-mouth, shared glasses, or a runaway sneeze. Just know she looked like death warmed over last night, and he said he couldn't get out of bed this morning."

Customers at the bar were pushing in three deep. The waitresses never stopped moving, sending in electronic orders through our tablet system, then picking up trays when the orders were filled.

"Next week, I'm holding a flu shot clinic here."

Lisa laughed. "Good luck with that. I won't go near a needle while conscious."

After doing a speed-pour round of shots on a tray, I dropped her a deadpan look. "Unconscious can be arranged."

Her eyes narrowed. "I'll be in line right behind you."

Damn. Did women know men hated needles? And the sight of blood. A natural aversion to being stabbed is built into male DNA.

Lisa stared out into the crowd. "Uh, Cade. Look to your three o'clock. You've got fans."

Glancing toward the dance floor, I spotted a quartet of

brunettes on the outer edge who turned heads through the crowd behind them like a wake behind a jet boat. I swallowed hard, shocked motionless for the seconds it took me to process who I saw.

Hannah.

Wearing a dress exactly as she'd described, she was a vision, all toned legs, high heels, and devastating curves. Flanking her were Kiki, Kristen, and Kendall.

"Forget the flu shot; I may not survive the night. Cover for me, I'm taking ten." Without waiting for a reply, I stepped out onto the floor.

Oblivious to the wrath she'd provoked, Hannah laughed at something Kendall said. Pissed the hell off, I strode forward with my blood boiling in my veins. Everyone in my path must've sensed the imminent danger, because people moved out of my way with every step.

What was it with women and pushing men's buttons?

I get that a woman wants to look attractive. News flash: you already do. We see it. But apparently to women, owning their own beauty isn't enough. They arm all the weapons in their arsenal to gain the attention of every Y chromosome within a ten-mile radius. Why do they go to all the trouble? Validation.

Meanwhile, biology dictates survival of the fittest; battles ensue, wars are fought, and somewhere amid all the carnage, a victor emerges to claim his female. All because said female just wanted to go out and feel pretty that night.

Well, if my females wanted to play with fire, they deserved all the heat they got from me.

By the time I reached the group that seemed intent on testing my limits, I'd gone DEFCON 1. With my hands clenched into fists at my sides, I didn't touch Hannah. Didn't trust myself to not throw her over my shoulder and run off, hiding her from all the men present...on the planet.

Yep. This was what women did to men. They brought out the caveman in our species.

I did nothing to restrain the fury in my voice. "What are you doing here?"

Innocent eyes blinked up at me, growing wider as she sensed my rage. A warning bell fired off somewhere inside my head, but it was drowned out by the rush of blood pounding past my ears.

She stepped closer, whispering between us as she gazed up with sparkling eyes. "I missed you, Cade. I couldn't go all night without seeing you."

Her soft words and sweet expression caused hairline fractures in my steel bravado. I pinched my eyes shut, taking a deep breath and counting to three. When I opened them, I scanned the faces of my three sisters. They all stood behind Hannah, expressions anything but innocent.

I growled, scowling at them. A stunt like this was classic Michaelson-Three harassment. Parade around the one sex kitten Cade couldn't have in front of him. Sisterly torture at its finest.

Only they had no idea Hannah and I were several steps ahead of them.

A twinge of guilt panged through me at deceiving them, at breaking my promise to them, hell, at fraternizing—the very thing I'd just been bitching about with regard to Cherise and Kyle.

My sisters' smug expressions obliterated any remorse I might've felt.

Holding my patience on a tight leash, I stared down at Hannah. "If you want to stay, if you want me to live through the night, I need you to come with me." I took her hand as her smile widened.

Okay. She was forgiven.

I looked back at the she-demons, glaring fiery daggers at them. They were not.

On my way back, the crush of the crowd forced us off to the side. I led the way, keeping a tight hold of Hannah's hand behind me as we crossed the room to my end of the bar. With no empty barstools, I did the only thing I could.

Turning to the two ladies warming the stools on the end, I addressed them. "I need your seats, ladies. How about a round on me?"

Their eyes brightened, and they nodded.

I looked at the sugar-frosted martini glasses with only an inch of yellow liquid remaining. "Lemon drops?"

"Yep. Two, please."

"Comin' right up. Give me just a minute."

They moved off their leather seats, stepping off to the side, and I led Hannah to the stool on the end. As she scooted her ass back onto the seat, my eyes drifted down to the bottom of the slinky black dress she wore.

"Jesus Christ, Hannah. You weren't kidding about that skirt. You better be wearing something under that." I forcibly swiveled her body toward the bar, so the only thing that would have a view beneath that dress was rusty metal sheeting.

Her eyes twinkled. "I sure am."

Great. Now my imagination ran the gamut of possibilities. I dropped my lips to her ear. "Something tiny, I hope."

She turned her head, her lips brushing against the shell of my ear. A shiver traveled down my spine. "Very."

Taking a deep breath, I pulled back, staring into eyes that had turned a dark emerald. "You look amazing."

She blushed. "Thank you. It's all for you."

I arched a brow. "No it's not. You're here displaying your sexy-as-fuck body for all to see and enjoy. Please. Protect me and stay here. That way I don't have to pummel any man stupid enough to touch you. Or look at you."

She cocked her head, laughing at my words, unaware of the incredible restraint in my tone. But she nodded, sparing me from having an aneurism right in front of her.

"You and I are *so* going to have a talk later about the birds and the bees."

On a single coughed laugh, she shook her head. "I've already gone way past that talk."

I leaned in fast, causing her to startle backward to avoid a banging collision of foreheads. "You need a refresher."

She scrunched her face at me in an adorable way.

I pointed a stern finger, glaring at her. "I'm watching you."

"That's the idea." She smirked.

"Fuck, woman. I'm beginning to think you need a spanking more than a talk."

Interest glittered in her eyes as she inhaled slowly.

"Orders are backing up! You coming back, Cade?" Lisa's distress call splashed ice water on the heated flirting.

"Don't move." I stared hard at Hannah.

"I promise to not even go pee without your permission."

I nodded, satisfied. "What'll you have?"

Her gaze traveled to the empty glasses of the two other girls. "Those looked good."

"Three lemon drops, coming up."

In the ninety seconds it took me to sugar dust the rims and mix the three drinks, Hannah had not only involved herself in a laughter-filled conversation with the girls whose place she'd taken, but had also been surrounded by my sisters.

As I slid the three drinks in front of Hannah and her new friends, I shot another frosty glare at my sisters. They'd caused this clusterfuck to happen. All my life, they'd made it their mission to cause me strife anytime opportunity presented.

"Awww, c'mon, Cade. We were just trying to cheer you up." Kiki dripped out the words with a sweet tone.

She fooled no one.

"Uh-huh. Just you remember, payback's a bitch. Kincade Michaelson's retribution is calculated and scarring."

All three of their expressions fell. Kendall turned white. Yeah. They realized how far they'd pissed me off tonight. And when I got this mad, I waited. I cooled off. I planned. And then, things got brutal. Wars were started in the Michaelson household in the aftermath.

Kristen wrapped an arm around Hannah as she took a first sip of her drink. "We were only helping out a *friend* and our brother. We didn't want you two to be separated because of a little ol' wedding."

My eyes narrowed at Kristen's smirk. They didn't know anything. They couldn't know.

I glanced at the three, who were doing their best to downplay their meddling. "Fine. You want to avoid my wrath? You're point on Hannah tonight. All three of you. Pretend like she's one of you tonight—like she's not just my friend I want to protect, she's my *innocent* sister. No man better touch her. And if one looks about to, one of you had better body check him before I see, or blood will spill. And it will be on your hands. And then, I will square a debt of revenge on each of you. Individually."

Hannah laughed, tipping her head into Kendall's. "I had no idea he'd go all possessive and protective. It's kinda hot."

Kendall scrunched her face while Kiki voiced, "Ewww."

I growled, unhappy none were taking this shit seriously. Then it dawned on me that I hadn't told my sisters anything about my date tonight, but Hannah clearly had said something for them to know about the wedding. Kristen had seen a glimpse of us together at the charity function, but hadn't confirmed anything.

How much did they suspect?

It couldn't be much. None of them knew the depths of what I felt for Hannah, because even Hannah didn't know. Fuck, even I was still trying to nail down that one. All they could possibly know was that we worked closely together and were about to go out for dinner, which was the truth of the matter.

But that they weren't jumping all over my shit for a potential breach in their "no doing the help" rule raised all kinds of suspicious red flags with me, not that Hannah was the help. Not even close.

Occam's razor: simplest explanation is always the most likely. And the simplest explanation? My sisters loved to fuck with me. And that's all this parading-Hannah-to-look-like-the-sexiest-fuckable-bombshell shit was about.

"Cade!" Lisa wailed her final plea before her mutiny.

"Go." Kristen shooed me off with waving hands. "We'll guard Hannah with our lives."

Hours flew by with barely a breathing break as drinks gushed forth from bottles. Our heads spun with the unrelenting and unprecedented demand. The line outside the door remained over a block long until well past midnight, when the crowd began to thin.

By 1:00 a.m., the dance floor cleared enough to allow

movement without mass body contact—actual dancing, rather than group up-and-down bobbing. Hannah and my sisters had popped up off their Cade-reserved barstools and made their way to a center opening on the floor. True to their word, they'd kept Hannah under a tight lock-and-key watch all night.

A slower dance song with a heavy downbeat began, and the four of them swayed their hips. Throwing their heads back and laughing, they moved in together, Kristen coming up close behind Kendall, and Kiki pressing her body up behind Hannah's.

My breaths shortened as I stared, watching Kiki grind into Hannah. When my cock twitched in my jeans, I scowled, thinking it was a thousand kinds of fucked up to get turned on by anything my sister did, regardless of the woman she did it to.

"Lisa, you got this?" I didn't glance back at her.

I couldn't take my eyes off of Hannah. Her gaze had dropped down and locked onto mine. Expression softening, her eyes had closed halfway in sensual invitation. Then she licked her lips and moved her flattened palms from her hips over her waist and up toward her breasts

"Yeah. I'm good."

I strode out from behind the bar as Lisa finished her reply.

A slow smile curved onto Hannah's lips. As I came closer, she reached her arms out to me.

I clasped hands with her, pulling her away from Kiki. Kiki had the nerve to smirk before she moved over to attach herself to the back end of Kendall and Kristen's bump-and-grind train.

Sighing, I shook my head. "You're all gonna drive me to therapy."

Laughter rang out from the reckless threesome, but the sounds of the club faded as I wrapped my arms around Hannah, focusing all my attention on her.

She snuggled into me, pressing her hips into my groin as we danced.

We were in full view of my sisters, but I really didn't give a fuck. They'd messed with me tonight to get me to want to touch Hannah, so let them earn those smug looks they'd worn earlier.

I growled. "*You* are a very bad girl."

On a slow lip bite, she looked up. "Is that a bad thing?" Her brow furrowed a fraction.

I gazed into dark eyes that began to sparkle. With the beginnings of tears?

I was usually an expert at reading people. Back as far as my memories stretched, I'd known when my sisters deceived, when a kid manipulated, when adults told white lies. In negotiations, I saw beyond ploys. When a person stood before me and "played a part" to cause a response in me, I detected their ruse the moment they began. And the woman in my arms right now? Had no idea what she did to me. Seemed to actually think she'd done something wrong.

Bending down, I buried my nose in the sweet tropical scent of her hair. "No, Hannah. It's a wonderful thing."

She pulled away and smiled at me, then leaned up on her toes, pressing her lips to my neck. "Good. I think I like being just a little bit bad."

I groaned. "My sisters are a horrible influence."

She laughed and turned around, pressing her ass into my groin, mimicking the movements she'd done with Kiki.

I sucked in a breath as she ground against my already hardening cock. Gripping her hips, I held her there, delivering back as much as she gave, no matter how much aching pressure hammered against the inside of my fly.

Her head dropped back against my chest, and she sighed, closing her eyes.

I swallowed hard, lowering my head down toward hers. "How long again do we have to wait?"

A smile lit her face, but she kept her eyes closed. "Third date. The musical rule."

I growled low, drawn to Hannah in ways I'd never imagined. Pressing my lips along the side of her neck, I grumbled, "Damned musical rule."

18. SUNDAY MORNINGS

Sunday mornings were a favorite lazy ritual at my place. Mase always had Laura stay the night and well into the next day. Lately, Ben showed up about 10:30 a.m. with his new girl, Stacy. And, after another night of closing down the bar at 2:00 a.m. and stumbling into bed by 3:00 a.m., I stayed in bed until almost noon, waking to mouthwatering smells of coffee, bacon, and something cooked by one of them on the griddle. Smelled maybe like French toast this time.

I stretched as images from Friday night of a very sexy Hannah flooded into my mind. I'd dropped her off at her place early Saturday morning after closing down Loading Zone, then went home and crashed from exhaustion. And after a grueling Saturday night tending bar, with no Hannah there to brighten my mood, the idea of waking up with her became more than tempting. Too bad I couldn't have talked her into staying the night this early in the game.

But Hannah wasn't ready yet for a sleepover. The three-date rule proved that. And maybe I wasn't quite all there yet either. We weren't talking just sex here. She knew it. I knew it.

Slowly, steadily, we were getting used to the idea of taking the risk, of moving beyond our friendship, for the reward of something more. And for two people who'd been blindsided by love so horrifically, damaged almost beyond repair, the wait was necessary. The slow dance of ours had become much-needed therapy.

Grabbing another pillow, I groaned, shoving it over my face, thinking I deserved a medal of honor for what would go down in history books as legendary restraint. No, not a medal. Sainthood. You know, for the whole lack-of-sex part.

Not one logical part of me wanted anything to do with the sticky-note list of eight, however, my body begged to differ. I was used to getting sex. Often. Like four, five times a week.

Now, I'd been left to soaping myself up in the shower, thinking of Hannah. Which, I had no doubt, was nowhere near the same as Hannah in the flesh. Even so, that tattered list paled in comparison.

Unable to deny the aromas of breakfast any longer, I dragged my ass out of bed. After a few minutes in the bathroom, and the coldest water imaginable splashed on my face, I pulled some flannel pants on and stumbled into the kitchen.

Bright. It was very bright in the window-filled room. I squinted.

Four faces turned toward me and burst out laughing.

"Nice hair, Trollhead," Mase mocked.

I shot my audience two stiff birds with a wide smile. "Good morning to you too."

A muffin sailed through the air at my head, and I caught it. "Nice. Blueberry banana." I stuck it on my plate and surveyed the spread. "Ha! French toast." I shoveled the last of the still-warm food onto my plate.

"What're you guys up to today?" I opened the fridge, grabbed the carton of orange juice, and poured it into a tall glass.

"We're headed up to Central Park." Mase tugged Laura onto his lap.

"Hey! I'm not done eating." She reached for her fork, but Mase flipped it out of the way. He then proceeded to feed her by hand. With narrowed eyes, she ate from his fingers, sucking them clean while he groaned.

I chanced a seat by the other couple, the ones who didn't look like they might bare all and fuck right there in the chair in spite of the audience. Stacy was quiet, but intelligent. Ben had gone exclusive for her, which was quite the feat. But I'd caught her occasional looks at him when she thought no one was looking, and there was something wilder that sparked there.

"Want to come?" Ben leaned back, sliding his hand under the table toward Stacy.

"Nah. I've got a paper due tomorrow." My phone started ringing from my bedroom. No one ever called me this early on a Sunday. Officially, I was still sleeping. I sighed and stared at my loaded plate.

Then suddenly, I realized who it might be. I raced to my room, made it to the phone, and pressed "answer" before it rolled over to voicemail. I grinned like an idiot when I saw the ID that'd flashed on the screen.

"Hannah." I strolled back toward the kitchen. I didn't give a flying fuck whether or not it was rude to talk on the phone at the table. They had their girls, now I had mine.

"Hey, Cade." Her voice was soft. Sleepy.

"You just wake up?" I sat down and folded half of a French toast slice covered in syrup and took a bite.

"Yeah." A sexy moan filtered through the earpiece.

I chewed once more, then swallowed the lump down my throat. "Did you just stretch?"

"Mmm-hmm..."

I looked up from my plate to the sudden silence in the room and found the entire table gawking at me. I narrowed my eyes and shook my head, ignoring them.

"What are you wearing?"

I swear I could hear her smile.

"What I always wear."

"Which is...?" I wondered if she was a flannel-pajama girl, or a T-shirt-and-boxer sleeper, or maybe naked...

Soft laughter. "What makes you think I'm going to tell you?"

For a second, I focused on the commotion at the table. There seemed to be a great debate over whose vehicle they would take on the ride up to New York: our Jeep or Ben's Escalade.

No one paid any attention to me. "Better than me imagining the possibilities: cotton...silk...burlap..."

A long pause. "Nothing."

"*Fuck.*" Sunday mornings just shot stratospheric. On a slow exhale, my plate finally came into focus again. "I can't wait to share a lazy Sunday morning with you." And it wouldn't be here at my house, either.

She hummed, but it broke midway through into a purr. Damn. I wanted to hear that sound again. My life's mission had suddenly become: make Hannah purr.

"Lazy Sunday mornings sound nice." Another slow moan.

I lifted a piece of crispy bacon into my mouth.

Hannah's stretching moans silenced. "What are you doing? Are you eating?"

"Yep. That was bacon."

Soft laughter now replaced the breathy moans.

Purrs and laughter. My favorite sounds from Hannah. I began a new list. The only list I would ever have.

The thought of lists reminded me of my calendar. "Oh, I meant to call you later today anyway. Kristen sent me an email. They want to go over the plans for our next event. Want to do dinner at Kristen's tonight?"

Ben dropped his fork onto his plate, clanking echoing out.

"What?" Ben and Mase both shouted in protest.

Blinking, I glanced up to both of them staring at me, looking slighted. *Figures.* Take away their gourmet food source, and they became all ears.

"Shut it." I glared at them. "You can have her Monday and Wednesday." The comment prompted an epic inquisition from their women over the secretive dinners they'd been told nothing about. Good. Serves those meddling fuckers right.

Hannah laughed. "That the boys?"

"Yeah." I rolled my eyes at them. "Babies."

"Awww, I think it's kinda cute. They're addicted to my cooking. And yeah, I can make Kristen's tonight after I close up the shop; I promised Chloe I'd close if she opened."

"Good. And they are addicted. They're also addicted to you. But not like how I am."

She laughed. "God, I hope not." A pause. "Because, if you recall, I don't do foursomes."

"Me either. I'm a twosome guy."

"Yeah? Never a threesome? Not even once?"

I snorted. "Not even once. Not my thing."

Had the opportunity presented itself? Sure. But I'd declined. I'm too dominant in bed for that shit. I take control, making certain every shudder and moan comes from what *I've* done to her, for her.

Two girls and a guy? Poor Y-chromosome sucker never stood a chance.

"Good. I like a guy whose full attention is on me."

I sighed. Sainthood had its trials. My breakfast had suddenly lost its appeal in favor of the woman on the other end of the phone. With a scrape of my chair, I abandoned the table to take the conversation private.

"Whipped!" Mase shouted at my back.

Yep. Totally whipped, but they were only harassing, guessing. They truly had no idea.

I entered my bedroom, growling, "You have my full attention now," to the pleased murmurs of a girl who I now needed to mainline daily.

With a wide grin on my face, I closed the door.

19. TIPPING THE XY BALANCE

The dinner vibe at my place was like the best poker night and game day all rolled into one, with Hannah being one of the guys right along with us. Dinner with Hannah and my sisters at Kristen's? The exact opposite.

It was hell.

The dynamic of one brother and three sisters had always been evened out by my level of antics, attitude, and absolutely no filter whatsoever. But the skill had been balanced and fine-tuned over a lifetime of noogies, swirlies, pink bellies, and drool-monster wrestling. I particularly prided myself on their teenage years, embarrassment taking on a whole new level when both popularity with other girls and attracting crush-of-the-month boys were at stake.

Tonight, I sat as a quiet observer at the table, realizing the scales had been tipped into the X chromosomes' favor. Perhaps irrevocably.

Silence evolved from a need for self-preservation. But the way this group bonded together, I wondered if I'd finally met my match.

And yet, seeing the smile on Hannah's face, how she

thrived among a newfound sisterhood she'd never had, I couldn't bring myself to ruin it for her with even one snarky remark. At my place, she'd found in my friends the brothers she'd never had. And now she had sisters too.

Kendall came over and took my face in her hands, pinching my cheeks together. She laughed as I narrowed my eyes. "Awww, why so glum, Cade? You don't have to lift a finger. You should be happy."

I arched my brows. "True. I don't think I've ever been waited on hand and foot before."

Laughter burst out from the kitchen, and Kristen leaned over the counter. "Please. It's like a regular beer-delivery service around here."

"Beers don't count. When you're getting up anyway, bringing one back for a guest is only common courtesy."

Kiki snorted. "Funny how you never 'get up anyway.'"

I shrugged, crossing my feet up onto the couch. "Hey, I can't help it if I perfectly time my beer drinking to your bladder emptying."

Kristen arched a brow. "You've honed that skill quite well."

I chuckled, closing my eyes. "Got it down to a science."

By the time we gathered around Kristen's dining table for dinner, I'd calmed down about being outnumbered, deciding to go with it. Hannah's presence didn't throw things as far out of balance as I'd imagined. My sisters seemed to be on their best behavior tonight.

In fact, if I didn't know better, after the club prank Friday night and now tonight, I'd swear the Michaelson Three were actually pushing me and Hannah together. I didn't know what to make of that. At first, instinct made me want to rebel, as anything those three wanted for me, I definitely did not. But for once, even if their motives were likely just to fuck with me, I agreed with them. I wanted Hannah, twinges of guilt be damned.

Unsure about the whole sisters–Hannah situation, I kept a close eye on everyone, waiting for some catch I'd missed to reveal itself.

Tonight's meal was actually a group effort, as Kristen also prided herself on her cooking. I'd been kicked out of the kitchen at the onset, but heard laughter and cooperation. They'd shared preparation tips and "reducing" techniques.

I glanced at the spread on the table, impressed. "What is all this?"

Kristen grinned. "Melon, stewed tomato, and prosciutto gazpacho; braised vegetable roots; and chicken two ways, stuffed and pan fried with shallots, haricots verts, and wild mushrooms."

The soup was already in individual bowls, but we helped ourselves to the rest from big platters in the center of the table. I held myself back from digging in until Hannah had taken what she wanted. She gave me a quick glance and held my gaze for a beat longer than necessary before handing me the serving spoons.

Kendall poured everyone white wine, then raised her glass. "I want to give a toast."

We all raised our glasses.

"To our new business tightening the bonds of family and friends." Kendall glanced at Hannah. "I know I speak for all of us in saying we're glad Invitation Only brought you into the fold, Hannah. We were great as a foursome, but having another girl in the mix (and helping us give Cade shit) makes us grateful we're now a fivesome."

I coughed hard, somehow forgetting how to breathe for a moment.

But the way Hannah beamed beside me made me sober up and be grateful too.

"I second that!" Kiki shouted.

"Hear, hear," I agreed. "I would just like to say, if anyone else has to give me shit, I'm cool with it being Hannah." I tipped my head toward Hannah before taking a swallow of the dry wine.

Kiki put her glass down. "So, tell us about the bakery, Hannah. You just opened it, right?"

Hannah nodded. "Two months ago. Sweet Dreams is doing well, I think. New customers come in every week from word of mouth. My two employees, Daniel and Chloe, are amazing. Daniel had an idea to solicit corporate businesses in the area for their office functions. Our latest big orders have come from financial firms, title companies, and real estate offices."

Kristen wiped her mouth with her napkin. "That's great. I'm happy things are going so well outside of the events with us. Makes me feel less guilty for demanding you be exclusive."

"Me too." I nodded. "Since we insisted on your exclusivity and *compromised* on no weddings, I'm glad your business is booming."

Hannah took a sip of wine, then put her glass down. "Don't kid yourself. The Invitation Only contract was to my benefit. Why work my ass off when I can charge top dollar to your clients?"

Kendall snorted. "Cade, have you been training her?"

Unwilling to share details about our dinner–study arrangement for fear my sisters would read into it, I kept my reply brief and shrugged. "I've given her a few valuable business tips."

The dinner conversation died down into small talk while

we ate the incredible meal they'd cooked. And for dessert, they'd made some kind of gelato.

They made a big production out of giving me a bowlful. The three of them stared at me.

I furrowed my brows and looked down. "What flavor is it?"

Kristen crossed her arms, shaking her head. "You have to take a bite before we tell you."

I stared at the three pale green scoops in my bowl with suspicion. "Kiki, did you sneak ganja into the gelato?"

She snorted. "No. And I don't know where to get weed." Her eyes sparkled with mirth.

Uh-huh.

Under the scrutiny of the girls, feeling like a lab rat under a microscope, I lifted my spoon, scooped up a brave amount, and shoved it into my mouth, closing my eyes, hoping for the best.

A creamy, mild flavor filled my mouth. I moaned. "Damn. That's delicious. What is it?"

"Avocado!" The chorus shouted their secret with excitement.

The only one with a bowl at the moment, I tucked it close into my chest, guarding it with my free arm as I ladled another hefty bite onto my spoon. "Go get your own."

Laughter ensued as they doled out the rest of their gelato into bowls. By the time they sat down, I'd taken my last bite. Then I proceeded to lick the bowl clean.

"Ugh. Animal." Kristen tossed her spoon at me, and it ricocheted off the back of my chair when I ducked, clattering onto the floor. She threw her arms up in the air. "Great. Now I need a spoon."

I grinned. "Use your tongue."

She did, sticking it out at me. Then she stole Kendall's

spoon, which had been buried upright into the top of her gelato mountain.

"Hey, give that back!"

A tug-of-war ensued. Hannah scooted her chair up next to me as we watched. "Wow. They're really serious about that spoon." She took a first small spoonful from her own bowl and stuck it in her mouth. Her eyes closed on a moan.

I smiled, glancing at her. "Right? That stuff's amazing. And, yep. My money's on Kendall."

"Why don't they just get another spoon?" Hannah whispered, opening her eyes.

I scoffed. "What fun would that be?"

She laughed, nudging me.

I nudged back. "You know it's serious when—"

Kendall yanked the spoon away, swiped her bowl off the table, and stabbed the tip of the spoon into her melting gelato, angling an elbow out for leverage as she took aim.

"—food starts flying."

"Don't *make* me do this." Kendall glared as Kristen bobbed and weaved, preparing to duck from anything launched.

"No." Kiki stabbed her spoon into Kristen's gelato. "You cannot waste that awesomeness. I'm stepping in."

I glanced at Kiki's empty bowl. "Well played."

She shook her pig-tailed head, wincing. "I have brain freeze."

"It was for a worthy cause." I patted her head.

When everyone settled down, each to her own chair, I settled back in mine, happy all the girls were getting along so well. And look at that, I didn't even have to lift a finger to cause chaos. Maybe Hannah's presence, with so much exposure around the guys, tipped the universal scales in my favor after all.

"Let's talk nuts and bolts about the McGinty's event." Kiki grabbed our empty bowls, steering clear of Kendall and Kristen while they finished their dessert.

I slid my laptop from my messenger bag on the counter and opened it to the file. "It's their first year open, and with our growing reputation, they want us to draw the crowd."

"Where are they at again?" Kristen made loud scraping noises with her spoon against the sides of her bowl to get every last avocado drop.

I glanced at her. "Couple of blocks down from Loading Zone, right where you turn toward the restaurants on Sixth."

"Music?" Kristen had her game face on now.

"I compiled a list. Classic Irish pub songs plus new popular favorites."

Hannah leaned in, spying on my screen at the titles and read one aloud. "'Fuck You I'm Drunk?'"

The girls burst out laughing.

"What? It's hilarious."

Kristen gave me the pointed look. "No."

"You can't overrule the music. That's why you brought me in. Music. Drink. Big-picture planning."

The other girls, one by one, turned toward me, a united front. "No."

Undeterred, I shrugged. "We'll see. Client gets final say. It's his bar."

Before they could argue, I moved on. "Cake?"

Hannah propped her elbows on the table and her chin on her hands. "I'm thinking beer mugs. Giant green beer mugs."

I chuckled and glanced at my sisters. "Thoughts?"

One by one they all nodded, which stood with sound

reason. Hannah had outdone herself with every cake project. Why would we doubt her creative talent now?

"Perfect. Let giant green beer mugs be your inspiration."

When we finally wrapped up the evening, I walked Hannah out to her car. She'd come over to Kristen's straight from her shop.

She turned and leaned back against her driver's door.

I planted my arms on either side of her, bending down until our foreheads touched. "I'm glad you agreed to come over here tonight."

She slid her hands under my jacket and T-shirt and up to my chest, staring into my eyes. "I'm glad you invited me. I like being a part of your world."

"Yeah?" Intelligent response, I know. But I couldn't find any real thought with her hands on my bare skin. I'd been reduced to caveman words.

"Yeah. I really love your sisters." She moved her hands back down my stomach, breaking contact before hitting the waistline of my jeans.

Pulling back before I pushed things too far between us, I took a deep breath. Fuck, I wanted to take us there, but I still sensed she wasn't ready yet. Even if it killed me, I would wait for her to be ready. To take that next step.

Instead, I smirked. "They seem to have taken to you. Do you know I was strictly forbidden to fuck you?"

She bit her lip and then nodded. "Yep. They told me Friday night."

My shoulders shook as I laughed. "I *knew* it. They're fucking with me. I've spent all my life with them telling me I can't have something, only to have them dangle it in front of me in torture."

A firm hand pushed against my chest. I glanced down, then back up into her eyes. Her expression was fierce.

"*I'm* not theirs to dangle. *I* decide."

I swallowed, turned on even more by the power behind her words. "I agree. You decide."

She turned slightly, angling toward her car, but kept her gaze locked onto mine. At the last second, she leaned into me and brushed her lips across my cheek, kissing me just below my ear. "You know I've already decided, Cade Michaelson."

My brain fogged with the sexy tone of her voice, but before I could respond, she turned, slid into her car, and shut her door. I crossed my arms over my chest, grinning until my cheeks hurt. She drove away with a final wave.

Minutes passed as I stood there unmoving, feeling like the luckiest bastard on Earth. The freezing night air didn't faze me with my blood still heated from her touch.

I felt an all-knowing presence approach seconds before Kristen moved to stand beside me. She stared off into the same direction I did, where the end of her drive stretched into darkness.

"She could be good for you, baby brother."

I turned, blinking at her.

She met my gaze.

All their meddling seemed like they'd been messing with me, but I now began to wonder if they were rooting for me deep down. Although I'd never shared the horrid details of my devastating Valentine's Day massacre two years ago, Kristen knew what the aftermath had done to me. Some things didn't need mentioning. And to have her support, their support, even through all the superficial shit we gave each other, meant a lot.

"What about the rule?"

She snorted, laughing. "When have rules ever stopped you?"

I stared at her a few beats more, floored at the conversation we were having. Having never spoken with any of my sisters in seriousness about my relationships before, the moment seemed surreal. However, I didn't want to give away my feelings just yet. Not about her suggestion, and not about what was developing between Hannah and me.

She didn't say anything more, and I didn't ask for clarification.

But something had been offered between us in the unsaid words, eldest sister to younger brother, and I recognized it for what it was—a gift of support, even though she didn't know the details.

Nevertheless, an enormous weight lifted off my shoulders with her veiled blessing, taking the troubling guilt I'd been feeling about breaching our agreement out of the equation.

After a deep exhalation, I nodded. "Thanks, sis."

20. CURSE OF THE IRISH

Music blared out the door and three blocks down, or so the cops informed us. We promptly turned it down (a decibel), then invited the officers to join us when their shift ended.

McGinty's had an unprecedented showing. Wall-to-wall people were well on their way to being shitfaced. The Irish sure as hell knew how to party. So did the rest of us who adopted the Emerald Isle as our homeland for the holiday.

Since we'd essentially lent our name as a customer draw, we didn't have much responsibility during the event. That was all being handled by the owner, managers, and employees of the bar.

Hannah's cake was a hit. She'd created a bar top replica with giant frosted mugs of green beer on one side, one of them knocked over, spilling beer and foam to form a sheet of cake down the "bar." But with most of the guests smashed by the time they dug in, that it was there and tasted good was all that mattered. Still, we made sure the local press got their photos early in the night, not only for publicity, but also for our portfolio and the bar owner's history wall.

When customers began eating the served pieces, they moaned, begging for seconds. Curious, I picked up a slice and sampled the chocolate cake with white icing.

As the first bite settled onto my tongue, I closed my eyes and groaned. "Bacon."

Hannah grinned, her eyes lit with mischief. "Hey, at least it's not ganja."

I blinked. I knew I'd downed a few beers, but my people-reading meter seemed way off. "Did you say there *is* or *isn't* weed in here?"

She snorted, then broke out laughing. "There is *not*. *No* ganja. Here, have another beer."

She handed me a frosted mug, and I gladly took it. It wasn't my imported favorite, but tonight wasn't about taste, it was about getting shitfaced. Damn. That rhymed. I made a mental note to make T-shirts for that.

It's not about taste, it's about shitfaced.

Mom would be proud.

I steered Hannah away from the cake toward a side booth that the Sisters Three had commandeered. Boisterous singing had been going on all night, but when Bondo came over the sound system, the chorus was shouted by everyone, including me.

"*Fuck you I'm drunk! Fuck you I'm drunk—*" I coughed out a laugh at Kristen's glare. "Don't blame me. It's his bar."

By the end of the song, Kristen defected, joining the rest of the world in wailing shitfaced profanity. She did me proud. I passed her another full beer.

When I looked down at Hannah, she smiled wide. She also vibrated, bouncing on the booth between me and Kendall.

"Having a good time?" I leaned toward her.

She gave me one of those megawatt smiles, crushing into my side. "The best!"

I laughed. "Are you plastered?"

"Pffft. No." She shook her head as if I'd suggested the impossible.

"How many beers have you had?"

Glancing up at the ceiling, she stared at a spot up there, biting her lip and frowning.

I looked up, wondering if she saw imaginary tally marks etched into the hammered tin ceiling tiles. "You know, if you have to carry the one, you're plastered."

She snorted. "I think I've had four. No, five."

I'd only ever seen Hannah have a glass or two of wine. "And that doesn't constitute plastered." My comment flattened into more of a statement than a question. Because arguing the levels of drunkenness with the drunk brought out rare forms of smartass in me.

Hannah shook her head. "Nope. The first beer is buzzed. The second, tipsy. The third one is drunk."

Kiki leaned around Hannah, pressing in. "The fourth one's hammered."

Kristen slammed down her now-empty beer mug. "The fifth is plastered!"

I barked out a laugh. "Which, clearly, you are. Have another beer, O Reserved One."

Hannah nodded once, as if an oracle had spoken through the mouths of beer-laced babes. "And shitfaced would be beer number six." She hiccupped. It was adorable.

Sitting in a booth surrounded by my sisters with Hannah by my side, I felt like the night couldn't get any better. Although Hannah had let loose with the guys and had settled in with my sisters like one of their own, I'd never seen her...filterless. The complete transformation was refreshing.

And she looked amazing.

With disheveled hair framing pinked cheeks and with those dark hazel-green eyes sparkling, she had this great messed-up look, like she'd just been thoroughly fucked. And damn, I wanted to give her that look. I wanted to give her the messed-up look of her life. Little Miss Ice Queen had irrevocably melted. And I loved every minute of it.

We all sang the last chorus to "I'm Shitfaced."

Kristen no longer hesitated, belting out the words at the top of her lungs, "And I only bought her one rouuund."

Her letting loose was golden, because I had turned on my phone's video, capturing it all. Moments like this needed to be relived, maybe at a family gathering, like Thanksgiving. Or Christmas. Again, Mom would be so proud.

"I have to pee." Hannah made the announcement like a newsflash. It was the third such bulletin in the last two hours, but her drinking pace made it a redundant given.

Before I could slide out, she knocked into me like a bumper car. I chuckled, shaking my head. "Hold on! I'm moving."

Of course, I'd had as many beers as the girls, plus a few shots of scotch. None of us drank this much normally, but I wasn't feeling much more than a slight buzz. I think mine was masked by the adrenaline of the night, of having Hannah attached to me by the hip while she had the time of her life.

When she stood from the booth, her body swayed and she tilted at a forty-five-degree angle, crumpling against me and the back of the booth.

I wrapped my arms around her from behind, my hands

sliding up just under her breasts. "Whoa. How about I escort you to the bathroom."

She tilted her head back against my chest, gazing up at me with half-lidded eyes. "You gonna help balance me over the toilet?"

My mouth opened. No words came out. I glanced back at the girls, but all three of them looked at me with wide-eyed expectant expressions, like the entire world's problems would be solved by my answer. I glared at them.

"Do you need me to?" I furrowed my brow at the limp girl in my arms.

Hannah burst out laughing. "Nooo, silly. Was bein' smartass." Not only were her words slurring, she missed a few as she spoke. "Worst case, I'll grab handicap bars. Did last pee."

She pushed against my hips with her hands, righting herself by spreading her arms wide. I stood there as she took a tentative step in those high heels, fully prepared to fireman-carry her ass to the bathroom, pull down her jeans, and hold her over that toilet, if necessary.

Her next two steps were faster, and I almost thought she was falling forward until I slammed into her back, nearly knocking her over.

I threw my arms back around her, righting her.

But she didn't need my support. Like a cement wall that had been poured and hardened instantly, she drew herself up and held there.

Some clean-cut guy stood two feet in front of her, staring at her.

And she stared back.

I shifted to her side to see her expression. She'd gone white like she'd seen a ghost.

"Wh-what are you doing here?"

Cocky expression on his face, the guy shrugged. "Saw your picture in the paper for the event. Thought I'd come down and see you."

Every ounce of protectiveness programmed into my DNA fired to life. It didn't take a rocket scientist to figure out that was her piece-of-shit ex. I took a step forward, ready to block Hannah and body check Dumbfuck, who had the balls to show his cowardly face now.

A hand on my shoulder held me. I growled, glancing back.

Kristen now stood by my side, serious as a heart attack and shaking her head. "Don't, Cade. Let her fight her own battle."

My brow furrowed. Had Hannah shared her past with my sisters? Or was it just blatantly obvious to any person who wasn't passed out cold that this guy bothered Hannah?

Fighting the urge to pummel the guy into the earth, I held fast. Kristen was right. The fight wasn't mine; it was Hannah's. And who knew, maybe it would help her get some closure.

Hell, maybe I could live vicariously through her. Maybe for all of those shredded and abandoned hearts out there, Hannah could give the uncaring fuck a piece of all of our minds.

Hannah crossed her arms and stepped forward, invading Dumbfuck's space. Her stance was suddenly steady as a rock, like adrenaline had spiked through her too, readying her to fight. "You don't get to 'come down and see' me."

I forced a calming breath into my lungs as Hannah took another step closer to him, getting right up in his face.

With Kristen's restraining hand on my shoulder, I took a step forward, leaning in, pushing to make sure I remained within a three-foot boundary, ready to strike the asshole if he so much as twitched.

Hannah's razor-sharp words were loud and clear over the music from where I stood. A wry smile twisted onto her face as she lifted her arms straight out from her sides. "Like what you see, Brandon? Well take a good look. This is me *happy*. This is me *moving on with my life*. This is me *so damn glad you left*, because I was only a shadow of my true self with overbearing you."

She dropped her arms to her sides, leaning in so far that Dumbfuck had to sway back on his heels to prevent their foreheads from smacking.

"I've stepped out into the sun and I love it. Go back into whatever hole you crawled out from. You're not welcome here."

Hannah turned toward the bathroom.

Dumbfuck shot his arm up, grabbing her wrist.

I launched forward, slamming open palms into the asshole's chest, sending him flying. The momentum knocked Hannah off-balance and I lunged sideways, grabbing and steadying her before tucking her into my side.

His body crashed into a couple of occupied tables. Glasses flew and shattered on the floor. Dumbfuck sat on his ass for only a few seconds before jumping up and charging me. I shoved Hannah behind me, into my sisters.

The music stopped and a low chant grew louder, escalating to shouts. "Fight! Fight!"

In a blur of movement, Kevin, the bar owner, tackled Dumbfuck from the side, obliterating another table. The crowd cheered, then sang yet another Irish song about drinking and brawling.

Before things got out of hand, Kevin's employees descended, lifting the asshole off the floor and forcibly removing him from the building. The entire time, he stared at Hannah with a psychotic grin on his face, like ruining her night had made his.

I spun around. Hannah stared at the floor where he'd been, her gaze unfocused. Tears brimmed in her eyes.

My sisters surrounded her from behind. We were a pack who protected our own.

Rage coursed through me that the idiot could pull her out of having such a great time and upset her to this extent. There was a special place in hell for the Dumbfucks of the world.

A few tears finally spilled over onto her cheeks. I lifted my hands to cup her face and rubbed the tears away with my thumbs. "Hey, Hannah. You okay?"

She stared up at me with a pained look on her face, then shook her head, breaking away. "I have to pee."

Before I had the chance to stop her, she barreled into the crowd and skimmed along the wall down the narrow hallway to the bathrooms.

Her panicked expression imprinted into my mind. Carefree Hannah had vanished. Determination rising hard and fast inside me, I took a deep breath and vowed to help her keep that bright happiness she had worked so hard to claim.

When my sisters began to make their way down the hall in pursuit of one of their fallen, I rushed to catch up. In the narrow space, I grabbed Kendall, pulling her back. I lunged forward, clutching Kiki and Kristen by their shoulders before they pushed open the door.

Kristen frowned. "What are you doing, Cade? Back off. This is a girl thing."

"No. It's not." My voice had gone gruff.

They turned to face me. Kristen looked at me. Then she *really* looked. Her eyes widened as understanding dawned.

The one who was most like me, who read people as well as I did, had connected the dots that I was the most equipped to help Hannah. I'd been there.

I took a deep breath, tamping down the rush of emotion. "Hannah needs me more than she needs any of you. I need to do this for her—and for me." My voice broke.

Kristen nodded and moved aside. The other two gaped at her, clearly confused, but they stepped back behind Kristen, letting me pass.

The bathroom door opened and two laughing girls stumbled out. I shot an arm out to stop the closing door, scanning ahead from the doorway. Three sinks lined the wall. An upholstered chair, a small round side table, and a couch sat empty in an entry area.

Searching for the unseen stalls that had to be somewhere on the right, I stepped inside. A toilet flushed. Another girl appeared and walked to the sink, flipping on the faucet.

"Hannah?"

Soft crying. A sniffle.

I followed the sounds to the last bathroom stall. The other two were now unoccupied. I stepped inside the stall beside hers, closed and locked the door, then leaned against it.

"Hannah, please talk to me."

"Fucking asshole!"

The shouted cathartic words made me smile. "I was going with Dumbfuck."

She sniffed. Her voice quieted. "That too."

I heard her stuttered inhalation. Silence followed.

A painted metal barrier stood between us, and I suddenly felt ridiculous. Not that I wouldn't do anything for the girl suffering beside me, but the way we were partitioned off like this felt like one of those Catholic confessionals I'd seen in movies. Only I was no priest. And Hannah had done nothing wrong.

No, in separate stalls in the ladies' bathroom of an Irish pub was not the way this was going down. I stepped out and walked to her closed door. My palm wrapped around the top edge and I rattled it.

"Let me in, Hannah." My words were layered with meaning.

Another loud sniff, then the latch on the lock slid, releasing the door. In the large handicap stall, there was room for the two of us. Barely.

She stood there looking sad and beaten, and I wrapped her in my arms, just holding her.

After an extended silence, she tightened her hold around my waist, speaking without lifting her face away from my chest. "Why now? Why after all this time did he have to show his sorry-ass face? I got over him. I *was* over him."

"I don't know, Hannah. Guys are assholes, some more than others. But he takes the prize."

I felt a nod against my chest. Her body shuddered.

Her words rolled over in my mind. This vulnerable girl who had opened her heart, only to have it stomped on by the same jerk who'd kicked it aside once before, was drunk. And large quantities of alcohol brought out the honesty in people like a lie detector.

"Hannah, are you *not* over him?"

It was hard to say when anyone let go of feelings for someone they loved deeply, no matter how badly they'd been hurt. Like Hannah, my ex had crushed my heart, then disappeared, never to be seen again. Only Hannah's ex had rematerialized. And the cascading emotions in the after-math needed to be sorted out.

"I hate him, Cade. After that day, I never wanted to see him again. Never. Look at me, Cade. I'm a mess. Does this look like someone who's over him?"

At that, I pulled away and looked down at her, seeing through all the hurt and pain. "Hannah, you went through a horrendous loss when he stood you up at your wedding, but you never got closure. He robbed you of that."

She snorted. "Was that supposed to be closure?"

I shook my head, resting my chin on top of hers as I squeezed her. "No. Closure is us dealing with our feelings on *our* terms. That egotistical fuck pulled a stunt, knowing full well he held the power to upset you. That was on his terms."

She nodded. Minutes went by in silence as we stood there in the bathroom stall.

After a while, she stirred in my arms, pushing away. I didn't like the feeling, nor did I feel good about the resigned look in her eyes, but I let her go.

"I have to get out of here. I need to go home." She looked at me as if from afar, distancing herself with a cold expression on her face. Only it was different than "Ice Queen" cold. She appeared to fall away from herself, absent.

"I'm going with you." I stepped forward.

She backed away from me shaking her head.

My heart thudded hard, my hands clenching into fists at my sides. I needed to be with her—no longer for her, but for me. An unseen tie that had formed between us began unraveling. I felt it happening. She was falling into an abyss and refused to grab my hand, preferring to fall and be lost.

"I need to be alone." Her words had deadened. "I'll grab a cab."

Terrified to let her go, but sensing that pushing her now was the wrong thing to do, I nodded, following her out.

Minutes later, I stood on the sidewalk with a fierce wind biting through my shirt as I shut the cab door, Hannah tucked safely inside. She didn't look up at me once, not even a glance. Hadn't said another word to me after we left the bathroom, either.

Helpless, I stood out in the cold on the sidewalk as Hannah disappeared into the night.

My throat locked up.

I couldn't find my next breath of air.

21. WHAT'S IN A NAME

Hannah hadn't returned any of my calls. When I'd shown up at her shop around noon, Chloe said she'd called in sick. Well, at least I knew she was alive.

But "alive" only meant you pulled oxygen into your lungs and your heart chugged along. It didn't mean "okay." I needed to make sure she was okay.

Sunday night came and went, but Hannah didn't call or show up at my place for dinner. My heart burned a hole in my chest while I isolated myself in my bedroom, staring at the ceiling. Her trauma had become my trauma, and I wouldn't have wanted it any other way.

Morning came and I still stared at my ceiling, as if the secrets of the universe lay written in the wrinkles of plaster, waiting to be unlocked.

I kept imagining what I would feel like if the roles had been reversed, if it had been my ex who had shown up out of the blue, smug look on her face. Those looks were the stuff of our nightmares, the fears that we had a weakness when it came to this one horrible person in the world, and they had power over us, over our emotions. But it was only because we gave it to them.

So as I waited for Hannah to deal, I handled my pain as best I could. If she had to trudge a path through hell and back, then I would too, because we'd both been there. Because I also had demons so entrenched into my psyche, I'd let them govern my life.

In fact, the hold my past had on me was so tight, I'd made a fucking rule to protect my heart: *no weddings*. Like hiding from all the fluff of someone else's best day of their life would erase my worst. No amount of bleach in the world could scour that shit from my mind as if it never existed.

A sudden epiphany lit up in my mind like a blinding light bulb. I pulled on jeans and a T-shirt and shrugged into my jacket. After scooping up my keys, I rummaged through the junk in my desk drawer. Then I grabbed a pair of pants out of my closet and stuffed them into a white plastic bag.

The ride over to Hannah's seemed to take forever. Left to my thoughts, they all came up blank. My only focus was Hannah. Finding her. Seeing her face. I'd checked her shop first, hoping I was wrong, but she'd pulled another sick day. Not surprising. The gut-wrenching, nauseating feeling hadn't disappeared for me either.

It would never go away. Not unless we made it go away.

Her street was quiet. When I pulled into her drive, loose gravel crunched beneath my tires, washout from her landscaping after the heavy rain overnight.

A dense fog had rolled in, humidity from the waterway behind her house intensifying the effect into a near-total whiteout. As I walked through the soupy air, the mist parted, spinning into little eddies on either side of me.

I jogged up the steps. Taking a deep breath, I pounded on the door.

As I waited, I scanned her two front windows. No lights were on. I debated the wisdom of creeping around back, banging on every pane of glass until she let me in, but quickly discarded the idea as the act of an insane man. The last thing I wanted was to be cast into the category of a stalker.

I knocked a second time with a bit less anger. Three hard raps on the wood.

Nothing.

Determined, I turned around and sat on the cold brick step, putting the plastic bag beside me. By the time little dewdrops formed on the plastic, I figured at least another twenty minutes had gone by. I leaned back and knocked again. *Rap, rap, rap.*

My steady knocking was repeated every thirty minutes or so.

As the sun broke through the dismal fog, I wondered if I should've brought soup. What if she really was sick? Chicken noodle was always my favorite. I calculated how far away the nearest convenience store was and how long it would take me to get there and back.

Although, what a sad offering to someone in need: soup in a can. I pulled out my phone and surfed the Net to find the nearest restaurants and eateries. It wasn't even 10:00 a.m. Most wouldn't open until 11:00 a.m. for lunch.

I rapped on the door again. It had been at least forty minutes since my last attempt. I didn't want her to think I'd given up.

My doorstep vigil continued. Noon approached. The thought of creeping around the perimeter of her house to find an open window, or at least peek inside, had been revisited and discarded. Three more times.

Legs suddenly cramping, I stood up and stretched,

walking down her pathway to work the kinks out of my muscles. When I turned around to return to the spot I intended to sit in all day if necessary, the door cracked open.

Like a starving man suddenly offered a bite of bread, I rushed forward, afraid I'd imagined the opening, or that the invitation would be taken away.

The door opened further, revealing a distraught Hannah in flannel pajamas. Her eyes were red rimmed, her cheeks wet with fresh tears. Her hair was a tangled mess.

I dropped the bag inside her living room and crushed her to me, inhaling the sweet tropical scent of Hannah.

She shivered. "You're freezing."

"Tough shit." I refused to let her go and, instead, pushed forward and kicked the door shut. Her stiff body eased bit by bit the longer I held her.

We said nothing. Just stood there, holding each other.

With great reluctance, I gently released her. We needed to talk. Absent a professional therapy session, Hannah and I needed to deal with our demons head on. There would be no way to move forward unless we exorcised the darkness from our past.

I took my jacket off and she backed up, staring at me the way she had in the bathroom at McGinty's—like she wanted to increase the distance between us, like I was dangerous. That look killed me, but I held back, giving her the physical space she needed.

Hell, I'd made it into her house. That was a first step. And nothing would make me leave now. Not even Hannah. We were in this together, even if I needed to play the role of both interventionist and commiserating victim.

She took a deep breath. "I need to get something to drink." Looking frazzled, she disappeared behind the column, closing the shutters over her counter.

I sat in one of the chairs. The thing was more comfortable than it looked. I scooted my ass back and forth, finding the sweet spot in the cushion, before relaxing back.

The chair faced the kitchen. Hannah banged around in there, opening and shutting cupboards. I heard a whirring noise.

A slow smile curved my lips. We'd been here before, and the familiar situation gave me a small amount of comfort. Only then, I'd been a cocky son of a bitch camped out in the front of her shop, while she, the Ice Queen, with her impermeable shields, got her bake on in her kitchen in the back. Now, we'd become two different people who'd cast off their armor, baring themselves. And no matter what else Hannah or I wanted from each other, in the midst of it all, we'd become friends.

The whirring died down. "Do you want something to drink?"

I was parched. "Yes. Whatever you're having."

Silence. "Are you sure? I have coffee. Pellegrino."

My mind raced through what else she could be making for herself. Tea? The last time I checked, tea didn't involve whirring. "I'm sure. Make it two."

A moment later, Hannah emerged with two giant coffee mugs. One she clutched through a handle, the other she balanced on her palm as she walked over to me. I grabbed the second one as she held it out. Then she backed up and took a seat on the couch across the room, curling her flannelled legs beneath her.

At a whiff of the contents, I looked down, furrowing my brow. I lifted the cup, taking a deeper inhale, examining the dark green mass with tiny bubbles sitting on top. "What is this?"

"A smoothie."

Every smoothie I'd ever seen was pink. Or orange. Not this putrid green color. I wrinkled my nose. "Looks like pond scum."

"How do you know it isn't pond scum?"

I glanced up. Her face was dead serious. She held a mug the size of mine, but I hadn't looked inside hers. "You wouldn't poison me to get rid of me, would you?"

She slowly shook her head.

"You've got the same thing in your mug?"

Her eyes gleamed. Challenge was there. "Yep."

"Do I want to know what's in this?"

The corners of her lips twitched. "Nope."

I nodded, taking a deep breath. When she made no move to lift her mug, I raised mine, waiting. In slow motion, she raised hers, watching me with a wary gaze, eyes narrowed.

On a steadying breath, I toasted the only thing that came to mind. Us. Now. "To friends."

She raised her mug in toast, then took a sip.

I lifted my mug to my lips, taking a hit of the hideous smelling smoothie like a strapping Russian would take a shot of vodka. Walk in the park.

Lumpy fluid dissolved into a gritty mess as it filled my mouth. I felt like I'd swallowed a compost heap. I forced down the first swallow. I hoped to God it was like hard liquor, which got easier the more you drank, because I wasn't moving from this chair in her living room.

"Okay, tell me what's in it." Maybe knowing would make it easier to swallow.

She'd been downing the thing and came up for air at my question. "Beets, cucumber, parsley, kale, tricolored carrots, and two apples."

"Well, thank *fuck* for the apples." I took another sip, fighting the urge to shudder.

Instead, I focused on the returning healthy color of her face. She looked better. No more tears, but puffiness still persisted around her eyes. Hair, normally shiny, was dulled and tangled. And still, she looked amazing.

Her eyes drifted over me. "You look like shit."

I fought a laugh. "Thanks. It's what happens when you party with the Irish and then get no sleep for two days."

Her mug paused halfway to her mouth, and she cocked her head. "You didn't sleep either?"

"No, Hannah. I worried about you. I would've been here with you if I could've been. But I didn't want to push you before you were ready."

Shifting her legs fully beneath her and crossing them, she lowered the mug back to her lap. "What makes you think I'm ready now?"

I took another sip of the putrid liquid, hoping something in it would fortify my nerves. I was a guy. We didn't do feelings. But Hannah did something to me on a visceral level. Around her, I felt myself change from the inside out, transforming into the person I'd always imagined I could be.

"Because I'm ready." Bold, I know. But I needed to warm up to the touchy-feely stuff.

Her brows arched high. "Ready for what?"

I took a deep breath, then slowly exhaled. *Suck it up, Cade. She needs the whole truth.*

Finding my balls somewhere in the green smoothie, I looked up, steeling my spine, meeting her gaze. "Hannah, you have to know by now that there is more than a physical attraction between us. You do know I care about you, right?"

Unafraid, she kept hold of my gaze and nodded once.

Good. At least we were on the same page about my... feelings.

Gaining momentum, I continued. "When you left the bar that night, I was devastated for two reasons. One, you needed someone to be there for you. I needed to be that someone. Seeing you shredded apart like that wrecked me, and I wanted to be the one to help take away that pain. Maybe I didn't know how to right then, but I sure as hell wanted to be the person to try.

"Two, I stood there on that sidewalk abandoned. The crushing wave that sucked you under dragged me down too. All the jarring memories of my nightmare flooded back in on me."

Her hands tightened around her mug. "So it's my fault that you relived your hurt too?"

Treading on thin ice, I shook my head, rerouting the explanation in my mind to get her to understand. "No. Nothing was your fault. I get it. I get you. We've both been there, even though your situation was a thousand times worse than mine. But we've both run before. We've both buried our feelings, lied to ourselves that we were actually living."

She took another sip from her mug, gaze holding mine, listening. Her expression was cool. I understood. She'd been burned deeply and wouldn't yield her position easily.

Nothing worthwhile in life comes without a fight.

"I'm only explaining all of this so you understand where I've been since you left. I've relived my agonizing destruction. Then I replayed yours in my head, putting myself in your shoes, feeling your pain. I let the two situations, yours and mine, intertwine in my head because I *wanted* to feel your pain to be able to help you."

Her face began to soften, tense muscles in her jaw relaxing.

"This morning, I knew you were ready, because I was ready. I could no longer stand to be apart from the one person who gets what I've been through. You get me. My patience snapped, Hannah. I needed to be here for you, and I needed you to be here for me too. It seemed asinine to continue to deal with it separately."

She snorted, her lips twitching at the corners. "And really, are we dealing? If this is dealing, we suck at it." An almost-smile appeared. At least I was on the right track.

I gave her a gentle smile. "Then it occurred to me that we didn't have to suffer anymore—separate or alone. By letting their selfish actions hurt us, we give them power. I refuse to let my ex have an ounce of power over me. And I definitely don't like Dumbfuck having any power over you."

Amusement lit her eyes. "Don't think I mentioned it earlier, but I like calling him Dumbfuck."

I grinned. "Feels good, doesn't it?"

She nodded and then regarded me for a few seconds. "We need to have a name for your ex."

A sudden weight crushed my chest as my ex's name burned through my mind. Fuck, I knew this wouldn't be easy, but therapy sucked ass harder than I thought. In order to get better, I supposed we had to rip our scars wide open, let them heal. I didn't know how we'd ever be able to move on until they were gone.

Hannah's steady gaze disarmed me. Under her watchfulness, a protection wrapped around me that I hadn't ever felt before with another human being.

I barely found my voice in my closed throat. "You name her."

She tilted her head. "Why?"

A smirk tugged at my lips. "Because I christened your asshole Dumbfuck."

The smile she'd been fighting finally lit up her face, and it was brilliant and contagious. I grinned as the two days' worth of suffocating tension eased off my chest.

Her fingertips tapped her lips as her expression turned thoughtful. "Are you sure you're ready for this?"

I straightened. At this point, Hannah could tell me to jump onto a sinking ship and I'd do it. I nodded.

"Well, I need to know, was she cruel?"

My eyes never left Hannah's, but memories of the night flooded in. "After I proposed, she said 'no.' Then she laughed at me."

Hannah's brow furrowed, her eyes sparking with anger. For me. "What reason did she give you?"

"She'd said she'd only ever been with me during our time together. But that night, she told me there were others —while we were together. She didn't want to settle down. She wanted to see the world and be with other men."

She exhaled hard, compassion washing over her face. "She cheated on you?"

I sighed, dropping my gaze, staring at the wood grain in the flooring for a few heartbeats before looking back up at her. "Yeah."

"So she obviously wasn't serious about you at all. She was just having her fun with you." Hannah scowled. "That's such bullshit, Cade. What a selfish bitch!"

For a few seconds, we sat there in silence—her digesting the latest details of my train wreck, me feeling a little better because she was outraged by them. Wounds two years' deep had begun to cauterize right there in Hannah's living room.

"Selfish Bitch."

I glanced up. Calmness descended over Hannah, like she'd gotten control over herself, over my situation. "What?"

"That's her new name: Selfish Bitch."

I grinned, feeling vindicated by a girl who hadn't been there, but seemed pissed off enough to bloody her hands and do battle for me. Then I arched my brows and nodded. "Nice."

Hannah laughed with me, and the whole room lit up. And I no longer cared about names or our exes. All that mattered was we'd each taken a step toward one another.

Her eyes drifted to the abandoned bag on the floor. "What's that?"

I glanced over at the white plastic bag. "That is an epiphany I had, and a way we can both move on."

Hannah stood from the couch and waited, watching me. "I'm ready."

"See?" I winked at her, confidence building in where this was headed. "I knew you were."

22. RULEBREAKING AND RITUALS

Hannah had a skeptical expression, but she came over to me anyway and removed the mug of sludge from my hand. She deposited both mugs on a small side table. Then, with a finger and thumb, she picked up the plastic bag I'd brought.

I stood there like an idiot, watching her. In the span of thirty minutes, over two crap-tasting vegetable smoothies, we'd become a team in something again. The baby step made me feel like Neil Armstrong on the moon.

"Well?" With the bag dangling at the end of her arm, she looked at me, her brows lifted.

I stepped closer and took the bag, then remained in place, inches from her. "It's important to note we're already properly dressed for the momentous occasion."

She looked down. "The pajamas I put on Saturday night?"

I grinned. "And the jeans and shirt I had on Saturday night. The dress code to exorcise Dumbfuck and Selfish Bitch from our lives forever is funky grunge."

She laughed. And the world tilted a few degrees toward right again.

Her expression grew serious. "But we get to shower after this, right?"

I arched a brow, exhaling slowly. "Is that an invitation?"

She shoved my chest, laughing harder. "No. Separate showers. Separate places."

"Damn." I took her hand in mine and led her toward the kitchen. "Come on, let's do this."

When we reached her center island, I ripped open the bag and dumped it upside down, spilling out its contents onto the marble surface.

The double-sided yellow sticky note stuck out from beneath a pile of fabric. Hannah plucked it free. "Your list?"

I nodded. "That list and all the shallow emptiness it represents, that was the old me. That piece of paper is the only physical evidence of how badly she fucked me up. You got a pan we can burn this in?"

After a slow nod with a dubious expression on her face, she bent down and pulled out a large pan with both hands. It had a metal lid with a glass insert in the center.

I tilted my head, reconsidering the idea. "It won't ruin the pan?" The last thing I wanted to do was destroy something of value as we obliterated items that had become worthless.

"Nope. It's a SCANPAN, fired in thirty-six-thousand-degree heat. We're good." She put it on the stove and lifted the lid.

I dropped the list into the center of the dark surface. "Excellent."

She dropped the lid down, her attention shifting to what remained on the counter. "Pants?"

I nodded. "New pants I'd bought for the infamous date

and wore that night, which had the pocket that held her ring in a velvet box. Don't know why I kept them. Everything else was tossed in the trash in a fit of rage. Every letter, card, movie stub, T-shirt, her favorite pillow, our favorite movie, her favorite CD—all of it was thrown into a giant heap on February fifteenth. Weeks later, I realized I'd forgotten the pants."

She lifted the lid off the pan again and tipped her head toward it.

I grabbed the pile of wool and dumped it on the list. The material spilled far over the edge of the large pan, making it seem woefully inadequate. "You sure we won't set fire to the place?"

Hannah set the lid on the counter, then bent over, opening a slim cabinet door beside the stove. She pulled out a fire extinguisher and placed it beside the lid.

I snorted. "Use that often?"

"Precautions of the trade." She crossed her arms. "What now?"

"Your turn. Do you have something from Dumbfuck to burn?"

Her gaze fell to my pants overflowing from her pan. She stared at them, blinking.

I waited, remaining patient, knowing that we walked this path together. My anguish was hers; her pain, mine. I hoped to relive this one last time, then banish it forever, finally moving on with our lives.

"Yeah." Her voice was quiet, but strong. "I have something."

Hannah turned and left the kitchen. I followed her into her spare front room where she disappeared behind the half-opened door of a walk-in closet. When she emerged, a large black garment bag was in her arms. She crossed the room and laid it flat across an empty table that was pushed against the wall beneath the window.

She took a deep breath. Then with slow movements, she proceeded to unzip it from top to bottom. A mass of frothy white material billowed out. The more it spilled out on its own, the faster she pulled, until a giant heap of silk and lace covered her table.

"That's it?" Staring at the dress, I tried to make light of the heavy tension in the room.

She nodded. "It's all I have."

When I glanced at her, she sighed. "I threw away everything of his and ours too. There were so many things, I had to stack five large trash bags and a chair out by the curb. I stripped the sheets, bared the walls, got rid of the big screen that he'd bought for the living room. All of it."

"But not the dress."

She shook her head.

"That you kept a dress and I kept pants should say something ridiculous about us, but I can't for the life of me figure it out right now."

I stared at the pile of white fluff—her wedding dress. The ultimate symbol of most girls' dreams and hopes for her future lay in a heap, once cherished, now discarded.

Gauging her mood as she stared at the pile with me, I said the first thing that came to mind. "A pan on the stove ain't gonna cut it. We're gonna need a bonfire."

She didn't even laugh. In a lunging movement, she scooped up the mass. Then she spun around and left the room. I followed her down the hall, watching as the outside edges of the bundle in her arms dragged along the walls, tiny beads scraping where they made contact with the smooth plaster.

Not wanting her to have any permanent marks to deal

with after this, I reached behind her and held the fabric away from the walls.

When we made it back to the kitchen, Hannah nodded to the stove. "Grab the pan."

I obeyed and followed her to her back door. While she slipped her socked feet into a worn pair of sneakers, she blindly fumbled with the latch, which was hidden by the mountain of material, until she turned the knob and pushed the door open.

A cold, damp breeze hit our faces. The mineral scent on the air felt cleansing, renewing, as if the universe conspired with us to set things right again.

We crossed her patio decking, then went down three steps and out into a sloping yard. Near the water, a grouping of teak Adirondack chairs surrounded a brick pit filled with ash.

I grinned as Hannah dumped her dress into the fire pit. With the humidity in the air, no ash flew up, but as the material settled, black soot marred the white fabric.

She glanced at me and began bouncing with energetic excitement.

I followed suit, dumping my pants onto her dress. Leaning over, I tucked the list into a folded area of material on the top, leaving three-quarters of the paper sticking out. The sadist in me wanted to see the damned thing burn.

"I'll be right back." Hannah tore off toward the house in a full run, waves of hair flying behind her.

Dark cloud cover hid the sun from view, but it seemed like twilight instead of early afternoon. All the neighboring houses and those across the water had their porch lights turned on, shining yellow beacons marking their presence through the foggy haze.

I turned when I heard Hannah running back. She now

wore a jacket and had a blue blanket folded over her arms. She gripped the neck of a Champagne bottle in one hand.

She held it up toward me. "To celebrate."

"Fuck, yeah. This is great cause for celebration."

I took the bottle, and she spread the blanket over two chairs. On one of the chairs, she left extra fabric on the end. She sat in the other, placing a Sunday paper in her lap. As I peeled the wrapper off the Champagne cork and worked the wiring loose, I glanced over to see the front-page story was from several weeks ago. She began crumpling pages into loose balls and tossed them onto our pile.

Other than an occasional car driving down her street, or the cry of a gull flying overhead, the only sound filling the silence around us was the tearing and crumpling of old news. How fitting.

Tucking the bottle into the crook of the chair, I took my seat and held out an open hand toward the paper. She handed me the *USA Today* Life section. I tore and crumpled, tossing page after page onto our pile. Inside, I'm sure, were wedding and engagement announcements.

Crumple.

Toss.

None of it mattered anymore.

All that mattered was the girl beside me who'd had her heart ripped to shreds.

Realizing the extra amount of blanket she'd left on the end was meant for jacketless me, I pulled it around me, appreciating the small gesture as we crumpled and tossed in companionable silence.

Once we'd amassed a paper mountain in the fire ring, I got up and grabbed a broken branch dangling from a neighbor's tree and ripped it loose. I returned to poke the papers around, tucking some into the folds, thinking there would need to be a lot more oxygen to burn our dense pile of fabric.

The list remained on the top, daring me. I glared at it. My dick didn't rule my life. Neither did those women. Nor my ex. I refused to lose myself in the addiction of numbing pleasure anymore.

It was time I felt again, even if feeling sometimes meant pain.

Ready, I turned toward Hannah. "How are we gonna light this thing?"

A gleam flickered in her eye. She seemed as eager as I was to light it up. Leaning to the side, she fished her hand around in her jacket pocket, then pulled out a metal cylinder: waterproof matches.

After burning through half a dozen matches and lighting the pile in various places, enough flames burned and started to merge. When the layered fabric of her dress caught fire, dark smoke furled too close to Hannah for my comfort. I grabbed the arm of her chair and dragged it flush beside mine. Then I altered the angle of my chair to match hers.

I took my seat again, pulling the extra fabric back over my lap. I grabbed the chilled bottle and gripped the cork with my left hand while I palmed the bottom of the bottle with my right. "You always have chilled Champagne on hand?"

She shook her head, staring into our growing blaze. "It was mine and..."

"Dumbfuck's?"

A slow nod followed, then a hard swallow as she gazed into the fire. "When I grabbed the matches, I remembered I'd buried it in the back of my fridge. We were supposed to drink it on our wedding night, before we left for our honeymoon the next day."

On that lovely note, I gave the bottle a hard twist and popped the cork. "What happened to the honeymoon?"

She glanced at me, grinning. "I turned the tickets to ash in that same SCANPAN."

I barked out a laugh. "Good. This Champagne will be all the sweeter today."

I lifted the bottle between us, and she wrapped her hands around mine, staring at me with absolute confidence in her gaze.

"To finding closure," I began.

"Saying good-bye to bitter endings," she added.

"And hello to new beginnings," I finished.

We raised the bottle in a toast, then I pushed it toward her. She took a sip before passing it to me, her face scrunching.

I took a mouthful and swallowed. "Uck." I nearly spit it out.

We both laughed.

I shook my head. "Not all Champagne is created equal."

Narrowing her eyes, she took another sip. "I'm still gonna drink it."

"Then so will I."

We continued to swallow down our medicine as we watched the fire burn. Noxious fumes rose up, but thankfully, the wind shifted to take the smoke away from us. We watched as my pants ignited. Layers of her dress peeled back one by one, the edges curling in the heat before bursting into flames.

The list on top singed on the edges, blackening in stages before it too caught fire. Without a single emotion, absent of any thought in my head, I stared at the list as it disintegrated into an orange flame.

Floodlights kicked on from her neighbor's roofline. A door opened and banged shut behind a large figure who stared at us. He was downwind from the smoke.

Hannah took another swig from the bottle, then passed it to me while she watched her gawking neighbor. "We won't get arrested for this, will we?"

I snorted. "They can haul me away with a grin on my face. No way in hell I'm stopping now. We'll tell them I coerced you."

She shook her head hard. "Uh-uh. We do the crime together? We do the time together."

I ruffled her hair. "Thanks for the solidarity, Bonnie."

"Anytime, Clyde."

The flames faded as the fire ran out of fuel to burn. Hannah's gaze grew pensive. All I could think about was how we'd taken another giant step toward each other.

I kicked a foot up onto the top of the brick wall rimming the pit and leaned back, grinning. "Good. I like us rule-breaking together."

23. ONE STEP BACK

As the fire died down into glowing embers, our past vanishing into nothing but ash and smoke, the air grew heavy between us. What used to be a comfortable silence among friends now carried a thread of tension.

I knew where mine came from. Thoughts about how to move forward from here rattled inside my head. With no road map, I didn't have a clear direction on how to proceed. But the woman sitting next to me deserved careful consideration about every brave step we took.

Hannah broke the silence with soft-spoken words. "I don't know if I can do this."

Dread filled me. I hoped she hadn't read my mind and I hadn't frightened her with the seriousness of my thoughts. I glanced at her, diving off the cliff. "Do what?"

She sighed, staring straight ahead into the smoldering pit. "Do...us."

Breathe. I closed my eyes, forcing air into my lungs. I'd already fallen too deep into whatever was between me and Hannah to come out of this unscathed. "How do you know until you try?"

"That's just it. I don't know if I'm even capable of trying. One shock from the past and I had a total meltdown. I...I think I'm broken, Cade."

My heart lurched, and I opened my eyes, twisting toward her. A lone tear tracked down her cheek. Her pain was a thousand times more devastating in person. It burned through my chest, and still, I preferred being here over the alternative. There was nowhere I'd rather be, even if it meant getting hurt again.

Setting my jaw, determined to break through to her, I slid my palm over her freezing hand that gripped the arm of her chair. I pried her fingers loose and turned her hand over, tangling my fingers with hers.

"You are not broken. Neither am I. Damaged? Yeah, we're damaged. We're survivors, though."

When several seconds passed with no response from her, I pointed dramatically toward the fire. In the best theatrical impersonation I could manage with absolutely no stage experience whatsoever, I gave it my all to lighten the mood while delivering a message. "Be a phoenix with me. From the ash at our feet, let's rise up, reborn."

"That's so corny." She glanced at me, a tiny smile breaking through the serious expression that had darkened her face.

I chuckled. "That's what you're gonna get with me. Corny."

She wrinkled her brow, pulling her hand away. Her hesitancy underscored how hard her foundation had been rocked. The road ahead was going to be a long and arduous one.

"I just...I can't." Pinching her eyes shut, she shook her head, dropping her chin to her chest.

"Can't? Or won't?" I reached over, tucking a finger under

her chin, gently lifting until she faced me again and opened her eyes. "You're scared. We can deal with scared. I'm scared too."

Her face softened. "You are?"

"Yeah. I'm scared to death. I don't want to get crushed again. I've been there before. It nearly killed me, and I'm not sure I could survive going there again. You want to know what gives me courage?"

"What?" Her eyes were locked onto mine, widening, full of hope and curiosity.

"You. You give me the courage to take the chance. Not only because of where you've been, but more importantly, who you've become in spite of it—the amazing woman I'm just getting to know. Out of all the women out there in the world, you're the only one I've wanted to burn the list for. You're the first person to make me feel alive again. You make me brave."

She took a deep breath. "What if I can't commit? I'm so scared right now, I'm not sure I can let myself go again, truly fall for someone and enjoy it without flashes from the past tainting it." She shook her head. "God, listen to me." Tearing her gaze away, she focused off into the distance. "I sound like a pathetic wreck."

Needing her closer to me, I pushed out of the chair and crouched in front of her. With my hands on either armrest, I caged her in, forcing her attention on me. "You are *my* pathetic wreck. And I'm yours. Fractured and flawed, beautiful and kind, you are mine, Hannah. I'm laying claim now. I don't care how long it takes us to get there. This is our journey, and we make it together."

On a hard swallow, she spoke, her words soft, her hazel eyes staring hard at me. "I can't lose you as a friend, Cade."

"You won't."

"But what happens if—"

I placed a finger gently on her lips, silencing protests that held no merit other than fear of the unknown.

But she didn't know me. I did. And nothing in this world would veer me off course.

"Nothing will happen. We will take this as slow as we need to, until each step of the way we feel confident enough to take another."

She sat there for a long while, staring at me. I held her gaze, more certain about the present moment than any other that had come before it.

"Okay." The word was soft, but echoed into my ears with the force of a thunderclap.

I smiled. "Okay."

A corner of her mouth kicked up. "Besides, I don't want to give up your friends yet. I'm kinda attached to them."

"Watch it." I narrowed my eyes. "I can only tamp down my jealousy for so long."

She laughed. "Your sisters too."

Rocking back on my heels, I glanced up at the graying sky, thankful for my family and friends. My gaze fell back to Hannah. "Yeah, sorry about that. Give those three time. They'll annoy you eventually."

Hannah leaned to the side, propping her elbow on the armrest and dropping her head onto her palm. "So I guess that means no third date."

I gaped. "No post-musical sex?"

With her other hand, she shoved at my chest. "How do you know it wasn't going to be during-musical sex?"

I blinked. "Woman, you continue to intrigue me. And turn me on."

She laughed.

But when the amusement fell away from her face, I could see she was genuinely concerned. I needed to fix that.

"How about we don't plan things out? No timelines. No pressure. We take things one date at a time. Maybe we should take the whole musical-third-date rule off the table. We'll throw it way out into the future and cross that bridge when we come to it."

She nodded. "I think I need that. One step at a time."

"Good."

"Ummm, Cade. Please don't take this the wrong way, but I need to skip tonight's dinner. Wednesday night too. I need a break for a bit to ground myself before being with the guys again."

My heart stuttered. "But *we're* still on. You and me. Slow and easy. Right?"

Without hesitation, she nodded. And I was able to pull oxygen into my frozen lungs again.

"What about something new for a change? Everyone usually gets together when Jason comes back into town after a long trip, and this Friday night we're all going out to Versailles for drinks."

A slow smile curved her lips, and she nodded. "Yeah, I'd like that."

"Good. It's a date that's a non-date." I tapped the tip of her nose with my finger, then stood, letting blood rush into my legs again before I lost all feeling.

Hannah downed the last of the Champagne as I stretched. She tossed the bottle into the ashy pit, and I pulled her up from the chair.

"That's not gonna burn."

"Don't care. It goes with everything else." She hiccupped.

I smiled, a calmness spreading through me. I finally felt

like I could breathe normally for the first time since Saturday. And I wanted to leave things on a good note while giving her the space she needed.

"Cade?" Her brows twitched then furrowed.

"Yeah?"

"Would it be okay if we still...teased each other, though? You know, go back to the flirting and fun with no pressure about how fast it has to go. Just take things as they come?"

I slid both of my hands into hers, squeezing. "Of course, Maestro." I sighed, feeling the world settling back down. "Why don't you take those hideous pajamas off and take a shower. I'm going to my place to do the same."

She almost pouted, like she didn't want me to leave. It nearly killed me.

Be strong, Cade. She'd asked for a little space, but clarified we were still good. I'd do my fucking damnedest to give her everything she needed.

All of a sudden, she broke our handhold and shoved my chest, the flicker of a smile on her face. She jogged up to the patio as I laughed at her unexpected outburst. But once she hit the steps, she whirled around, plucking the fabric of her pajama bottoms away from her thighs.

"Wait. What's wrong with my PJs?"

I arched a brow, snorting. "Seriously? They have flying toasters on them. Toasters. Wings."

She grinned. "They're soft and snuggly."

Wicked thoughts flashed through my mind of her tossed on the bed, stripped in seconds by my impatient hands. I smirked. "Burlap bag, baby..."

Before my foot hit the first step, she disappeared into her house, squealing.

Then I heard another door inside slam, and I laughed.

24. UNSTABLE GROUND

Spending another night without Hannah was like going through the motions of life as a dazed zombie. And I wasn't the only one. The living dead had infiltrated my house, everyone mourning the loss of Hannah's vibrancy.

"When's Hannah coming back?" Ben poked the grilled cheese with a fork, looking uncertain about the food on his plate.

"Don't know. Not this week." I took another bite of my sandwich. Mase actually made a killer grilled cheese. Sourdough bread with a shitload of butter slathered on either side and grilled until golden brown, a thick slice of Tillamook sharp melted in between. But it paled in comparison to anything Hannah created.

Mase leaned back in his chair, fingernails peeling back the corner of the beer label that he'd half removed. "I miss her."

"So do I." Ben sighed.

"Her, or the food?"

"Both," they mumbled.

The lovesick saps in my kitchen were quite the sight, me

included. We should call *Big Brother*. Reality TV would make a mint off the ongoing phenomenon.

Like a teenage girl, I'd put my phone beside me on the table, waiting for a text. I had it on vibrate, but it hadn't moved all night. Occasionally, when too much time had passed, or I went somewhere in the house without my phone (because taking it everywhere, hoping not to miss a text would be lame), I'd hit the control button just to make sure the thing was still on. No alert showed on the screen.

"Yeah, I'm out. Gonna study." The kitchen was more depressing than a funeral home, and I needed some air and time away from the mourners. Geez, you'd think a beloved dog had died.

While I dropped my plate into the sink, the guys dispersed as well. Mase cleared the table, and Ben left. I grabbed another beer out of the fridge and went back to my bedroom.

Debating whether or not I should make first contact, I tossed the phone onto the bed, needing to think things out. The room was stifling, heat blowing from the register, and I already felt like I couldn't breathe. I went to the rarely used window and fumbled with the latch until the lock released. I had to shove twice before the frame unstuck with a loud *pop!* and slid wide open.

Cold air rushed in, blowing the curtains onto the back of my desk. Inhaling the crisp air, I closed my eyes, forcing myself to think about things from Hannah's perspective.

Because all I could think about was everything I needed and wanted. Which was her. Here. Happy and laughing. In my arms. Us secure. No doubts.

I didn't have that. What I had was uncertainty. Hannah wasn't yet on stable ground with us. Yeah, she'd agreed to try, but I knew what spiraled through her head. I'd walked the frightening path. I was further along in this than she was, in our healing after the devastation, but I needed her to catch up. Badly.

Pacing, I rubbed my chest. The more I thought about Hannah, the more I worried about what she was or wasn't thinking. Then I hoped she wasn't overanalyzing the situation. Until I realized I was doing just that.

"*Fuck.*" I sat on the edge of my bed, scrubbing my hands over my face. I shoved my fingers into my hair and gripped it, dropping my head onto my knees.

Lost in a state of panic with no easy way out, I closed my eyes and took a deep breath. This was ridiculous. Given our pasts, I had good reason to worry, but making myself sick wouldn't help.

And of the two of us, Hannah needed me to be stronger. She was the one who'd gone through recent trauma. She was also the one who'd gone farther into a relationship before her world crashed down around her. She'd been *in* that white dress she had burned. It hadn't been only hope and belief that had been shattered like mine—promises and dreams had been destroyed.

So I needed to calm the fuck down. If I couldn't toe the line, how could I ever expect her to?

Glancing at my phone once more, I picked it up. I needed some kind of sign from her that she was doing okay. For her. For us.

It was the only way I would get any sleep tonight.

I fell back onto the bed, tapping the phone on. After typing the passcode with my thumb, I went into my text app, hoping maybe I'd missed a text from her. There was nothing there. But I sighed in relief that I hadn't missed a message with her worrying why I hadn't replied.

Fuck, grow some balls, Cade. I shook my head. All the

time I'd spent being raised by females had clearly altered my makeup. Tomorrow, I needed to pump testosterone through my veins—lift a car or pull a tree out of the ground.

I typed a message. Then erased it.

Something less deep.

I typed again. *Backspace, backspace, backspace.* I held it down, trying to clear my thoughts.

In my mind, I battled between texting what I wanted to say and sending words I thought she wanted to hear. *Christ, I seriously need therapy.*

Going balls out, I typed what I really needed to say and hit send, forcing myself not to second-guess my instincts. Then I reread the message from her perspective.

> The guys missed you tonight. Me included.
> Me most of all.

I waited. Nothing came. Five minutes passed. Ten. I gave up looking for the text bubble to show her actively there on the other line.

Really needing to study for an upcoming exam, I put the phone on the nightstand and grabbed my laptop and research notes. With tremendous focus, I buried myself into all things Consumer Behavior, even though I would've rather spent the night theorizing business with Hannah like I did every Monday after dinner.

Still, even with the study distraction, I couldn't concentrate and kept looking over at my phone. As a matter of pure discipline, I refused to check the damned text box more than once an hour. But did so religiously, every hour.

Each time I put the phone back down, I hoped she was okay. That none of the nightmares from her past were haunting her. That she thought of me too, even if she couldn't bring herself to text me back. Even if she'd turned her phone off to give herself space.

Hours blurred together until the words on my screen did. When my eyelids drooped and my head fell forward, I snapped both back, startling to awareness.

My throat was raw, my eyes dry. I blinked several times trying to process the lights on in my room, the laptop open with the screen dark, and the loose notes spread all around me on the bed. Maybe I'd actually fallen asleep.

A buzzing noise sounded above me, then stopped. The gears in my mind turned until my brain caught up with reality and I flew upright, scattering the nearest papers onto the floor.

The screen on my phone was illuminated for a split second longer before it went dark.

I turned it on. Three texts. All from Hannah.

I took a deep breath and clicked into my text app.

The first came in at 5:37 a.m.

> Hey Cade. Sorry didn't reply last night. Fell asleep after shower.

The second a minute later.

> I missed the guys too.

The third came in with the same time stamp.

> Missed you most of all . . .

I let out the breath I'd been holding. I re-read the trio of texts. By the third time, I couldn't hold back the huge grin on my face.

And she'd sent me those three naughty little dots.

25. MUTUAL TORTURE

At last count, a week had seven days, a day twenty-four hours, and each hour had sixty minutes. The stretch between when I last saw Hannah until the next time I laid eyes on that beautiful woman had been the longest week of my life. It had only been four days. But those five thousand seven hundred and sixty minutes had felt like forever.

Now, I couldn't tear my gaze from her as she stood in her entryway, looking fucking magnificent. Her long hair hung down around her face in waves. A low-cut tank top cupped the upper swell of her breasts. Dark shredded jeans clung to her thighs. And her toes peeked out beneath the frayed denim at the hem, covered in a green polish.

My breathing grew shallow, just shy of outright panting with my tongue hanging out. "Fuck, you look edible."

Her easy smile twisted into a smirk as she pushed a flat palm against my chest. "Back up, horny boy. You don't get to lick the frosting tonight."

Tonight.

I did get to lick it at some future time. That incredible

point was not lost on me. I wanted to say "soon"—I was *dying* for it to be soon—but I knew Hannah needed my patience. And I would be patient as a rock for her.

Her brow furrowed. "You sure we can't take my car?"

I glanced at the fastback. Bet she purred like a dream. My thoughts immediately went to Hannah's jeans and the seam that stroked up between her legs where I couldn't wait to be. I *knew* my bike sent vibrations hard enough to cause a friction there for her. But would the bass vibration of the muscle car be more intense?

On a snort, I shook my head. Wild car rides would be saved until I actually had access into those jeans. For now, I settled for the next best thing.

"No," I growled low. My meager control around her had slowly unraveling threads. "I need you wrapped around me, even if it's only on my bike."

She pressed her lips together and then her tongue flicked out, wetting the lush bottom one. My eyes dropped there, staring as she bit it. Her neck flushed, and she took a deep inhale, doing wonderful things to her cleavage.

My mind raced. Intuition told me she'd guttered her thoughts as her gaze drifted down my body. I clenched my fists and released them, unable to stop myself from asking. "Whatcha thinkin' there, Hannah?"

Her gaze flew up from my crotch. Her blush deepened, lips twisting into a smirk. "Something very naughty." She passed me by, motioning to the bike. "Well, you getting on, or what?"

Too many retorts flew into my mind, tangling into a jumbled mess. Damn woman had short-circuited my brain.

Instead of taking our flirting dance further and risking her being uncomfortable by my ramping up the sexual innuendo, I climbed onto the bike. Over my shoulder, I muttered, "Hannah, please have mercy on me. If you don't, I may not survive the night."

She climbed on behind me, soft laughter ringing out in my ears. The wonderful sound calmed me back into a man more in control of his faculties, even if only by a few degrees.

As she adjusted though, I had to breathe deeply, pinching my eyes shut. Her flattened palms spread up my back, then down and around my waist, settling on my chest while her body pressed flush against me. I nearly blew a gasket, but slowly exhaled, grateful. I'd become the luckiest man alive with heaven wrapped around me.

She trusted me. Even if only with her life for this brief moment in time as we drove the twenty minutes to the bar. My heart thudded hard over the fact. After a week of not knowing which way was up in my world, her holding tight to me was an incredible start.

Although recent March nights had been unseasonably warm, there was still a slight bite to the air, and I worried for an instant whether or not she'd be warm enough. But with her pressed up so tight against me, intensifying the heat between us, I made it my personal mission to keep her plenty warm.

By the time we arrived, the front parking lot was almost full. I eased my bike into a slim space in full view of the packed front patio and cut the engine.

I helped Hannah off the bike. She removed her helmet and then looked up at me with bright eyes and a huge smile. Her cheeks were pink, and the soft waves of her hair had a windblown look, rendering her relaxed and naturally gorgeous.

She looked a little wild, in fact, and the effect knocked the wind out of me.

Because it resembled the just-been-thoroughly-fucked look she wore in my fantasies.

My body had been aching far too long for the woman smiling up at me. All week, my thoughts had drifted at random times to wonder what she was doing then, how she felt, and when I thought about what she might be wearing (or *not* wearing), which positions were her favorite.

And after all the torture of being away from the very thing I wanted most in this world, there she stood, here with me now, taking another tentative step toward me.

She smirked, a gleam sparking in her eyes.

My heart raced. I'd become the excited kid who got the exact toy he'd wished for all year for Christmas. And all I wanted was to run off to my room, lock the door, and play with her all day. And all night.

Shaking my head clear of the riot of dirty thoughts she incited merely by being naturally sensual Hannah, I put my hands on her shoulders and turned her toward the door. "C'mon. Let's get inside before I do something stupid and go caveman on you."

With a fiery look in her eyes, she bit her lower lip. "Is that something you do? 'Go caveman?'"

I growled, lowering my mouth to her ear. "Don't tempt me, Hannah. Remember, I'm hanging on by a frayed thread here. Play nice, or I'll take it as a sign you want to be thrown over my shoulder and then down onto my bed."

Her dark eyes widened, and she sucked in a fast breath. The pulse at the base of her neck jumped faster. When her gaze dropped to my lips for a fraction of a second, and she licked her own, I knew we were in trouble on the whole "take things slow" plan.

Desire pulsed inside her just like it raged through me.

I crooked the tip of my finger under her chin until her

gaze locked onto mine. She blinked. "In. Now. Before we start something neither of us can handle yet." Not entirely true on my part. I was ready to take the leap with her. Even if I hadn't yet dealt with all of my demons, something deep in my gut told me they would work themselves out.

With Hannah, I believed anything was possible. She made me a stronger man in all the ways controllable and made me want to smooth out every other rough edge.

I ushered her forward and into the club, nodding at the doorman I knew well. A subtle buzz of energy hummed in the atmosphere inside the club. Which meant, as charged as we already were, we needed to calm down a notch or two with a drink—STAT.

When we crossed the dance floor, I spotted our group. The girls all sat to one side of a VIP section huddled together, laughing. Kristen glanced up and waved. I tipped my chin up toward her in greeting.

We worked our way through the light crowd, and every male turned his head toward Hannah, staring at her with blatant hungry expressions. The hairs rose on the back of my neck and I growled. Alcohol and testosterone made guys stupid assholes. A gorgeous girl magnified the effect tenfold, making the idiots blind to the fact that my arm was around her.

I tightened my hand on her shoulder, and she instinctively leaned closer as we walked. Her natural calm to my possessiveness chilled me a fraction.

We climbed the few steps into the private area our party had reserved for the early part of the night. The bouncer unfastened the velvet rope as we approached with a small nod.

"Cade! You made it." Kiki sprung up from the red uphol-stered couch, launching herself into me with a body-bouncing hug and a squeal, accidentally knocking Hannah away from my side.

I winced. The bubbly girl on steroids, who I swear had kidnapped my sister, looked up at me with bright eyes and a huge smile. I raised my eyebrows, directing a look at Kristen and Kendall. They pressed their lips together, but lost it seconds later, laughing.

I glanced back down at her, squeezing her shoulder. "Kiki, how many drinks have you had?"

She furrowed her brow in concentration, sliding a glance back to the table. Her finger bobbed as she tallied on her midair imaginary chalkboard. "Three. But I got here early. And Tiffany introduced me to their new house special. It's *sooo* good."

I laughed, shaking my head as I guided her back to the couch. "I can see that. Maybe ask Tiffany for something milder for your next round, before you start inspecting floor fibers." I nodded to Kristen's husband. "Hey, Jason. This is Hannah, the cake designer for our team. Hannah, this is Kristen's husband, Jason." I paused, tilting my head. "You may have met each other at the Super Bowl party."

Hannah gave him a warm smile and reached over to shake his hand. Jason snorted, pulling her in for a big hug. That's how we did things in my family. No half ass about it. You were friends and family, or you were other.

"It really is good." Kendall gestured to the green frothy drink beside Kiki. "You should try one, Hannah."

I glanced at the drink, wondering if she'd take the recommendation. "And these two party girls are Stacy, Ben's girl, and Laura, who Mase belongs to."

Laura laughed as both of them waved from the couch.

A dozen martini glasses sat empty, collected on their tabletop. Inside each was a green, curled glow stick and a pineapple wedge on the rim. When Tiffany returned, I beckoned her with a curl of my fingers. "Let's do a round of club sodas for the girls." I pointed to the group while they laughed a little too loudly over something Laura shared. "I'll have a Konrad's Stout. And Hannah will have..."

"Single vodka tonic in a chilled draft glass with lime."

I glanced at her, tilting my head. "I didn't know you drank vodka tonic." Aside from the lemon drop martini I'd made for her at the bar, all I'd ever seen her drink was wine, beer, and Champagne. I liked learning another small thing about her.

"Tonight I do." She grinned. Then she leaned up and pecked my cheek before joining the group sitting on the couch, splitting the difference between the girls and the guys.

I turned my head to find the guys staring at me like some stranger who'd crashed the party, which was almost true with how different I felt being the guy whose world was rocked when his girl pecked his cheek.

Fuck. I should've ordered a scotch for that beer to chase.

Glaring at the nonexistent space between Mase and Hannah on the couch, I weighed out how much I needed to be near her tonight with how much shit they'd give me if I shoved him out of the way. Not giving a rat's ass what the guys thought, I moved toward them. Hannah saved the potential scuffle by scooting closer to the girls, glancing at me with a smile.

When I sat down, she eased closer to me, pressing her thigh flush against mine. Thank fuck, because it calmed me even further.

Irritated with the guys' continued scrutiny, I growled, "What?"

Mase held up both hands. "Nothing, man. Just didn't

realize you and Hannah were a thing beyond studying and work."

Ben's eyes gleamed with challenge. "Yeah. What happened to your rule about no fraternizing in business?"

Fuck. The guys giving me shit in public hadn't been something I'd considered. They'd had ample opportunity to witness little things and suspect more, had even accused me of being whipped, but I'd never confirmed or denied.

Kristen sat diagonal to me; Hannah sat across from her husband, Jason. With laser-beam focus, Kristen zeroed in on the conversation. "Yeah, Cade. What happened to your rule?"

Sure. Figured. She wouldn't pass up the opportunity to give me shit too, even though she was the one who'd suggested Hannah could be good for me, insinuating rules were made for me to break them.

I glared at her as all the girls leaned closer, wanting in on the news.

And I sat in the hot seat.

Used to being on the receiving end of harassment from three unrelenting sisters all my life, this bullshit didn't faze me, but Hannah sat right beside me. What she felt and thought mattered to me a great deal, and we hadn't discussed the pressure of the microscope we'd be under.

I pinched my eyes shut and took a deep breath, calming my reaction. How the hell could I define what Hannah and I were when she and I were still figuring it out? The last thing I wanted to do was spook her. We were in a fragile place right now, and her comfort with where we were at was more important than what any of these armchair quarterbacks thought.

"No rule was broken. We aren't a 'thing.'" In full view of at least Kristen and Jason, I put my hand on Hannah's knee, squeezing lightly as a measure of consolation. "We're friends who came together tonight. So chill the fuck out."

I glared at each of them until they all gave in, laughing, nodding, holding their hands up in surrender. Kristen gave me that knowing look, like she suspected more was going on. Let her look, assume whatever she wanted. Nothing to see here. Not yet.

Hannah pressed in close, leaning up to my ear, grabbing my full attention—which, to be honest, was the only place I wanted it to be tonight, scrutiny be damned.

"Will we come together every night?" Her whisper had the heat of a nuclear blast.

I swallowed hard, closed my eyes, and dropped my face onto my hand, sweeping my fingers together over my brow to pinch the bridge of my nose. Frustrated beyond definition, I forced myself to remain patient.

I tilted my head toward Hannah and opened my eyes. Mischief glittered in hers. I narrowed mine, trying to send menacing vibes her way. "*Behave.*"

Hannah laughed, and I couldn't help my smile. She was having a good time, and since that was the goal of tonight, I sighed and decided to let her have her fun. Even if it was at my expense.

"Troublemaker," I growled low at her.

Animated conversation resumed around us. Jason and Ben were embroiled in a heated golf discussion over the latest adjustable Cobra drivers, spurred by watching last weekend's PGA Valspar Championship. Mase philosophized about the merits of golf as a sport, and I interjected a random comment here and there on both topics.

But we'd had this discussion dozens of times. Philosophy of golf didn't interest me tonight.

Only the brave woman drinking the vodka tonic beside me did.

While I half listened to the guys, I eavesdropped on the girls. Kristen had booked us another gig, but she was gossiping about the host of the party, which was uncharacteristic of her. Before I could delve into that thought, Kendall brought up the subject of a hot new intern at her architectural firm. I think she said his name was Toby.

Then they all leaned in close, whispering. I heard snippets about Toby's hot ass, the carved abs Kendall visualized beneath his thin cotton shirt on casual Friday, something about spilled coffee and licking.

I blinked, scrubbing and bleaching my mind of all thoughts having to do with Kendall and licking.

Hannah laughed, leaning back, resting her hand high on my thigh like it belonged there. Warmth from her touch went through the denim, scalding my skin beneath. Then thoughts of Hannah and licking followed. I groaned, gritting my teeth.

Through the torture, I focused on Hannah. She seemed to be having a great time. In the middle of all the people who infiltrated my daily life, she felt comfortable. She belonged.

Tiffany had rotated in and out through the conversation and now appeared with a tray holding six green-glowing martini glasses. When one was handed to Hannah, I arched a brow at her, surprised.

Nudging me with her shoulder, she laughed. "I'm experimenting; it's a girl thing."

She hummed with pleasure after the first sip and licked her lips.

And I now liked that drink.

I also became hyperaware of everything to do with

Hannah as she grew more relaxed. Her windblown hair, low-cut top, and glistening lips were only the start of it. The way she stretched her legs out, then pulled them back and flexed her calves. The way she curled her fingers into my thigh, scraping lightly with her fingernails while she listened to the girls.

As the level of frothy drink went down in the martini glass, her sensuality went up. Her entire forearm now rested on my thigh, and her hand had fallen to the inside, her fingers drawing small circles.

My body went bowstring tight, and I had to focus to breathe steadily. No longer interested in staying at the club, I turned my attention to the guys. They seemed to have written me off, absent as I was, and two other guys had joined in on their conversation. They were in a heated debate over something to do with baseball.

Before I lost my mind, I slid my hand into Hannah's, pulling her up from the couch. "C'mon. Let's get out of here."

Her eyes sparked with amusement. I set my jaw, trying not to smile. She'd known exactly what she was doing to me, getting me worked up beside her. Pride radiated in her expression.

I gave her a stern look and mouthed the word "*bad*."

She grinned back at me, clearly pleased.

I shook my head. If only I could give her a proper punishment tonight for her crimes. I started a mental list. That kind of fun would have to wait, but I intended to fully collect not long from now. Payback for teasing me mercilessly would be a delicious bitch, and I couldn't wait.

Ben pegged me with an accusing stare. "Leaving *together* so soon, Just Friends?"

I shot Ben my best don't-fuck-with-me glare.

Hannah shrugged. "I have to get up early. Gotta make the cupcakes." She flashed a warm grin and waved to everyone before turning and colliding into my side.

I righted her, holding on to her shoulders for a moment to be sure she had her balance. "You okay to walk out of here?"

She arched a brow. "What's the other option? You gonna finally go all-out caveman and toss me over your shoulder?"

When the corner of her lower lip disappeared behind her teeth, I'd had enough of her teasing. Faster than she could process, I shoved my shoulder into her waist and grabbed the back of her thighs, hoisting her up. Hannah squealed and struggled, but I clamped my arms around her legs, holding her tight.

"Put me down, Neanderthal!"

As I turned toward the door, Mase shouted behind us, "You are *so* a thing!"

I chuckled. Now I was the one pleased with myself.

The bouncer at the rope grinned, winking at me as he let us through.

I smacked her ass when she began to kick. "Stop flailing. You're going to hurt someone."

What felt like her fist pounded into my lower back. "Put me down!"

"No. You started it." I smirked.

Cool air rushed around us as we stepped out from the covered entrance, and it was a welcome relief to the stifling air from all the warm bodies in the club. By the time we made it to my bike, Hannah had stilled on my shoulder, accepting my control for the time being.

Taking care, I bent with my knees, lowering her down until she found her balance on the pavement in those high heels of hers. A hard slap stung my back the moment I released her.

When I stood up enough to lift my head, she stared at me, indignant. A mix of fury and passion sparked in her eyes, and her wild hair matched her expression. Her chest heaved up and down.

My gaze dropped to the tempting rise and fall of her breasts. Feeling a little wicked, and a lot Neanderthal, I blasted a scorching look at her, thinking about several of the animalistic positions I wanted her in.

Her gaze heated in seconds. Then she swallowed hard, backing up a step. "Stop looking at me like that." Her voice was breathy, low.

I took a step closer. "Like what?"

"Like...you want to devour me right here."

I exhaled a slow breath. "I do."

And she did too. Hannah had actually come farther than she realized, but the safety of her denial made her blind to the signs.

I saw it clearly from her unfiltered actions. She let go the moment she got out of her head—when she lost herself in the fun of my friends and family; each time she focused on her baking. And in every verbal sparring match we'd ever had, she let down her guard and let me in without recognizing her defenses had vanished.

She sucked in a shaky breath, took a deep, considering look at me, then gave me a small smile. "Okay, I cry uncle. I know I started it, but I was just having fun in there." She smirked. "You're fun to tease."

I inhaled deeply, but it did nothing to cool the heated blood in my veins. I was well aware she'd put the brakes on, but I didn't want to stop the playful banter between us. "Fair warning. I'm keeping track. I'll play nice for now. But you have no idea what teasing is. I intend to teach you that lesson. With pleasure."

Her eyes widened, and she licked those kissable, very fuckable, lips again. She wanted to be taught a lesson. It was written in her dilated eyes, in the visible pulse at her throat.

But we weren't ready to go there.

Yet.

26. MEASURED TRUST

The twenty-minute ride back to her place buffered us back into reality. Hannah thought we needed a little more time. Which *meant* we needed a little more time. And I would give her all the space she needed while seducing her slowly.

Over the last couple of months, we'd become great friends, but we'd also become so much more. And although we hadn't defined what exactly we were yet, classifying it was only a technicality. All of which would rectify itself in time.

But even when she made small unconscious strides, her brain kept interfering, fear pulling her back from where she naturally wanted to be—close to me.

Both of us remained quiet as I helped her off the bike. She said nothing when she unfastened her helmet. After she pulled it off, she set it on the seat and shook her head, ruffling her hair back into sexy disarray. *Fuck.*

Then she lifted her gaze to mine, and so many things were said that didn't need words. Want and need flickered in her eyes, along with a dose of doubt and fear.

She was a mess. But she was *my* mess. And fucked up as I felt at times, I was hers.

As if sensing I needed body contact, she stepped up against me, sliding her fingers into my belt loops as she tugged me against her.

I swallowed hard, staring down at her, uncertain what to do.

There was no protocol for how to handle a woman walking a tightrope between what she wanted and needed, and what she thought she was capable of handling. Nor was there any instruction manual on how a damaged man should proceed in courting her when her fears were his own, his grip on them only slightly tighter than hers.

We were writing the groundbreaking handbook together as we went.

Her brows furrowed. "I wish this wasn't so hard."

"Me too. Hey, I get it, Hannah. More than you realize. But we took two different approaches to recover from our heartache."

She tilted her head. "How did you do it differently?"

"After destroying everything I touched for days, then wallowing in self-pity for another week or more, I buried all the bullshit and threw myself out there, ready or not. This is the first time you're putting yourself out there with anyone else. When I did it, I lowered the stakes, took my emotions out of it. But through the difficult process, shallow as it may have been, I learned to trust myself again. That's your problem now. How can you trust me—trust us—when you don't even trust yourself?"

She shook her head, brow furrowing. "What do you mean?"

"When I got hurt, it wasn't simply a gut punch. My heart was in deep. She didn't just hurt me; she almost destroyed me. And she didn't care one fuck about how I felt. Sound familiar?"

She exhaled. "Yeah."

"Afterward, for months, I doubted myself. I'm normally the one who's skilled at reading people. Yet she'd cheated on me multiple times while we'd been together, and I'd had no fucking idea. If I couldn't make the right decision about the person I wanted to spend the rest of my life with—if I *chose* the wrong kind of person to begin with—how in the world could I trust myself to make any good decisions about people at all?"

She nodded, eyes widening. "That's how I feel."

I sighed, my heart clenching in pain for her. "I know... you're still scared. You don't trust your decision-making abilities."

"So, you aren't scared anymore?"

"Sure I am. It's natural for us to be afraid. Putting blind trust, our very heart, into someone else's hands takes an incredible amount of faith. We have to go through a dark tunnel, hoping the light on the other side remains and a cave-in doesn't happen midway through. We have greater fear because we've been there. All the walls already collapsed in on us. Yet for us to ever have a chance at love, we have to walk through it all over again, knowing the worst-case scenario."

Silence followed as my words sank in. A cramp formed at the base of my throat, and I gulped in a breath. Her hand slid down my forearm to my hand, and I turned it over, locking my fingers together with hers.

"So we shore up our tunnel." She nodded once, making the decision without an ounce of doubt in her voice.

Brave girl.

I smiled. "And we walk through together, hand in hand, focused only on the light at the end."

She gave me a half smile. "I can't promise I might not freak out and look at the walls and ceiling now and then."

"Fuck, Hannah. I'm claustrophobic. I might stop breathing."

She laughed. "Really? I'm claustrophobic too. But I promise to give you mouth to mouth."

Her gaze drifted to my lips, and her smile faded. Her tongue flicked out, wetting her lips before she pressed them together.

It took all my willpower to remain still, waiting. "I'd like that." I let out a slow breath. "I'd like that *a lot*."

A smile played on her lips again, and she looked up into my eyes. "You would, huh?"

"Yeah." I squeezed her hand, taking a deep breath.

A lock of hair fell into her face as she leaned closer. I lifted my free hand and swiped it away from eyes that glittered with amusement and something more. When I tucked it behind her ear, brushing against her soft skin, she shivered.

She stared at my lips and exhaled. Then she gazed up into my eyes, stilling. She swallowed hard. "What are we doing?" she whispered.

Feeling like the green "go" light was shining, even if it was faded and flickering in her uncertain expression, I wrapped my arms around her. I dropped my gaze to those luscious lips and licked mine. "You're about to kiss me."

"I am?" She laughed, easy and carefree.

"You are." I tightened my grip, but merely stared down at her, waiting.

"Right here on my driveway, next to your bike?"

I laughed softly. "Would you rather it be in your bed?"

Her eyes widened. She shook her head once.

"Your shower?" I gazed up into the night sky, pretending to ponder it. "Because I think that's a tad fast, but I'm willing to go with it."

A soft laugh escaped those devastating lips. "No."

Unable to stand the suspense any longer, I turned her and walked her backward with careful steps, never loosening my grip as I stared down into her eyes. "On your kitchen island?" I grinned. "Will there be food involved?"

Her shoulders shook as she laughed harder. "I don't know. What kind of food would we use in kissing?"

We stopped before her front steps, and I pushed gently forward. She took them slowly, one leg bending back and her body rising in the close quarters of my embrace, one at a time. I took a deep breath, making a feeble attempt at calming myself, as I considered her question.

"Do you have chocolate sauce?"

She nodded.

"Caramel?"

Another slow nod.

"Honey...?" My voice fell lower, sounding rough to my own ears, as I imagined the slow drip of honey from her peaked nipple and the kiss I would place there before I sucked it off. I would drizzle more in other places on her body as I explored with my mouth, learning her reactions.

I wanted to know what made her gasp. I needed to discover what made her scream. In the darkness of the night at her front door, I pressed her body against the cold wood.

When I braced my arms above her, gripping the doorframe to hold my shaking body upright, she leaned away from the door, molding her body back into mine. The moment spun slowly around us; time seemed to slow, suspend. All I could think of now was her on her kitchen island covered in honey, her legs spread wide as I dipped down, tasting all she had to offer.

"Cade?" Her voice trembled.

"What?" I rasped out, my voice lost.

She blinked heavily. "You're looking at me like that again."

"Like what?"

"Like you want to devour me."

I swallowed hard, glancing from her eyes to her lips and back again. "I do."

There we stood, her clinging to me, begging me with her eyes. To do what? Take charge...but be gentle? I couldn't. If I leaned down to kiss her, I couldn't be sure I would stop. I was afraid I would burst into flames, break her door down, and tumble down with her to the floor.

Trying to hold it together, I gripped the doorframe harder. With great effort, I focused on my breaths as I stared at her lips.

They moved to form the shape of an O, and her eyes widened a fraction before they softened, as if she hadn't understood my body cues at first, but now spoke the language.

With flattened palms, she spread them up my chest, then stopped midway, holding them there, as if her gentle pressure reinforced my restraint, and together we held back an avalanche.

Searching my face, she leaned up. Her tongue peeked out, wetting her lips the way she did around me a lot lately, as if she wanted to devour me too. As if she couldn't wait to have a taste.

I kept my eyes open, unable to believe this was finally happening, not wanting to miss one second of it. Her breath was soft and warm against my chin, then my cheek.

She moved forward, brushing her lips along my jawline. I felt her pause, place a tender kiss there. She glanced up into my eyes again, keeping our gazes locked until she moved to the other side, doing the same.

For a brief second, I shut my eyes and swallowed hard. "Tease."

I opened them again to find a wicked smirk on her face. "You have no idea."

She was right. I didn't. The more I was around her, the greater a mystery she became. I couldn't wait to find out what made this intriguing woman tick, even if she teased out the unveiling of all that was Hannah from now until eternity.

Her face grew serious in concentration as she stared at my mouth.

My breathing grew shallow. My pulse raced hot through my body, thundering into my cock with aching need.

In slow motion, she tilted her face upward, and her eyelids drifted closed. I closed mine too, needing to feel everything as she did.

Soft brushes feathered across my lips. Then using more pressure, she molded them softly to mine. Her hands slid to my lower back, and she pressed her pelvis into my groin.

I moaned, overloaded with sensation.

Her tongue flicked out, teasing before she sucked on my lower lip.

I gave in to her tender pace and kissed her back with all the restraint I had. When she started to pull away, I leaned in, sucking on her lower lip.

One sip and I was drunk on this incredible woman, swimming in a sea of her. I was a drowning man, and I never wanted to come up for air.

After several seconds of hungry exploration, Hannah

eased back, breaking contact. Our hot puffs of breath fogged across our lips. Hers were pink, glistening.

Wow. Just fucking *wow.*

I took a shaky breath, and she did the same. We stared at each other for long seconds while I remained still, muscles tensed, not trusting myself to move.

She finally smiled, biting her lip, then sucked it in, as if tasting me on her skin. Pulling her keys out of her pocket, she took a step back before turning to unlock her door.

When she shifted back toward me, I leaned forward, unable to let her go. She reached behind her, grabbing on to the door handle. The action jutted her breasts out like an engraved invitation. I bent down, staring, growling.

She bent down, her face interrupting my detour to meet my gaze. I fought the urge to look down at the even more spectacular view.

"Good night, Cade." She smiled.

Pure happiness radiated from within her. *I'd* put that feeling there. And she'd let me.

I groaned as she backed into her house, feeling helpless. And very much in need of more of everything she had to offer. "You can't leave me here like this."

"Can you wait until tomorrow night?"

Confused, I searched her face. "What's tomorrow night?" I needed specifics here. Did she mean the bed? Or the kitchen island? Were we talking chocolate sauce or honey?

"If you don't have plans, would you want to go out on our first date?"

My heart soared. This brave girl was taking the leap, giving me a chance with her heart. I wouldn't let her down.

"Fuck yeah, I would!" Her startled look humbled me. "I mean, yes. I'd love to."

Her expression softened. "Then, c'mere, you. How about one last kiss to tide you over?"

This time I met her halfway, losing myself in Hannah with every moment she granted.

Happily Ever After
for now . . .

Cade & Hannah's romantic adventures continue to unfold in the **No Weddings** series...

No Weddings
One Funeral
Two Bar Mitzvahs
Three Christmases
For Valentine's

Thank You!

Thank you for experiencing Cade and Hannah's romantic adventure with us in *No Weddings*.

If you enjoyed the story, please express your love for *No Weddings* by recommending it to friends in person, by email, on Goodreads, and through book clubs and reader groups.

And if you value reviews to help guide you into your next book, as we do, please help other readers by sharing your review of *No Weddings* on your favorite retailer and book community sites.

Incredible thanks to everyone for extending your love of *No Weddings*.

Reviews are cherished love notes to authors
and tantalizing invitations to readers.
Appreciated by all. ♥

Want to Read More?

Dive into the steamy romantic comedy of the
No Weddings Series...
No Weddings
One Funeral
Two Bar Mitzvahs
Three Christmases
For Valentine's

Read more of your favorite characters from the No
Weddings series in the steamy spinoff
Unbreakable Series...

Kiki & Darren's romance ignites in...
Heartbreaker

Mase & Leilani's passion flares in...
Rule Breaker

Ben & Shay flirt with danger in...
Lawbreaker

Escape into award-winning time travel romance
in the steamy novels of the
Highland Legends Series...
Forged in Dreams and Magick
Bound by Wish and Mistletoe
Born of Mist and Legend
Found in Flame and Moonlight

Adventure in paranormal short stories
in a spinoff of Highland Legends
THE TRAVELER: Initiate Years ...
Veil of Realms
Secrets of Alexandria
Panther Rising
Stones of Power
Highland Magick

Want to Read EVEN More?

Icebreaker **and** *Ball Breaker*
AND
an epic romantasy series are all coming soon!

Be the first to receive preorder alerts, exclusive bonus gifts,
and occasional free stories...
Join our Bastion Family Adventurers!
katbastion.com/email-subscription

ALSO BY KAT & STONE BASTION

No Weddings Series

No Weddings · One Funeral

Two Bar Mitzvahs · Three Christmases

For Valentine's

Unbreakable Series

Heartbreaker · Rule Breaker · Lawbreaker

Forthcoming: *Ball Breaker · Icebreaker*

Highland Legends Series

Forged in Dreams and Magick

Bound by Wish and Mistletoe

Born of Mist and Legend

Found in Flame and Moonlight

THE TRAVELER: Initiate Years

Veil of Realms · Secrets of Alexandria · Panther Rising

Stones of Power · Highland Magick

Half-Baked Holidays

Half-baked Holidays:

A Romantic Comedy Holiday Collection

Sneak Peek of our Unbreakable Series Novel

Heartbreaker

Kiki...

For a blessed few hours, I forgot.

Loading Zone did that to me. The nightclub's Industrial Grunge feel, which I'd helped design with its exposed brick and rusted steel, wrapped itself around me like a comfortable blanket. Heavy bass thumped, vibrating into my bones. My thighs burned from dancing back-to-back songs. Three lemon drop martinis in the last two hours hummed warmth through my veins.

"C'mon," my sister Kendall shouted above the loud music as she grasped my hand, then tugged me forward. "My toes are numb."

Out of breath, I nodded and we headed toward the corner booth the eight of us had crammed into earlier. I dance-walked in the narrow path through the crowd behind her, each step a hip shake and head toss to the pulsing rhythm.

The moment we reached the table, our oldest sister, Kristen, pulled her husband from the booth. "Time for us to go. Jason has an early flight tomorrow."

Cade, our brother and silent partner of Loading Zone, guided his new wife, Hannah, out right after them. "Last dance, Mrs. Michaelson?"

Which left Cade's two best friends: the scruffy prodigy surfer Mase, his former roommate; and clean-cut businessman Ben, the other owner of Loading Zone. I slid over the black distressed leather before landing in the center of the wide, shallow booth to face the dance floor while Mase abandoned his spot on the opposite side to anchor the end next to me.

I grasped the stem of my martini glass, sipped the last bit of the tart lemon drop, then let out a happy-buzz sigh. Being around these three—including rising-star architect Kendall—all of them with their shit together, lent some grounding *yin* to my artistic *yang*.

"Sex on a stick, twelve o'clock," Kendall announced.

My heart suddenly slammed into my ribs. But I exhaled slowly, trying to hide my reaction.

I'd been excited about tonight for several reasons: banish my secret problems from my head, surround myself with my favorite peeps, and *Darren Cole*.

Ben snorted out laughter while Mase dropped me a deadpan look. "'Sex on a *stick*'?"

I shot Mase a sidelong glare and elbowed him in the ribs.

He grunted and nudged my arm away.

By the time I glanced up, corded forearms shot over the outer edge of the table. Large hands planted with a hard smack on the brushed metal tabletop. A familiar folded strip of paper skittered out from his fingers, sliding in a wide arc toward Ben.

My breath caught as I stared into Darren's dark green eyes. A lock of his shaggy black hair fell over his forehead as he tilted his face downward. He set his jaw, expression hardening, as a scuffle between four guys unfolded right behind him, the apparent cause of his sudden hand-plant. He gave me a piercing look. "Twenty minutes."

Then he turned and grasped the nearest offender by the scruff of his shirt. Security arrived an instant later and manhandled the others into submission.

As Darren flexed his left arm while leading his guy toward the exit of the club, the tapered point of a tribal tattoo peeked out from the back collar of Darren's black T-shirt. My imagination began to paint what lay hidden from view: thick black ink arcing across sculpted back muscles, a woven design that twisted downward toward his tight...

"What's that?" Kendall leaned over the table.

I tore my gaze away from Darren and reached for the note, but Kendall snatched up the slip of paper first. She unfolded it and read its message aloud, "'*Gimme a* ride? *K*.'"

"Oh, sure." Mase took a long pull from his beer, then swallowed. "Kendall gets to innuendo the fuck out of this, but I don't?"

Ben arched a brow. "Twenty minutes. That's one helluva ride."

"Shut up. Both of you. Guys objectify women. We can do the same. And it's a ride home, smartass." I tried to shoot Ben an annoyed glare, but the corners of my mouth twitched into a smile and ruined the whole thing.

"*Suuure*...a ride home." Mase winked at me, then glanced over to where Darren strode along the edge of the room as he headed back toward his DJ booth. "I suppose he qualifies."

"Worthy of objectifying? Darren more than qualifies." I pinched the message *meant for Darren's eyes only* and ripped it from Kendall's grasp. "He doesn't say much," I continued. "Leaves the club with different women. Built like the perfect male specimen..."

Ben choked on his beer. "And what are we? Male rejects?"

"Ewww." Kendall scowled. "That's incestuous."

"You're like our brothers. Can't even..." I scrunched my nose and blanked out my mind, willing myself not to visualize it.

"Not looking for love?" Ben asked, tone softening.

At that, all of our gazes drifted toward the dance floor. One of the last songs of the night streamed a fast tempo from the speakers, but in the center of a thinning crowd, Cade and Hannah stood oblivious. Wrapped together, they swayed to a slow rhythm only they seemed to hear. The look of adoration on their faces as they stared deep into each other's eyes spoke volumes.

"No," I said with absolute conviction. "Heartache lies down that road."

Mase laid a gentle hand on mine. "As your pseudo-brother, I'm warning you: Be careful."

I had no idea whether he meant Darren specifically or men in general. It didn't really matter. I'd learned my love lesson early. And I'd never trusted a guy enough to let one hurt me since.

Darren? The only kind of guy I was willing to play with. A beautiful man I refused to form any attachment to—easy to leave.

The quintessential heartbreaker.

In Darren's truck. Again. A vast awkward distance between us. *Again.*

The drive took only about ten minutes. But the ride home from Loading Zone in Philly's Old City Arts District to the outskirts of sleepy Glenhaven—the third since last summer—stretched eternal.

Why? A hookup shouldn't be this difficult.

My gaze shifted toward him. Powerful hands gripped the steering wheel, thumbs knocking some unheard drumbeat into the silence of the cab. Sculpted forearms stretched up toward cut biceps that vanished under the thin black fabric of the T-shirt that hugged them. His expression was serious, but relaxed. As if he didn't feel the weight of the moment like I did.

Now or never, Kiki.

I took a deep breath and ran a flattened hand over the gauzy material of my skirt, trying to calm myself. Then I inched closer to him, needing some sort of validation that whatever tenuous thing we had between us was moving toward something...fun...instead of away from it.

Tonight didn't have to be a big deal. He either wanted me or didn't. Two other platonic drop-offs didn't mean anything significant. Maybe he was shy. Or a gentleman.

As we drove, yellow pools of light from wrought iron lampposts marked the passing time in a visual cadence. *Light...dark. Light...dark.* The streetlights soon began to feel like a countdown, as if they mocked me for just sitting passively in their spotlights.

Yet how to breach the uncomfortable silence? My mind tumbled over the possibilities: *How did your sound board glide tonight? Wow, how 'bout the heavy bass on that last song?*

He cleared his throat, beating me to it. "Sooo...talk to me. How's the art going?"

"Good." *Good? Really?* I winced at my pathetic attempt at conversation.

We made the second-to-last turn, my time running out, as he gave a single nod in reply.

Buck up, Kiki. You either want him or you don't. Stop being a pussy. "Actually, it's a smaller sculpture. A single orchid sprouting from a rocky riverbed."

He glanced my way. "You work with metal, right?"

"Yeah." I leaned back, staring out the windshield, finally calming a bit as I thought about my art. "This piece is bronze. The lone color is the violet on the flower."

"Sounds cool." His voice lowered. He cleared his throat again.

Had he moved closer?

Impossible. He was driving. Behind the steering wheel, as always.

Yet our legs nearly touched. The rough denim, tight over his thigh, had slid over the tan leather seat to within an inch of my bared knee; he'd spread his legs wider.

The man already consumed most of the space in the truck with his commanding presence. But instead of moving away, I automatically drew closer. My thundering pulse throbbed heavier, warmer...lower.

I swallowed hard, attempting to find my way back to the conversation. "How did your night go?" Maybe his sound board was a medium for his art, like metal was for me.

"Good." The corner of his mouth twitched into a barely perceptible grin, then relaxed.

He dropped his right hand from the steering wheel and floated it in the infinitesimal space between us. Gentle pressure rubbed through the flimsy fabric that covered my upper thigh.

My gaze lowered from the dashboard at the exact moment the knuckle of his index finger trailed in slow motion up the skin under my hem.

I held my breath.

I haven't *been imagining things.*

But then his hand suddenly lifted and fisted. His expression hardened as he stared straight ahead. We made the final turn onto my street, and he eased off the gas, letting us coast. The ride I'd been waiting all night for—six long months and two failed attempts for—appeared to be over.

We rolled to a stop in front of the white picket fence that surrounded the darling butter-yellow Victorian. Then he shifted the truck into park, letting it idle.

Refusing to give up, especially when I sensed him struggling with an attraction we both knew was real, I made a final direct attempt. "You don't have to drive right off. You could come in for a drink."

"No, I can't."

"Why not?" The two words tripped out flippant in my pitiful effort to sound nonchalant.

"You're Cade's little sister."

"No, I'm n—" I blinked.

The pad of his finger pressed to my lips. Warm. Firm. Suddenly, I thought of nothing else. My whole world became our tantalizing first contact.

He didn't move. Simply stared at me.

I closed my eyes. My head eased back against the headrest, but the contact remained as my lips pursed into the gentlest kiss against his fingertip. I wanted to flick my tongue out, taste him. But then he pulled away.

I blinked my eyes open.

He'd half-twisted on the seat toward me. "You deserve better than a one-night fuck, Kiki."

"What I deserve," I muttered, then snorted.

Damn right, I deserve better than that.

But one night was all I could handle.

"Doesn't matter." What I continued to tell myself. "What

I want right now is you." There, I'd said it. Out in the open. Bold and direct.

"What you deserve *does* matter. Don't ever forget it." His voice hardened with every word. His dark brows furrowed to the point a deep crease marred the tanned skin between them.

Without thinking, I reached up and pressed my thumb along that vertical line, massaging until his face began to relax.

He stared at me with renewed intensity. "What are you doing?"

"Trying to get you to chill out." I let my thumb slide a fraction to the right until I found a pressure point, then I spread the rest of my fingertips across the line of his eyebrow. "Is it working?"

"No." The corners of his mouth twitched again.

"Liar."

"Okay. A little."

"Seriously, though," I continued as if I hadn't been distracted by his impressive scowl. "I'm an excellent one-night fuck."

He jerked his head away, then lapsed into a coughing fit.

I arched a brow. "What? Don't think so?"

He shook his head. "No." His mouth fell open. "I mean, I'm sure you are." He blew out a heavy sigh, cheeks puffing from the effort. "You just…"

"Unnerve you?"

"*Yes.*" He thrust a splayed hand into the open air between us with the curt word. "Are you trying to kill me?"

A smile began to curve my lips. "No, I'm just trying to—"

"Don't say it."

The word hung on the tip of my tongue. "You know I'm thinking it."

"Stop thinking it." He took a measured breath, his chest gradually rising, then falling.

Enjoying the loaded tension between us, I remained still, waiting.

When he turned toward me again, I leaned closer and deeply inhaled his earthy scent. "Look. This doesn't have to be complicated just because I'm Cade's sister. You're an adult. I'm an adult. Aren't you attracted to me?"

Every telltale sign he'd shown suggested that he wanted me. But I'd never encountered so much resistance in a guy before. Then again, I'd never had one in my sights so long before either. I ignored the implications in that.

"Of course I am." He draped an arm along the top of the seatback.

His warmth lured me in, and I edged even closer until my entire side crushed against his. He made no move to stop me and didn't flinch away, but his lengthy pause indicated that he resisted committing to anything.

"All it has to be is one night," I whispered, my lips nearly touching the warm skin of his neck.

Another heavy sigh ruffled the hair above my ear, shooting chill bumps down my side. "You gotta know, if I could...I would. It *is* complicated. I can't explain. But no matter how badly either of us want to, this can't happen."

I blinked, confused and lost in uncharted territory. Never had a guy not taken the bait I'd offered. And he was being so nice about it. My mind couldn't process what was happening. "You want me."

"Fuck, yes. I mean, no." He growled in frustration. "God-dammit, Kiki. Just get out of the truck. Please."

I pulled away from him and straightened in my seat, almost laughing at the desperation in his tone. Then I dared a glance at him. His expression grew tortured. A tiny part of me felt bad for putting him in a position I didn't understand. The rest of me beamed that I wasn't the only sexually frustrated one in the vehicle.

Not yet willing to admit defeat, I gave him a smile and grasped the cold metal door handle. "Thanks for the ride, Darren."

I wouldn't ask for one again. But I didn't need to. The seeds had been planted. My work was done. Either he wanted me enough to get past whatever obstacle was cockblocking his way, or he didn't.

Meanwhile, I'd go back to the life I'd been trying to forget, once my mind-numbing buzz wore off.

I wanted to glance over my shoulder as I unfastened the painted wooden gate, double-check to see if he was still watching, but I fought the urge.

The low hum of his idling truck engine remained unchanged. But had his mind?

This lonely girl can only hope.

———

Enjoy the rest of the romance...
Heartbreaker

Found in Flame and Moonlight

Eight minutes was all Chelsea Smith had. All she needed. *Hopefully.*

The heavy wooden door to Professor MacLaren's private office snicked closed behind her. With a subtle suggestion from her mind, the tumblers reengaged within its lock, a deadbolt she'd "picked" with similar mental ease mere seconds ago.

On her next inhale of cooler undisturbed air, the distinctive scents of age washed over her: that certain spice of centuries-old leather, a mustiness of layered dust, the sweetness of yellowing paper in a prized collection of ancient books.

The room's furnishings echoed its owner's passion for antiquities. Within a sizable entry, a vintage coffee-colored Chesterfield sofa with matching wingchairs hovered at the edge of a burgundy-and-gold Aubusson carpet. Along the side and far wall, relics from exotic locales perched from various niches between precisely stacked scholarly tomes in massive bookcases. And beyond a sizable polished wood desk and its stately leather chair, within tall display cases that flanked a large window, treasured discoveries from historic digs rested on glass shelves.

Yet one particular artifact stood apart from the rest. The

sole reason for her break-in. And the item occupied the nearest corner of his polished wood desk, exposed. No bookcase niche. No protective case.

"Such unfathomable *power*," Chelsea murmured toward the rectangular object, at once fascinated and intrigued. More than she'd been about anything in her first twenty-two years of an immortal life hiding-in-plain sight among "normal" humans.

Her excitement even eclipsed what she'd witnessed from the other side of that window while walking to MacLaren's lecture less than an hour ago.

Though her mind still reeled about that discovery as well.

Because something very *not human* had stood near that power-drenched box, partially transparent, as if not fully materialized into the human world. And that shirtless muscular something had resembled artistic depictions of male angelic warriors, only skewed darker and more sinister with its dusky olive skin, inky black wings, and blue-green prismatic eyes.

And the enigmatic creature had stared directly at her, eyes narrowing, puzzlement twisting his sharp features as Chelsea blatantly stared back. He'd seemed surprised. That she could detect him? Or perhaps that their paths had intersected in the first place.

Yet inside the professor's locked office, no sign of the dark angel remained.

Seven minutes.

The forceful vibration of the artifact's unique power was what had caught her attention from the other side of the window. It had radiated an exhilarating and complex energy, beckoning her like a siren's call.

"Invitation accepted," she whispered.

With slow breaths, Chelsea banked her excitement. Not hard to achieve. Her kind, further evolved humans, born-and-bred assassins, had been trained through millennia to suppress emotion.

"Yeah." She let out a soft snort. "Look how well *that* turned out."

Members of her race had recently evolved again. And an underground faction had organically formed. One that no longer sought to squelch their emotions. That strong minority yearned for something greater, a deeper meaning to their eternal life.

Months ago, Chelsea had been secretly contacted by them. The founders had detected her tendency to operate on the fringe of acceptability. Of course, she'd joined their cause without hesitation.

In the hours and days following that pivotal decision, she'd eased the cognitive restraints that had hobbled her. They had warned her that she would suffer unimaginable internal struggle. Yet nothing had prepared her for the cascade of emotions. One in particular had caused an enormous dissonance with her inherited vocation.

Empathy had bled into her black-and-white world.

An *assassin's* world.

And that problematic emotion had caused a thunderstorm of chaotic gray.

Six minutes.

Focus, Chelsea. She took measured steps toward the charged artifact, noting its unusual features. A foot long, half that wide and tall, a rectangular box sat encased in layers of elaborate metallic latticework. The gleaming designs that adorned its corners and edges were comprised of various metals from differing artistry. But beneath those ornate motifs, simpler flat sides were fashioned from a beautiful bluish-silver metal with a slight sparkle to its sheen.

Indirect bright light glowed in from the large window, but as Chelsea approached, an aura of energy haloed around the box. Infinitesimal particles glittered beyond its surfaces, flashes of silver and gold visible to her preternatural eyes.

Five minutes.

Which meant MacLaren's lecture in his beloved Advanced Theories in Archaeology had concluded. Earlier, Chelsea had obediently endured the graduate-level course with fifteen other classmates until she'd politely excused herself at the last and most opportune moment. A correct amount of respectful time from a valued student. The perfect window of plausible deniability should her burglary plans go awry.

Students typically waylaid him after his lectures, but to be certain, she extended her superhuman hearing. Down a wide sidewalk between buildings, across a grassy quad, and into the cozy window-lined room that the tenured professor claimed as his own, she detected the voices of eager students who had indeed detained him. Which enabled him to wax eloquent about the week's series and his latest obsession: prehistoric artifacts handed down by gods, breadcrumbs to the secrets of mysterious civilizations.

"But you've been keeping the biggest secret of all right here in your office, haven't you?" Chelsea murmured as she paused within reach of the object.

Four minutes.

Plenty of time to abort, to walk away without detection.

"I don't *need* to be here." Sound reason.

And yet, need had become relative.

For in the months following her recent evolution, an

undefinable hunger had begun to grow that nothing satisfied. A craving for a deeper purpose. Not the deadly one mandated by her ancestry. Not even the glimmer of hope that her emerging faction offered.

"Something personal," she murmured, staring at the box. She'd been hunting a cause that matched her sudden passion for life. Unique and special. Sparked by her newfound awakening. "Worthy. And all my own."

Because every action she'd taken in life, from actual missions to basic periphery cover, had been by her race's directive. Even attending university. Particularly MacLaren's courses.

But for the first time, she operated on her own volition. Because before that morning, she hadn't been privy to any details of *why* MacLaren had become a person of interest. Until one shining detail had made itself known, flashing its undeniable energy straight toward her.

Therefore, the risk of exposure? While investigating an object as exceptional as what she hoped to discover about herself?

More than acceptable.

While she continued to listen, the distinct voices of six fellow grad students dwindled to two hardcore disciples. They peppered the professor with questions, theories, and offers of assistance on his next expedition. Groveling, as usual. But MacLaren had their number. And only a couple of minutes remained of his scheduled patience.

Chelsea drew a deep breath to calm her riotous—clearly *not* suppressed—emotions.

Instinct screamed the intricate box held her destiny. Even if she had no idea why.

But as she took a final step and reached out a hand to touch, its unique power reacted to her proximity with accelerating vibrations of energy—plenty of evidence to back up that gut feeling.

Three minutes.

MacLaren shooed out his fan club with his parting excuses and locked up the classroom.

Right as Chelsea hovered a hand over the artifact.

Energy emanated upward from that bluish-silver top, charging the air with electrons that sizzled and sparked. Warmth bathed her palm. Friendly. Inviting. *Intoxicating.*

Until a sense of grave danger spiked in those scant inches between the mysterious metal and her skin. And an unfamiliar feeling of trepidation tripped down her spine. Like some cosmic warning.

Chelsea paused, then blinked heavily, thrown by the sudden unfriendliness of the box and her own emotion about it. She wiggled her fingers within the box's charged aura and considered her impulsive actions. And their unknown ramifications. With the artifact. And MacLaren.

An extensive list of potentialities scrolled through her advanced mind. But the calculations magnified when she removed the laws of the known universe and input alternate realities. Involving energized boxes. And dark angels. And supposedly regular professors that capture the attention of a race of assassins.

Ninety seconds.

"So many possibilities," she murmured about the upside. *Too many variables to calculate.*

Chelsea snorted and shook her head with a slight smile. "I've never been afraid of anything in my life." Headlong into the adventure. The only way she saw the world.

The leather heels of MacLaren's loafers clicked down the nearest sidewalk.

Less than a minute. Before her trespass was discovered.

Urgency fired through her veins. She tensed her arm and lowered her hand, ready to touch no matter the outcome. To finally complete some circuit she'd begun to sense, as if the dark matter hovering between the spaces in the universe needed her help.

The charged air rippled with a stronger dose of caution.

Chelsea narrowed her eyes at the box.

Are you trying to communicate with me?

That the inanimate object had sentience, as opposed to some other force out in the ether, gave her pause. Deadly animals and insects often displayed vivid warnings of their lethal venom.

But why lead me here with such clear invitation? Do you not want me to touch?

The warning vibration wavered back and forth in response as the additional questions crossed her mind. Not quite a yes, not quite a no. That it wanted her there, perhaps. But not to touch? *Orrr...*

"Not yet?" Barely an inch existed.

A hot glow sparkled into existence between her and the artifact, golden and shimmering. The box's energy extended an exquisite representation of agreement in its special language.

"Fascinating." Mesmerizing.

The artifact's seductive power continued to astound.

Have you taunted MacLaren with such scandalous invitation?

No sooner had she posed the mental question, than an answer rippled forth. Only that message vibrated not from the artifact, but from somewhere out in the ether. *No.* Crystal clear. Not as any legible word, but a negative in resonance.

The energized box did not wait on that desk for the professor.

At that moment, the artifact existed for a singular purpose: to join its immense power with hers.

MacLaren's footfalls began to click down the tiles of the building's corridor.

Energy spiked from the box again. Even while its power rippled another caution: *Not yet.* The message clearly vibrated from the object, not the ether.

But unraveling the mysteries of a higher consciousnesses in matter and space had to wait.

Adrenaline surged through her. "Out of time."

Golden sparks fountained up from its metallic top, singeing her palm. *Not yet!*

"When?" Chelsea choked out a laugh at the box. "*After* he has campus security cuff me?"

MacLaren's key slid into the lock.

Her pulse raced, the thump of her heart a drumbeat in her ears.

Now or never! she argued to the unseen gatekeepers.

Tiny clicks echoed as tumblers released in the lock's mechanism.

The door edge scraped over its frame, the only means of a clean escape swinging open and her window of opportunity closing right along with it.

Half-assed alibies spun through her mind, all utterly ridiculous: *I followed a burglar in, I needed to lie down and only your pin-tucked sofa would do, I saw a black-winged angel with sparkling blue-green eyes staring out your window.* Voicing that last factoid? Bordered on certifiable insanity.

But at the last split second between clean infiltration and utter discovery—right as her anxiety skyrocketed—a powerful vacuum slammed her hand down that remaining inch.

A scorching current charged up through her palm from the metal. Blinding power and incredible pleasure flashed through her being.

MacLaren's office vanished.

And a realm of absolute nothingness descended.

Gawain Brodie sucked in a stunned breath as the inside of his chest...*boomed.*

Thunder? Confused, he frowned but refused to break stride. He raced down an earthen footpath in the shadowy forest to rejoin his warriors; he'd been ambushed while scouting. And since no cloud marred the late-afternoon sky, he shook off the jarring sensation.

Faster! Scant seconds remained. Clan Brodie had been exposed. Their castle's centuries-old secret somehow breached.

Blood from three attackers speckled his arms and chest. Yet the last one's dying words bore evidence of the exposure: *Your magick castle is ours!*

A tang from the skirmish coated his tongue, pungent earth and the coppery taste of blood. Anger churned in his gut. Ferocity pumped through his veins. Single-minded determination overcame burning muscles as he sought to vanquish whatever enemy they faced.

Intent on cutting time, he broke into a sunny glade, ran across rippling purple blooms of heather, then rejoined the well-worn trail. Yet as he rounded the gnarled trunk of an ancient yew, a sudden awareness made him veer wide in the turn.

Alongside the path, lacy fronds of bracken trembled. Then a blur of motion burst forth.

Dark garb registered in his peripheral vision. As did the gleam of a swinging sword.

He unsheathed his own sword, then blocked a strike meant to cleave his neck.

Never pausing his momentum, Gawain twisted his body and shifted forward, swinging his weapon over. Then he tightened his blade down at the last moment for the killing blow.

To his surprise, the swords clashed. Punishing vibration jarred his bones from hand to arm, shoulder to neck, till they rattled a final quiver down through his teeth.

The attacker—a male with flaxen hair, of similar height and breadth to the threesome he'd more easily dispatched —merely sounded a low grunt.

With greater determination, Gawain thrust.

In equal measure, his opponent parried.

Fury darkened his attacker's eyes.

Exhilaration fired through Gawain's veins.

Their deadly battle-dance continued with strikes and blocks, thrusts and parries. Each next metallic crash rang out with echoing menace.

"At long last, a worthy opponent," Gawain murmured.

Gawain arced his sword back around, but once the tip swung skyward, he twisted, tucked, then thrust from a lower angle.

The soldier deflected then stepped aside, just as well trained, equally gifted.

"Aye. An 'opponent' who'll impale yer bloody arse like a stuck pig," the soldier replied in an English accent. A sick hunger gleamed in his eye.

Amused, Gawain relaxed his stance and drew back his weapon. He tilted his head and narrowed his eyes. "Why eat pig when you can dine like a king?"

The man's expression fell. As did the tip of his sword while he gave a heavy blink and furrowed his brow. "What're you on about?"

In the next heartbeat, Gawain lunged with incredible speed. The tip of his sword led the way, piercing the man's heart before he was able to draw a full gasp of surprise—or reengage his sword.

"The differences between us," Gawain whispered into the ear of the dying man.

Severe lack of emotion and abundance of wit.

What Gawain possessed and most did not.

With a quick jerk, Gawain freed his sword. As the body crumpled to the ground, he swiped both sides of his weapon on the cleanest patch of the soldier's woolen tunic. He believed in letting fallen men keep their blood. *Off my sword.*

English! The revelation of how far and wide their exposure had traveled still stunned him.

No time! He charged back toward the footpath and raced on.

After another few hundred yards, the clear sounds of combat filtered into the dense forest: the clatter of weapons, shouts and grunts from men.

Seconds later, he burst upon a greater battle. Or what little remained of it.

His brethren carved and sliced through their own tenacious dark-garbed attackers. One Brodie to five English. But the last of their foe fell in rapid succession, one after the other, none prepared for the skill of the unique clan of Highlanders.

With no immediate threat left to eliminate, Gawain sheathed his weapon.

A second strange thunder boomed through his chest.

And its fading vibration carried the aftertaste of something imminent...*weighty.* As if an event of great import was about to transpire. *Involving me?* Or the clan.

Dismayed by the inexplicable and unnerving sensation, Gawain stared toward the western horizon as a fiery sun dipped below jagged mountain peaks.

Two warhorses suddenly appeared below his line of vision, one snow white, the other coal black. Both materialized seemingly from nowhere. And knowing their riders as Gawain did, they likely had.

Another powerful vibration reverberated through Gawain's chest so hard, he stifled the urge to cough as his family approached.

Astride the white mare was Isobel Brodie with her long blond hair flying back in the wind. Clad in her custom deerskin hunting outfit, she braced her toddler son between her arms.

On the black stallion rode Iain, Isobel's husband, Gawain's older brother, and Laird of Clan Brodie. He cradled their lad's twin sister with a father's protective hand.

Clutched in Iain's other hand was a magickal box whose surface sparkled even in gloaming's waning light.

Yet that box had *never* left Brodie Castle.

Not in all the years of Gawain's life.

Nor in any of the legendary tales of generations past.

An unmistakable sense of foreboding washed over him as his fellow warriors gathered to watch their leader and kin draw near.

"*All* approach the battlefront?" their commander, Robert, inquired to his right.

"With the wee ones?" Duncan asked at his left.

The warriors were part of Iain's elite guardsmen. Twelve in total. Closer than brothers.

"Nay." Naught was as it seemed. A great change had begun. Those facts rang true with every heavy beat of his heart. And he'd somehow landed in the center of its shifting tides. "They'll be but a moment," he murmured.

Even if Gawain failed to comprehend *how* he knew what was about to transpire, he sensed why they'd come.

Fate had descended upon him. Though the circumstance made little sense.

"I'll not take your place!" Gawain objected to the notion. The magickal box may as well have been scepter, orb, and crown. For of the many powers it wielded, foremost among them had long been to ordain the next Brodie male as chieftain of their clan.

"*Aye*, you will." Iain lifted the hallowed box high, reaching back.

"You remain hale and whole." Fit to rule. No reason to shift the obligation.

"We've no time to explain." Isobel tightened her legs to bring her mount alongside Iain's as she glanced at her husband. "Danger abounds. And we've been summoned"— at the last word, she directed Gawain a pointed look, heavy with meaning—"*away*."

Gawain sighed. *Away through* time itself. *No explanation needed.*

A strange feeling quivered in his gut. Akin to uncertainty. And a more familiar one: dread. Of the unknown. Of the burden of a reign he had never expected to shoulder.

The obsessive focus of battle had served him well all his life, had helped him overcome childhood demons. Even to the detriment of relations with close family. Namely his sister, Brigid, who he'd wrongly blamed for the cause of those demons so long ago. But Gawain had already come to accept how he'd done Brigid a grave disservice and labored to make amends.

Of late, he'd grown more noble. Worthy of the reign.

And his brother well knew it.

"'Tis the way of it," Iain bellowed for all the guardsmen to hear in witness of the historic moment. "You'll lead the clan through."

"*Aye.*" Gawain gave a clipped nod to his brother in dutiful acceptance of the role.

Iain dipped his chin with satisfaction, punched his arm forward, and released his grip.

The box arced through the air.

With narrowed eyes, Gawain thrust his hands up to catch it.

Yet at the exact moment his fingertips made contact with its cool metal sides, several monumental events happened at once, in plain sight of their guardsmen.

A bright bolt of lightning shot from ground to sky with a true boom of thunder.

Isobel touched a hand to Iain's shoulder and Clan Brodie's former ruling family vanished, warhorses and all.

Heat sparked from the box to his fingers and flashed through his entire body.

And a raven-haired woman appeared out of thin air. Vibrant blue eyes stared straight at him. Her slender hand rested atop the box.

"*Nay!*" Gawain growled, furious.

In his disgruntled shock of becoming laird, he'd forgotten the *other* burden the ancient box bestowed.

A soul mate.

Enjoy the rest of the adventure...
Found in Flame and Moonlight

ACKNOWLEDGMENTS

An incredible team of people were directly involved in making of *No Weddings* and are mentioned below; however, any errors within the published novel, whether existing there intentionally or not, are ours alone.

Enormous appreciation goes to Kristi at Picky Editor. She was the first developmental editor and the last proofreader. But in between, she went above and beyond, providing additional editing, support, and advice in areas that far surpassed the traditional author–editor relationship. Kristi, we enjoyed the journey all the more because you were an integral part of it. You are a rare treasure, and we're immeasurably grateful for you and all you do.

Thank you to Claire and Bryan at Finish the Story for helping us polish the book. We appreciate the time you spent, especially your perseverance, patience, and understanding to get the story just right.

Huge thanks to Heather and Misty, our close friends and cheerleaders, for fielding all of Kat's random texts and for providing valued opinions about the opening of the book.

To our social media friends, fans, supporters, readers, reviewers, and bloggers, both those we've interacted with thus far and those we look forward to meeting—we are immensely grateful for all you do. Your unending enthusiasm for reading our stories fuels our excitement to write them.

Stone, what in the world could I say here to cover the

depth of my gratitude to you? Not enough. But I will say that I'm so glad we took a wild idea over pizza out one night and turned it into a labor of love and laughter. I'd shout out some of the hilarious moments to make you laugh, but I have a feeling you're already thinking about them...and smiling.

Kat...Wait, what? Is this like wedding vows? You know what you mean to me. The journey. The love. The laughter. *Squirrel!*

ABOUT THE AUTHOR

Kat Bastion won several awards for her bestselling debut novel *Forged in Dreams and Magick*.

Kat & Stone Bastion's bestselling first novel *No Weddings* and the No Weddings series were named Best of 2014 by multiple romance review blogs.

When not defining love and redemption through scribed words, they enjoy hiking in vivid wildflower deserts, ancient tropical forests, and historic urban jungles.

Join our Bastion Family Adventurers!

Be in the know with preorder alerts, exclusive bonus gifts, and occasional free stories:

katbastion.com/email-subscription